Praise for the novels of Sheila Roberts

"No one is better at expertly fusing small-town charm and holiday cheer than Roberts, and her latest...is the literary equivalent of watching *It's a Wonderful Life* with a mug of hot chocolate and a plate of cookies."

—*Booklist Reader* on *Christmas from the Heart*

"A deftly crafted and delightfully entertaining novel from the pen of an author with a genuine flair for originality and the creation of memorable characters."

—*Midwest Book Review* on *Christmas from the Heart*

"A lovely blend of romance and women's fiction, this insightful holiday treat hits all the right notes."

—*Library Journal* on *Christmas in Icicle Falls*

"Roberts engages readers from the first page with her colorfully distinctive characters and her amusing storytelling. She expresses the pitfalls that occur through the holiday season with flair and fun. A delightful read."

—*RT Book Reviews* on *Christmas on Candy Cane Lane*

"The ultimate in feel-good family drama and heart-melting romance. Plus there's the added bonus of getting to celebrate the season with a community that couldn't be more devoted to Christmas."

—*USA TODAY* on *The Lodge on Holly Road*

"This amusing holiday tale about love lost and found again is heartwarming. Quirky characters, snappy dialogue and sexy chemistry all combine to keep you laughing, as well as shedding a few tears, as you turn the pages."

—*RT Book Reviews* on *Merry Ex-Mas*

"Roberts' charming holiday-themed contemporary story set in the Seattle area offers hope, comfort, and a second chance for those who believe, and a nudge to change the minds of those who don't."

—*Booklist* on *The Snow Globe*

"Witty characterizations, slapstick mishaps, and plenty of holiday cheer."

—*Publishers Weekly* on *The Nine Lives of Christmas*

Also by Sheila Roberts

CHRISTMAS FROM THE HEART

Moonlight Harbor

WINTER AT THE BEACH
WELCOME TO MOONLIGHT HARBOR
THE SUMMER RETREAT
BEACHSIDE BEGINNINGS

Icicle Falls

CHRISTMAS IN ICICLE FALLS
STARTING OVER ON BLACKBERRY LANE
THREE CHRISTMAS WISHES
HOME ON APPLE BLOSSOM ROAD
CHRISTMAS ON CANDY CANE LANE
A WEDDING ON PRIMROSE STREET
THE LODGE ON HOLLY ROAD
THE TEA SHOP ON LAVENDER LANE
THE COTTAGE ON JUNIPER RIDGE
WHAT SHE WANTS (also published as
ROMANCE ON MOUNTAIN VIEW ROAD)
MERRY EX-MAS
BETTER THAN CHOCOLATE (also published as
SWEET DREAMS ON CENTER STREET)

Look for Sheila Roberts's next novel
SUNSET ON MOONLIGHT BEACH
available soon from MIRA.

ONE *Charmed* CHRISTMAS

SHEILA ROBERTS

Recycling programs for this product may not exist in your area.

ISBN-13: 978-0-7783-6092-6

One Charmed Christmas

This edition published by arrangement with Harlequin Books S.A.

For questions and comments about the quality of this book, please contact us at CustomerService@Harlequin.com.

Mira
22 Adelaide St. West, 40th Floor
Toronto, Ontario M5H 4E3, Canada
BookClubbish.com

Printed in U.S.A.

For Jana,
let's take another

ONE *Charmed* CHRISTMAS

1

"YOUR KIDS ARE TWITS," CATHERINE PINE'S friend Denise informed her. "They shouldn't be leaving you at Christmas, not after what you've been through."

"It's been a rough year," Catherine admitted.

Coping with widowhood and then, right after her sixtieth birthday, getting hit with uterine cancer. Not the best year of Catherine's life, for sure. And chemo and radiation awaited her in the new year.

"All the more reason they should be with you," Denise said.

"They have lives of their own," Catherine said in her children's defense.

Denise gave a snort and took a gulp from her latte. "Which they're happy to make you a part of when it suits them."

Catherine frowned. Denise was her best friend and best

friends were like sisters. Not that Catherine had a sister—only a brother who'd never bothered to marry—but that was what she'd always thought. Still, there were times when best friends and probably even sisters needed to keep their mouths shut. Morning lattes together at Starbucks and diet accountability didn't give a woman the right to diss her friend's children. Even if they were twits sometimes. Denise's daughter wasn't so perfect. She'd gone through two husbands in twelve years.

Denise pointed an acrylic-nail-tipped finger at Catherine. "They were barely there for you after your surgery."

"They both had to work."

This inspired an eye roll. "And now they're both abandoning you at Christmas? They should be buried up to their necks in lumps of coal."

Catherine had so hoped to have her children with her. "Mom, last year was torture," her daughter, Lila, had informed her when Catherine brought up the subject of the family gathering for Christmas. As if Catherine were planning to give them a repeat performance.

No, their celebration the year before hadn't exactly been a happy gathering. Not a "We Wish You a Merry Christmas" moment anywhere in sight. It had been their first one without Bill, and Catherine had cried through everything, starting with the opening of presents and going clear through Christmas dinner. Her misery had infected her daughter, making Lila cry, as well. William's wife had teared up, too, and poor William had looked miserable and at a loss for what to say or do. Even the grandkids had been miserable. Catherine's youngest grandchild, Mariette, had sat under the tree and sobbed, and Aaron, the oldest grandboy, had muttered, "This sucks."

Yes, it had sucked. Catherine had tried not to turn on the waterworks again when the kids and grandkids gathered their presents and put on their coats to go home, but she'd failed. *Ho, ho, ho.* They'd all left like people anxious to leave a funeral.

But this year Catherine was in a better place, and she'd wanted to make new memories. Still regaining her energy from her hysterectomy, she hadn't felt up to preparing a big meal at Thanksgiving. But now, with the year coming to a close, she'd been feeling more energetic and ready to ring in the holidays. She'd never imagined doing that by herself.

"We're going to Park City with James's parents for Christmas," Lila had said when Catherine called her. Where there would be skiing and spoiling aplenty. James lacked for nothing and, after marrying him, neither did Lila.

Not that she'd lacked for much of anything growing up. Catherine had done her best to make sure of that.

"You'll be fine for a few days, won't you?" Her daughter's tone of voice added, *Of course you will.*

"Yes, but what about your presents?" Presents were always a good lure. Maybe they could get together beforehand.

Sadly, no. Lila had sooo much to do. "You can send them along with us," she'd offered.

William had beaten Catherine to the punch for Christmas plans as well, mentioning when she'd checked in on him that he and Gabrielle were taking the kids to Cabo for the holidays. "We need to get away," he'd said.

So did Catherine. Nobody had offered her the opportunity to get away with them. But then, who liked a tagalong, anyway?

"You spoil the kids," Bill used to say. He'd especially said it whenever Catherine went over to their daughter's house to help with the babies or unpleasant cleaning chores. "Lila can clean her own house. Hell, she can afford to hire someone to clean her house. And she sure can afford to pay a babysitter. It doesn't always have to be you."

Yes, but Catherine had wanted to help her daughter. Wasn't that what you were supposed to do when you got older, help the younger generation? And besides, she liked spending time with the grandkids.

If Bill had been alive to witness her loaning their son that chunk of money for the bathroom remodel six months earlier he'd have had a fit. William now had a new position in his company and was making a boatload of money. So far there had been no mention of paying her back. He would, though. Eventually. Hopefully.

"Why don't you come with me on my cruise?" Denise suggested.

"Oh, I don't know..." Catherine hesitated.

"Come on," Denise urged. "This Christmas cruise is going to be fabulous. We'll hit all those European Christmas markets, drink Glühwein, eat gingerbread..."

"Blow our diets."

Not that Denise needed to worry about that. She never went more than five pounds over svelte. Catherine, on the other hand, rarely made it within twenty pounds over her ideal weight. If only she didn't like to bake...and eat what she baked.

"We can get back on them in the new year." Denise pointed out the coffee shop window at the gray Seattle sky. "Don't you want to get away?"

Catherine did, indeed, want to get away, not just from the Seattle rain but from her life. But you were stuck in the skin you were in, and no matter where she went she'd still be going through what she was going through.

"I don't know," she said with a sigh, and shoved away her to-go cup and the last half of her muffin.

"I really don't want to be in a stateroom all by myself. That darned Janelle, backing out at the last minute." Denise shook her head. "It won't be half as much fun if I have to go by myself."

She wouldn't be by herself for long. Unlike Catherine, Denise instantly made friends wherever she went.

"And who's going to keep me from eating too much kuchen?"

"Kuchen?"

"Cake. German pastries are the best, trust me. Just think, Amsterdam, Heidelberg, men in lederhosen."

Catherine raised an eyebrow. "In December?"

"Okay, maybe not. But who knows who we might meet?"

Denise the merry widow. She'd been on her own for ten years. Carlisle, her dead husband, had been her one true love, but that didn't stop her from enjoying a string of boyfriends or traveling with girlfriends. Denise had adapted well to being on her own. Catherine wasn't sure she ever would.

Denise brought out her brochure with pictures of the towns and cities where the ship would stop. "Isn't it magical?"

It did look magical. The brochure showed her town centers with fountains and cobbled streets, stately ancient churches with their spires piercing the sky, pictures of the Christmas markets all lit up and thronged with happy shoppers. And there was a picture of the boat, all decked out in lights.

It was indeed. And tempting.

"We can split the cost of the room," Denise continued, "and I'm sure my travel agent can work things out with the cruise company to get you on the plane since Janelle only pooped out on me yesterday. Your passport's up-to-date, right?"

"It is." Catherine had been looking forward to using it after Bill retired. She'd never gotten the chance.

"Then dust it off and let's go. After we get back you can have Christmas with me and Carrie and the girls."

A trip down the Rhine River, checking out scenic towns and bustling Christmas markets or sitting home alone, yearning for the past, being miserable in the present and worrying about the future—decisions, decisions.

"All right," said Catherine. Why not? "You talked me into it." Suddenly, the month of December was looking much brighter. Almost merry.

"Should you be traveling?" asked her daughter when she mentioned it during a phone conversation later that night.

Lila had called to see if Mom could come stay with the kids the night of James's office Christmas party and had been shocked to hear her mother wouldn't be around.

"I think I'll be fine. I'm feeling pretty good."

"It's only been three weeks since your surgery."

"I know. But my energy's starting to come back. I'm fine. Anyway, it will have been over a month by the time we go."

"You shouldn't be traveling halfway across the world all by yourself," Lila said firmly.

"I won't be by myself. I'll be with Denise. Anyway, I want to do something fun this December."

There was a long moment of silence. Did Lila think Catherine was guilting her? Hmm. Maybe she was, just a little.

"I still think it's a bad idea, but it's your decision."

No kidding. "Yes, it is."

Lila heaved a sigh. "I'd better start calling around for a babysitter."

"Yes, you had." Because Catherine was going to have a life.

Fifty branded Christmas ornaments successfully ordered online and shipped to the office of Tilly's Timeless Treasures for their annual Christmas party; holiday chocolate sampler boxes found for a wedding planner who needed them for an upcoming wedding; twelve special gifts bought for Harry Davis, Realtor, for his upcoming office party…and a partridge in a pear tree.

Sophie Miles set aside her laptop and stretched. All in a day's work for a professional shopper. She sneezed. Was she coming down with something? This would not be a good time to catch a cold, with the holidays right around the corner. Not that she had any big plans other than hanging out at her parents' house for Christmas.

Of course, hanging out at her parents' was a good thing. Hanging out by herself, well, at this point in her life it wasn't exactly what she'd planned. She'd figured she'd at least have a boyfriend in tow.

Being thirty and single at Christmas, with no hub, no kids, sucked. Being thirty and single sucked, period. She was pretty, she knew that. Blonde, blue-eyed, nice butt. She didn't have the biggest boobs in the world, but they were okay. She had good teeth. She was kind. She liked kids and football and wasn't too bad in the kitchen. Or the bedroom. Yet here she was, still single. Just because she had some health concerns sometimes.

"Sometimes?" her last boyfriend had echoed. "Everything's an emergency with you, Sophie. You've always got something. Or you think you're getting something. Or you're worried you're gonna get something."

That was an exaggeration. And it was only natural to worry. New viruses popped up all the time and people needed to take their health seriously.

"He does have a point," her sister, Sierra, had said when Sophie tried to cry on her shoulder. "You can get a little squirrelly. That's scary to some guys. I mean, I get it, but—"

"I am not a squirrel," Sophie had insisted. "I'm just in touch with my body."

"Right. That's why you thought you had throat cancer last year when all you had was acid reflux. Then there was the time we all stayed at that cabin in the mountains and you were sure you'd been bit by a tick and had Lyme disease, and the time you swallowed that corn nut and—"

"Never mind," Sophie had said, cutting off her sister before the list could grow any longer.

Just because a woman was vigilant about her health, it didn't make her squirrelly or a hypochondriac. Cuts could get infected. So could insect bites. Colds could turn into bronchitis and bronchitis into pneumonia. You could pick up the flu virus simply by touching an elevator button. (Which was why Sophie always pushed those buttons with her knuckle. Or better yet, her elbow.) It was important to be aware of your environment, especially after what people had gone through when COVID-19 hit. That wasn't squirrelly. That was preventive medicine.

Speaking of, she went to the shelf in her kitchen cupboard dedicated to her many bottles of vitamins, minerals and herbs, and took out her chewable vitamin C. Sneezes turned into colds in a heartbeat.

Her work was done for the day and her immune system was now boosted, which meant there was no putting it off any longer. She had to go to Costco and purchase those food supplies for her friend Camilla, the caterer. Camilla almost always did her own shopping but she was swamped and one of her employees was out sick, so she'd begged Sophie to help her out. The big warehouse store would be a zoo, full of people carrying all kinds of germs. This time of year people were walking petri dishes. No one stayed home when they were sick anymore. She'd take more vitamin C before bed.

She was reluctantly moving toward the closet to get her coat when her sister called. "Are you working?" Sierra asked.

She usually worked straight through lunch, eating an apple (an apple a day and all that) and some yogurt (probiotics, good for the digestion) while she surfed the internet on behalf of her clients. Today she'd gotten done early and once she'd braved Costco she was going to curl up on her couch with a cup of rooibos tea and stream a Hallmark movie.

"Just finished," she said. "You on your lunch break?"

"Yeah. Thought you might have a minute to talk."

A minute to talk. Obviously about how Sierra's plans for the night before had gone. There wasn't any excitement in Sierra's voice. That wasn't a good sign.

"Sure," Sophie said cautiously. "What's up?"

"Murder."

"Oh, no. Mark didn't like his Christmas surprise?" How could he not?

"He can't go."

"Can't go? Why not? Is the Grinch holding him for ransom?"

"He says he doesn't have enough vacation time left and, anyway, he's swamped."

Sophie frowned in disgust. Really, Mark was such a waste of man sometimes. "Why can't he, like, talk to his boss, borrow from next year's vacation time or something?"

Could you do that? Sophie had never been Miss Corporate America. Before she turned her shopping passion into a business, her jobs had been the kind that involved plates of food and tips. So what did she know?

"I don't know. I talked to his boss months ago, told her what I was planning. She said she'd be fine with it."

"Maybe his boss forgot about your conversation and needs him. Maybe he really does have too much work to do."

"Or maybe he just doesn't want to go with me." Sierra's voice was threaded with insecurity.

"What man in his right mind wouldn't be working every angle to go on a glam holiday cruise? With his wife," Sophie hastily added.

"Mine, I guess. I mean, I know things haven't exactly been perfect these last few months, especially with him working so much, but we still love each other."

Correction: they both loved Mark.

This conversation was going to take a while. Sophie took a bottle of juice out of the fridge and settled on her living room couch, put her feet on the coffee table and looked out the window. Her studio apartment had a great view…of the apartment across the street from it. That was what you got when you lived in Seattle and worked not at Amazon.

"I'm sorry, Sissy," she said. *Sorry your man is turning out to be such a subpar husband.*

Mark had a selfish streak that had been widening over the last four years. He was constantly frustrating Sierra by blowing their budget on expensive toys—a new car, that fancy watch he'd just had to have, pricey tickets to football games, which he attended with his buddies, a bigger and better TV. Sierra, the budget-conscious one, had tried to rein him in, but they were now five years into their marriage and the reins were pretty much broken.

Which made it all the more mystifying why he wasn't moving heaven and earth to take this trip. It should have appealed to him, considering his family's German roots and his love of extravagance. Sierra had been paying for the cruise for months.

"I swear if I wasn't such a good wife I'd poison him," Sierra said, the insecurity replaced with anger.

"Well, there you go. He senses danger and he's afraid to be alone with you in a stateroom," Sophie teased in an effort to lighten the moment.

"He's afraid to be alone with me in the bedroom, for sure," Sierra grumbled. "Afraid I'll poke a hole in his condom."

"TMI. Pleeease."

"Sorry," Sierra muttered.

"You guys talked about this stuff before you got married. Didn't he say he wanted kids, or am I misremembering?" Sophie took a drink of her juice. Orange juice. A little extra vitamin C never hurt.

"Yeah, eventually. But I'm thirty-four and he's thirty-five. Eventually is here."

"You still have time. Thirty-four's not that old."

"Yes, it is."

"No, it's not." If thirty-four was old, then thirty was middle-aged, and Sophie wasn't ready for that. "I'm sure you can convince him to change his mind."

"I've been trying, believe me. He thinks we can't afford a baby."

Maybe not, with the way he liked to spend money. Poor Sierra.

"It seems like we've been arguing so much lately. I was really looking forward to us getting away. I thought he was going to love this."

Sophie knew that Sierra had been excited to present her husband with the gift of a Christmas cruise the night before. She'd planned to make a recipe for Rouladen, a German dish she'd found online, and then serve him German chocolate cake for dessert as a warm-up for the big moment. She'd been so sure that this cruise was just what they needed to get back that honeymoon high.

"Not that things are that bad," she insisted. "But we need more time together. We need to get on the same page."

Sophie fumbled around for the right words. "Maybe he was just shocked. He needs time to process, figure out how to make it work." Lame.

"He should have jumped at this." Sierra's voice began to wobble.

"What happened when you gave him the envelope?" Sophie asked.

"He stared at it and asked, 'What's this?' Like I'd given him a raw onion or something."

The rat. "That's all he said?"

"No. He said he was really sorry. We can do something next summer. Blah, blah."

Sierra let out a sigh. "Looks like this wasn't one of my better ideas."

It seemed that, lately, Sierra and Mark spent more time apart than they did together. He did have to work long hours. The price of success.

If you asked Sophie, it was priced too high. She loved her work—what was not to love about shopping for people?—but she also loved hanging out with family and friends. You had to make time for that. She could have understood Mark's long hours better if he owned his own business or was doing something he was passionate about, but from what she could tell he was only a cog in the corporate wheel, working for a paycheck he could blow.

"What are you going to do?" she asked.

"Throw out the leftover Rouladen."

"No, I mean about the trip."

"I'm going. I paid for this and I'm going. I *can* take the time off."

"You're gonna go without him?"

That sure didn't seem like a good idea.

"He said I should since I already spent the money. He felt bad that he can't come with me and he didn't want the trip to be wasted. In fact, he even suggested I take you with me."

Very noble. Except Mark wasn't that noble and his offer made Sophie suspicious. Did he have some selfish hidden agenda? Did he welcome the idea of a week away from his wife?

"I'm not sure that's a good idea," she said. "I mean, you guys are already having problems."

There was a moment of silence. "I know," her sister said in a small voice. "I thought this would be good for us. I'd been hoping all morning he'd text me that he got the time off, after all. I finally texted him."

Having to nag her husband to go on a trip with her. This was sick and wrong.

"He said he really can't take off. My surprise sure backfired."

"I'm so sorry, Sissy."

There was a lesson in this somewhere, like never spend a small fortune on a trip you didn't plan together. At least, not if you were married to Mark.

There was another moment of silence, then Sierra said, "Maybe he's seeing someone."

Gaack! "Then you definitely shouldn't go!"

"Like staying home would stop him? A man can always find

ways to cheat. Anyway, he's always working. When would he get the time?"

Sophie thought of the old saying you always find time for what you really want to do. Mark was selfish, but surely he wasn't downright evil.

"Maybe we need this time apart," Sierra reasoned. "Maybe it will make us both realize how much we love each other."

Or how much he doesn't love you. Sophie frowned and set aside her juice, which suddenly wasn't sitting so well on her stomach.

The diagnosis for this tummy trouble was easy. She worried about her big sister. Sierra was a typical firstborn—a real caregiver, watching over everyone, including Sophie.

Sophie still had the card Sierra had made her when she was nine and had to spend the night in the hospital. The angel on the front showed the talent of a young, budding artist. Inside Sierra had written, *I'll watch over you.* She'd kept that promise, telling Sophie stories at night to distract her when she was scared that the invisible monster that had sent her to the hospital would come back and sit on her chest so she couldn't breathe. In high school she'd gotten Sophie through algebra and geometry, shared makeup tips and clothes.

She still watched out for her sister and everyone else, as well. She was always the first to offer to help their grandma decorate the Christmas tree and bullied Sophie and their brother, Drew, into putting up the Christmas lights for their parents every year. When Mark's mom had broken her ankle the year before it had been Sierra who took her to her doctor appointments and physical therapy. She loved with all her heart. Sophie didn't want to see that big heart of hers get stomped on.

"Anyway, I was stupid and didn't get trip insurance."

"You didn't get trip insurance?" Sophie repeated, shocked.

"I know. I should have. I'd just been so sure… Anyway, if I don't go I'll have spent all that money for nothing," Sierra continued. "So I'm going." She might as well have added, *So there.* "Want to come with?"

"On a cruise."

It had all sounded so glamorous and romantic when her sister first told Sophie what she was planning; she'd actually been a little jealous. But not for long, not after she remembered all those poor people quarantined on those cruise ships.

"It'll be fun."

"Yeah, until some disease breaks out."

"Cruise lines are being extra cautious now. You could be safer on a boat than you are here at home. Think of it—quaint German villages, beautiful scenery, sister adventures. Shopping."

The magic word.

"It's all paid for."

More magic words.

"I don't want to go by myself," Sierra confessed. "It'd be too depressing."

"That would be hard. You'd look like the loser of the high seas."

"We won't be at sea. We'll be on a river."

"Oh, yeah. Right."

"It really does look like fun and I know we'd have a good time. So what do you say?"

"Um."

"Come on. The only time you've used your passport was when we did that family trip to Canada. Don't you want another stamp in it?"

Actually, she did. And a weeklong cruise with her sister would be a fabulous way to start the holidays.

Um finally turned to *yes* and Sierra ended the call sounding happy instead of miserable. Sophie, too, was feeling a little swell of excitement. She and her sister always had fun together and she was sure they'd both enjoy this trip. Well, as long as neither of them got sick.

She went to Costco to shop for her friend. While she was there she bought a giant bottle of Airborne gummies. And on her way home she stopped and bought pills to prevent seasickness, several bottles of hand sanitizer (even though she already had three in her bathroom cabinet) and a mask to wear on the plane. Okay, let the fun begin.

2

TREVOR MARCH AND HIS BROTHER, KURT, SAT IN Pok Pok, the only restaurant to go to in Portland, Oregon, for great Thai food. It was also where they'd been meeting every Black Friday evening since their mom died five years earlier.

Now it was a tradition, and about the only one they had left. Dad had moved out when they were in their teens and started some new traditions of his own with the big-boobed, small-brained homewrecker down the street. Dad never got invited to Pok Pok.

Kurt stuffed a piece of kai yaang in his mouth. "Come on, change your mind. There's plenty of room in my stateroom. It'll be good bro time."

Trevor pointed his chopsticks at his brother. "You're not

looking for bro time, you ass. You're looking for a sucker to help you babysit."

"Huh-uh. I just want to be able to talk to someone once in a while whose frontal lobe has fully developed. Of course, in your case, who knows?"

"I thought Misty was going with you."

"Can't. Her grandma decided to come out for a visit the same time as the cruise and she has to help entertain her. That means I'm stuck on my own with an extra plane ticket."

"With a dozen college kids who'll get lost, get drunk and make trouble or fall off the boat. Yeah, sign me up."

"Come on, man. I need help."

"You sure do. What were you thinking?"

"That it would be a good experience for my German class. Easier than renting a bus, and someone else will be on hand to help with the head count."

Trevor shook his head. "You're lucky all twenty-five didn't decide to go." He signaled their waitress, who he'd been enjoying flirting with, and she hustled over. "I think I need another drink," he told her.

"Whatever you want," she said, and hurried off to fetch it.

Trevor grinned. "I like the sound of that."

"Don't get your hopes up. She didn't mean it that way," Kurt said.

"Jealous," Trevor teased. "You don't have the gift with women."

"I also don't have a chocolate company and unlimited bribes at my fingertips."

"You also don't have any charm."

"Hey, who's got the girlfriend?"

"Poor woman. She has no taste. You sure lucked out."

"No, I just got smart. Which is more than I can say for you with some of the women you've picked."

"Hey, I'm not psychic," Trevor said in defense of his poor choices.

"Like you had to be psychic to figure out that Angela was a loser? I never saw a grown woman pout so much. Talk about manipulation."

"She wasn't like that when I first met her."

"Yeah, she was," Kurt said. "And Sarah." He shook his head. "What a leech."

"Okay, already. Are we done talking about my love life?"

"We are. It's too damn depressing. You gotta quit being so shallow. Look for someone with some heart."

"Thank you, Dr. Phil."

"You're welcome. Now, back to the cruise. Are you coming or not?" Kurt demanded.

"Give me one good reason why I should."

"'Cause I want you to."

Well, shit. Playing the brotherly love card was hitting below the belt.

"We can see Heidelberg, where Gramps was stationed, drink all that good German beer and eat soft pretzels."

"It might be fun," Trevor said.

"Who knows? You might even meet some nice German Fräulein you can fool into thinking you're sexy."

"I am sexy. I got all the sex appeal in the family." Trevor had no problem getting women. He was tall and worked out enough to look good in a shirt and jeans. Like his brother, he'd inherited their lousy dad's movie-star face—square chin, right-size nose, good eyes. Women fell for him like a ripe apple from a tree.

Sadly, his brother was right. He never seemed to pick the

good ones. The women he dated always turned out to be more interested in going out to flashy clubs and being seen rather than seeing what else he had to offer beyond a good time. He guessed that was what he got for chasing women who walked through the world like the perfect, candy-colored boxes he sold his chocolate truffle collections in. Unlike those candy boxes, though, they were all shine and hard edges with very little inside to recommend them. Why weren't there more out there like his mom, who was kind and generous?

Or who liked to cook. Nobody wanted to cook anymore, at least nobody he'd found. He'd known his way around the kitchen better than the last two women he'd dated. Not that he minded cooking for a woman. He was a foodie, after all. Still, it would be nice if someone wanted to make a meal for him once in a while instead of the other way around.

And there was the bottom line. Relationships should be give-and-take. It seemed like Trevor always fell into ones where he was doing all the giving and she was doing all the taking.

At least his company was doing well. Cupid's Chocolates had grown like a weed in a pile of manure and the long hours he'd been putting in lately didn't leave a lot of time for any relationships beyond what he already had with his brother and his closest friends. The old saying was true: you didn't own a business; it owned you. Still, could he make room in his life for the right person? Damn straight he could.

"Okay, that settles it," Kurt said, and adjusted his glasses.

"Settles it! Since when?"

"Since you haven't said anything for the last minute."

Their waitress was back again, all smiles, with Trevor's drink. He barely noticed.

He frowned at his big bro. "I've got a business to run, you know."

"The business will be fine. You've got a capable manager and employees who are stupid enough to love you."

It was true. His people were the best. But Cupid's Chocolates was Trevor's baby. He'd poured his heart and soul into it, and like any good parent, he was always nervous about leaving Baby for very long.

"They can handle cleaning the chocolate vats."

Trevor lifted his glass, pointing his middle finger at his brother in the process. Cupid's Chocolates was more than a bunch of costly equipment. The company offered premium chocolate treats made from organic, fair trade cocoa beans. He and his people worked hard to make the best and most exotic chocolate to be found anywhere in Oregon. In the Pacific Northwest. In the world. Not that Belgium, Switzerland or Germany would agree.

As if reading his mind, Kurt added, "You can OD on German chocolate, check out the competition. Heck, you can bring samples along and pass 'em out to the other cruisers and probably pick up some new customers."

There was that. He could stuff a lot of chocolate bars in his carry-on. That, a pair of slacks, some jeans, a sweater and some boxers and he'd be good to go. Shaving kit, toothbrush...

Wait a minute. How had he gone from not going to thinking about what he was going to pack?

"You could maybe even find your dream woman there," Kurt finished. "A nympho chocoholic."

"Yeah, hiding in the middle of all those fifty- and sixty-year-olds."

"What? Now you're age biased?"

"Only when it comes to who I sleep with."

"You'll find somebody. You always do. Come on, what do you say?"

"I say I don't want to fork out for a plane ticket."

"You can have Misty's."

"You can't just change someone's name on a plane ticket anymore."

"My travel agent will take care of it. She'll cancel it and rebook. She's got connections. I'll even eat the cost of rebooking. Merry Christmas from your big bro."

How did you turn down an offer like that? "As long as I don't have to babysit."

"You can do your own thing. And I don't have to be with them 24/7. It'll work out."

Trevor finally said yes, leaving his brother to get the German 201 class from Portland to Seattle and driving up on his own. It would be fun to hang out with his brother. And who knew? Maybe Kurt was right. Maybe Trevor would meet somebody. Although he doubted it.

Kurt's prediction about finding someone proved right. Trevor met someone at the airport, all right. Not the kind of someone he wanted to meet, though.

He was sitting at Gate 20 at SeaTac International, checking his messages on his phone while his brother checked on his herd, when one of the herd broke away and plunked herself down right next to him, dropping a bulging duffel bag in front of her. She was a skinny kid in a winter coat and a long, black sweater that hung over blue leggings with a pattern that made him dizzy. Her feet were in boots that looked like she should be on parade with a drill sergeant yelling at her. Unstyled brown hair hanging to her shoulders and a face scrubbed clean. No makeup. No piercings, no tats to be seen.

No perfume. No nonsense. Snap judgment: nerd girl. If they ever did a reboot of *The Big Bang Theory* she'd be a perfect Amy Farrah Fowler.

He could almost hear his mother scolding, "Look at the heart, not the outward appearance."

"Guten Tag," she said. *"Sind Sie der Bruder von Herr Professor March?"*

Why wasn't she over there with the herd, practicing German with someone her own age?

Mom had taught him to be polite so he didn't ask.

"I am," he said, and looked to where Kurt stood talking with a hefty kid in ripped jeans and a black leather jacket, with blue hair and gauges in his ears. Had Kurt sent this girl Trevor's way just to mess with him? After their conversation at Pok Pok he'd better not have or Trevor was going to drown him in the Rhine.

"Sprechen Sie Deutsch?" she asked.

"What?" Seriously?

"Do you speak German?" she asked in English, looking almost exasperated that he hadn't caught on.

"Sorry," he said. "I barely *sprechen* English." He tried to sic her on the hefty kid with the blue hair. "I bet that guy does."

She rolled her eyes and snorted. "Hugh? He's pretty but he's dumb. He's on the downside of a C in class. Anyway, boys that age are so immature. I'm Harriet," she added.

"Trevor," he said in return.

"This is my first trip outside the US. I still can't believe it's happening."

That made Trevor smile. Little Harriet with her big brain sounded like a little girl who'd just been promised she could stay up late on New Year's Eve.

"It's happening, trust me," Trevor said.

"It's so awesome of Professor March to do this trip for us."

"Always good to learn the people and their customs as well as the language," Trevor said. His German grandma would have been glad to see that he was finally getting his butt over to the fatherland.

"Have you traveled very much?" Harriet asked.

"Some."

While Kurt's studies had taken him to Germany, Trevor's interests had sent him places like Ecuador and the Ivory Coast. The two of them hadn't traveled together since a road trip to the Grand Canyon after Trevor's high school graduation. They were past due.

"I intend to travel a lot," Harriet informed him. "I'm going to be a citizen of the world."

Trevor had his hands full being a citizen of the US. "Go for it," he said.

"Do you believe in the propinquity effect?"

The switch in topics about gave him whiplash. "Pro what?"

"Propinquity. It's one of the main factors leading to personal attraction. The more we interact with individuals, the more likely we are to form friendships and romantic attachments with them."

"What if someone doesn't want to spend time with you?" Trevor asked.

"Oh, they will eventually," she said, confident in P-power. "People think you form attachments just seeing someone across a room full of people. You know, love at first sight. But it's much more complicated than that."

He nodded. "Interesting." Oh, shit. Wrong thing to say.

"Isn't it?" she said, warming to her subject. "It's a scientific fact." She pulled a cheap supermarket chocolate bar from her backpack.

Trever watched in disgust as she broke off a piece, and popped it in her mouth. Okay, she was young. You had to make allowances.

She offered the bar to him. "Want some?" *Have some chocolate-flavored wax.*

He held up a staying hand. "Uh, no, thanks."

"You don't like chocolate?" She gaped in amazement.

"I'm a chocolate snob."

"Oh, Godiva." She rolled her eyes.

"No, more like Cupid's Chocolates," he said, unable to resist dropping his company's name.

"That stuff is expensive," she said with a frown.

"Ever hear the saying you get what you pay for?"

"I'm a student. I can't afford to pay that much."

She was on this trip. She couldn't be that broke. Still, generosity urged him to zip open his carry-on. *Give the kid a treat.*

Was this the equivalent of feeding a stray? He was aware of her looking over his shoulder, like someone standing over a guy panning for gold, eager to see what he came up with. Yeah, this probably wasn't such a good idea.

Too late. He heard the little gasp and knew she'd seen the gold nugget. A suitcase stuffed with gold nuggets. Now there would be no getting rid of her.

Oh, well. Convert them when they're young, then you'll have them when they're older and they have money. He pulled out an Orange Blossom Special, a three-ounce bar—55 percent dark chocolate infused with orange and loaded with almonds.

"Are you allergic to nuts?" he asked.

She wiped saliva from one corner of her mouth and shook her head, too awed to speak.

"Well, then, this is for you. But you have to hand over that poor excuse for chocolate first."

She did and practically snatched the bar out of his hand. "Where did you get all that? Are you a salesman?"

In a way. "Something like that."

She unwrapped the chocolate, broke off a piece and put it in her mouth. Closed her eyes and let out a groan. Chewed a little and groaned some more. Sounded like a woman working her way to an orgasm. Trevor looked around, hoping not too many people had heard it.

"OMG." Another groan.

Okay, this was getting uncomfortable. "Excuse me, I'm just gonna..." *Run away*. Trevor zipped his carry-on back up and bolted. The men's restroom. She couldn't follow him there. He found a stall and shut himself in.

"I'm so glad it worked out for me to come," Athena White said to her father as they towed their carry-on suitcases through the crowd at LAX, heading for the Lufthansa gate. "This is going to be so much fun."

"Yes, it will," said her father agreeably.

It was the first trip they'd taken together since her mother's death, which had been six years and one second wife ago. Athena was an only child and she and her father had always been close, even more so when her mom was ill. They had faced the hard time and terrible loss together.

Then something even more tragic had happened. Nicole. The very memory of that sneaky little gold digger still was enough to make Athena's blood pressure spike. Nicole had been forty-one, only one year older than Athena. Daddy's old tennis buddies had finally lured him back to the racket club and there had been Nicole in her short little tennis skirt, needing help with her backhand. That tennis club membership had been an investment that sure paid off for her.

Daddy had been easy pickings—widowed and lonely, and after no longer having a sick wife to care for, drifting and purposeless. Athena had tried to point out that Nicole was after Daddy's money. A nice-looking doctor with a healthy financial portfolio—every greedy woman's dream. But Daddy, it turned out, was as human as any man, and vulnerable to flattery. Nicole had convinced him she was more interested in his tennis game and his brilliant mind than his bank account. They were soul mates, so what did the age difference matter? It had worked out fine for Michael Douglas and Catherine Zeta-Jones.

So Nicole had led him to the altar like a sheep to slaughter and, once they were married, proceeded to throw around his cash like it was Monopoly money. Spending someone's money was one thing. Marrying him for his money was quite another. It soon became apparent that Nicole enjoyed spending time with Daddy's American Express card and her girlfriends more than she did spending time with him. The bitch. She spent their short-lived marriage making demands on him, doing everything she could to put a wedge between him and his daughter and then, finally, leaving him for a heart surgeon. How appropriate. Maybe he could give her a heart.

Daddy had been devastated. But he'd survived the devastation. The last few months he'd begun to ease into a social life. Some doubles at the racket club, drinks with an old friend here and there. Attending an occasional party.

Wondering about checking out one of those dating sites for seniors.

No! Athena had almost had a heart attack the moment he mentioned it. Those sites were shark-infested waters. She'd convinced him he wasn't ready yet and he'd settled back into seeing his old friends, staying home on a Friday night with a good book or streaming a movie. Meeting his daughter for lunch every Saturday. It was a good life. Who could ask for anything more?

Her father apparently. He'd been reading about cruises online and thought a holiday river cruise sounded kind of fun.

A cruise. By himself. No one to protect him. Oh, no. She'd quickly enthused over what a nice thing it would be to do together. He'd been pleased at the suggestion and made the arrangements, and now here they were at the airport, Daddy under the illusion that he was footloose and fancy-free, his daughter walking by his side, holding the invisible leash tightly. No one was going to get him this time. Daddy had endured enough unhappiness. The marriage gate was closed.

"Not everyone is a fortune hunter," her son had told her when they'd talked on the phone before her departure.

"Only the ones who go after rich people."

"Mom, you're such a cynic," he'd said in disgust.

Cynics weren't born. They were made. And Athena's rotten ex had certainly done a good job of turning her into one—hiding women, hiding assets. The only good thing she'd gotten from him was their son, a starving college student who was majoring in history. He was the one thing they'd gotten right.

"I'm not a cynic. I'm a realist," she'd insisted. She'd seen firsthand how twisted relationships could get when people married for the wrong reasons.

They got to the gate and saw a crowd of people, most seated, some milling about, many speaking to each other in German. Several couples sat side by side, drinking lattes and reading books. An older woman in a nice coat who looked like she was pushing ninety, a middle-aged woman sitting next to her. Maybe a daughter. Here came another couple, retirement age. There was a pair in their forties and a couple who looked like newlyweds. If these people were bound for Amsterdam and their cruise ship, she'd worried for nothing.

She caught sight of a new arrival, a slender woman in a red wool coat with a pretty face accentuated by eyelash extensions and plenty of makeup. A blonde.

Nicole had been a blonde.

This woman was at least a little older than Nicole, but that didn't make her any less dangerous. She smiled at Daddy, a speculative, hungry kind of smile.

Innocent that he was, he smiled back. Oh, no.

"I'd sure love a coffee," Athena said, improvising fast.

"You know, that sounds like a good idea. Why don't I get us both one?"

"Thanks, Daddy. You're a doll," she said, and stood on tiptoe and kissed his cheek. Maybe the shark in the red coat would think they were an item and look somewhere else. Athena looked over at the woman, cocked her head and lifted both eyebrows. A challenge. *Still want to try for this one?*

The woman frowned and turned her head a different direction.

That's right. Look somewhere else. My father is not on the market.

Ten minutes later Daddy returned, holding two cups of coffee and walking beside a short, middle-aged woman with salt-and-pepper hair. They were smiling and chatting away like old friends. Good grief, guarding her father was going to be a full-time job. She wouldn't be able to leave him alone for a second.

"This is my daughter, Athena," he said, handing Athena

her coffee. "Athena, this is Mona Gardner. She's on her way to Seattle to see her daughter."

At least Mona wasn't going on the cruise. Oh, and what was this? A ring on Mona's left hand. Athena relaxed and smiled at her. "Nice to meet you."

"I think it's great that you and your father are taking a trip together," said Mona. She shook her head. "My Gregory hates to travel." She nodded to where a heavyset man sat, reading a paperback novel. "It's a good thing our son and his family only moved to Seattle. We'd never have seen them otherwise. You're so lucky your daughter lives near you," she said to Daddy.

"Yes, I am," he agreed, and smiled at Athena.

Good Lord, how much information had the woman pried out of him when they were in line at Starbucks?

"Well, it was nice talking to you," Mona said. "Have a wonderful trip."

"We will," Daddy said. As Mona walked away he said to Athena, "Isn't it interesting how many friendly people you meet at the airport?"

"Most of the people I've ever met have been stressed and cranky," she replied.

"They probably weren't in vacation mode. Travel is different when you're doing it because you want to and not because you have to. There's something about travel that loosens people up."

How many loosened-up women were they going to meet before this trip was over?

"I'm sure we're going to make lots of new friends on this cruise," Daddy said. He sounded terrifyingly hopeful.

Athena smiled back and sighed inwardly. This was going to be a challenge.

★★★

"This is going to be fun," Sierra said to Sophie as they towed their carry-ons toward Gate 20 at SeaTac airport.

It was about the twentieth time she'd said it since Sierra committed to going with her. Which one of them was she trying to convince?

"Beautiful sights, happy people."

Who had better not be traveling if they were sick.

"Elegant dinners."

Dinner on board a ship. Sophie hoped she wouldn't get seasick. She always got sick in the back seat of a car. She patted her little red backpack purse for reassurance. If somebody rocked the boat she was good. She had Dramamine.

But even Dramamine couldn't guard you against food poisoning. "I hope I don't sick," she muttered.

"On the kind of five-star meals they're going to serve us? Don't worry. Anyway, if you do I'm sure they'll have a doctor on board."

"They don't. I checked. But the cruise line at least has a doctor waiting at each of their ports of call." And since those happened on a daily basis, Sophie figured she'd be okay.

Sierra gave her a teasing grin. "I'm sure you'll manage to meet one of them. Maybe he'll even be single. A doctor would be the perfect husband for you."

Yes, he would. If only.

3

"OF COURSE, JANE AUSTEN PERFECTLY CAPtured the everyday life of her class and time," Harriet said to Trevor. "I wrote a paper on it for my Women Writers of the Nineteenth Century class. But I prefer the Brontës. All that sexual repression unleashed, spilling out in such passion on the page," she rhapsodized. "Not that *Fifty Shades of Grey* is lacking in passion, you know. But I like subtlety. Don't you?"

"Oh, yeah."

And little Harriet the nerd girl was as subtle as a charging rhino. Smart kid but not smart enough to know she was charging the wrong guy. Trevor was no cradle robber.

Even if they'd been closer in age he wouldn't have been interested. Harriet was Wikipedia on two legs and she never shut up. A little of that went a long way and they'd passed long way an hour ago.

How on earth had he wound up assigned the seat next to her? Oh, yeah. It would have been Misty's. Now it was his, and Harriet and propinquity were gunning for him.

"Of course," she continued, "sometimes you have to come right out and say, *'Ich bin heiss.'*"

I am hot. And not in the sense of *Open a window, please.* More like, *Give it to me now.* One of the German phrases he did know. She was probably hoping he'd either catch on and ask, "Are you?" Or, even worse, ask her to translate. That would take them no place he wanted to go.

"Think I'll stretch my legs," he said, and about trampled Kurt, who was on his left, enjoying an aisle seat, in his haste to escape. He knew he should have booked himself a seat in business class instead of taking that ticket his brother had offered.

He walked to the middle of the plane and stood around by the bank of lavatories for a while, pretending to wait for one. He got in a conversation with an old lady who was going to Germany to visit her sister. He talked football with a Seattle Seahawks fan. He walked up and down the aisle a few times. If he was gone long enough Harriet would turn to good old C-average Hugh and start spouting facts at him. Harriet couldn't abide a conversational void. She'd have to fill it.

Yep. He came back to their row of seats to find her talking at Hugh. But she had built-in radar. She turned her head and smiled at Trevor.

He crouched down next to Kurt and hissed, "Trade seats with me."

"What? Why?"

"Don't play dumb," Trevor growled through gritted teeth.

Kurt dismissed Harriet with a wave of his hand. "Harmless."

"Good. Then it's your turn to be unharmed."

"That could look inappropriate."

It was BS and they both knew it. "Inappropriate, my ass. How about if I strangle you? Under the circumstances that would be appropriate."

"I need the leg room. Sit down and shut up before I have to beat you up," said Kurt, unruffled.

"You're only an inch taller than me."

"That inch is in my legs and I need to be able to stretch out in the aisle when I can." He nodded and smiled at the old woman Trevor had been talking to who was trying to totter past. "Sit down. You're blocking people."

There would be no uprooting his brother without a scene, which would bring whatever TSA agent was lurking on the flight. Trevor gave up and sat down.

"Think I'll try and get some shut-eye," he said to Harriet, then closed his eyes.

Harriet didn't take the hint. "I'm too excited to sleep," she said. "You know, most people can't sleep on a plane. Too many distractions."

Trevor knew. He was sitting next to one.

"I read that the best thing to take if you want to sleep is melatonin. It's what your body naturally produces. And magnesium. Did you know that it's an anti-stress mineral?"

"Got any on you?" Trevor asked, his eyes still closed.

"No. I never get stressed."

Of course not. She was too smart for that.

"I think a lot of people stress about flying. But statistically speaking, it's the safest form of travel there is. The odds of dying as a plane passenger are one in two million."

Unless somebody gets tired of listening to you and throttles you. Trevor squeezed his eyes shut more tightly. Only seven more hours to go.

★★★

The first class fliers were already settling in with their newspapers and their drinks when the peons in coach shuffled onto the plane. Someday, Catherine had thought, looking longingly at those cozy nests. Her husband had left her well provided for, but not well enough for her to justify that kind of extravagance.

It didn't matter, really. She wasn't a tall woman and she had enough leg room. If she had to use the bathroom (which she would, several times) she only had to climb over Denise, who would also be making her share of trips there. Meanwhile, a very nice middle-aged woman was seated to Catherine's left and happy to chitchat about travel and life in general.

Catherine was, too, until it came to that inevitable moment when the conversation turned to families. The woman had the perfect husband (seated on her other side), who loved her dearly and had given her this ring of silver-and-gold entwined bands encrusted with diamonds before their departure. Wasn't it pretty? (Pretty expensive, for sure.) Of course, he was also a wonderful father. In fact, they were taking the same cruise as Catherine and Denise, courtesy of their three lovely children, who had all pitched in and given it to them as a present for their thirtieth anniversary. Did Catherine have children?

"Yes, two. Oh, look, here comes dinner."

The arrival of food distracted the woman, who dug right in. Catherine lost the desire to dig. Instead, she nibbled on her chocolate dessert and contemplated her own life. She had no husband to shower her with expensive anniversary rings anymore. Not that he ever had. The only rings Bill had ever given her had been her engagement and wedding rings. And the biggest anniversary celebration they'd ever had was a trip to the Space Needle for their twenty-fifth. Lunch. Much more practical (and affordable) than dinner. No big gift from the children for any anniversary. But so what? Her husband had loved her, and her children weren't bad. They were both responsible adults with good kids.

Yes, they were a little on the selfish side, and spoiled. Especially Lila. Bill was right. She had indulged them too much growing up and then enabled them once they were grown. What was it the experts called that? Codependent. But did anyone have a perfect family, really?

"I can imagine what her Christmas letter reads like," sneered Denise, who'd been in on the conversation with their fellow traveler at the beginning and quickly opted out.

Catherine sighed.

"I can see where you're going," Denise said. "Don't let her fool you. Nobody's life is perfect, you know that. You have a lot to be thankful for, Catherine. You're beating the big C and you're having an adventure. Your kids have their faults but at least they're not on drugs or in jail. And you've got grandkids. Plus you have friends who care about you. That's more than a lot of people can say."

Of course Denise was right. "You're such a good friend."

"I certainly am." Denise smiled and gave her a shoulder bump. "I'm one of the good things in your life."

"One of the best," Catherine said. Yes, she did have much for which to be grateful.

The plane landed and the weary travelers were met by a uniformed employee of the cruise line who was holding a red paddle. Like so many ducks, they followed her out of the airport and climbed onto buses, which then shuttled them from the airport into Amsterdam.

Catherine took in the charming old buildings, the seventeenth- and eighteenth-century canal houses, narrow and huddled close together, jutting up like teeth, the houseboats parked along the banks, the hordes of cyclists zipping along the streets in the nippy, drizzly air, and could hardly believe she was actually there.

"Pinch me," she said.

"I would but I'm saving my pincher in case I meet a cute steward on board," Denise quipped.

Their bus pulled up at the dock area and Catherine saw three river cruise ships from different lines, all lit up for the holidays. Theirs, the *Heart of the Rhine*, was the most elegant of all, glowing white with tiny white lights strung from stem to stern, poinsettias lining the entry off the gangplank. She felt like a little girl on Christmas morning as she followed Denise up the gangplank. *Look what Santa brought!*

The reception area inside with its check-in desk was as festive as the outside, decked with boughs of greenery embedded with silver ornaments. A Christmas tree decorated with gold-and-silver balls and ribbons sat to the side of a short flight of stairs leading to the next level. In front of it was a small table covered with a snowy white linen tablecloth, and on top of that sat a huge gingerbread house complete with candy stained-glass windows. In front of it ran a gingerbread train, with jam thumbprint cookie wheels. Looking up to the next level Catherine could see a cozy seating area and a small library off to one side and, toward the bow on both sides of the ship, two stations with fancy coffee machines, tea supplies and serving bins stocked with cookies.

Doors beyond that led to who knew what? She could hardly wait to explore and find out.

The ship was abuzz with people checking in, chatting, laughing, excited for their big adventure to begin. A troop of college students came in behind them, noisy and exuberant, shepherded by two men who looked to be somewhere in their thirties. Nice-looking young men, one of them wearing glasses and a tired smile. The other one standing next to a chatty, plain girl. He, too, wore a smile, but his looked a little strained.

Catherine had to chuckle, remembering how exhausting her two children had been when they were that age. The chuckle died. It wasn't going to feel like Christmas without them.

But what was Christmas supposed to feel like, anyway? Did it have to be the same every year? And really, wasn't the celebration about more than family?

She and Denise were given key cards for their room and pointed down the hall. Their bags would be delivered soon. Meanwhile, the ladies were welcome to enjoy a light repast up in the lounge at any time. Dinner would be served in the dining room at seven.

Their room was large enough for two single beds, a bathroom the size of Catherine's shower at home and a closet. It had a counter running along the wall opposite the beds, which gave them a phone, a writing tablet and pen and plenty of plug-ins for a computer, iPad and cell phone. Under it were drawers for their clothes. Above it stood a long mirror, which reflected two smiling women, not young but not that old, either. Two women still young enough to enjoy life.

And Catherine intended to. A twenty-minute rest would be just what she needed to charge her batteries. They definitely needed charging. She was exhausted.

She sat on her bed and looked out the French window at their view of the bustling city. "This is perfect," she said to Denise.

"Yes, it is," Denise agreed. She smiled at Catherine. "I'm glad you came."

"Me, too," Catherine said. This trip with her good friend would be her Christmas Day. And it would be a good one.

What brain-fogging drug had Trevor been on that had made him stupid enough to let Kurt talk him into this?

The first leg of their journey had been torture. On the plane, on the bus, up the gangplank—he'd felt like an engine, reluctantly pulling along a string of cars. Directly behind him had been Harriet, talking all the way. Behind her had come the hulking Hugh, who every once in a while would break in on Harriet's pontificating with questions like, "How the hell do you know that, Harriet?" or comments such as, "I think you're full of shit." Behind Hugh had come a girl with a nose ring and a tat above her right boob (showed off by the low-cut skin-hugging black top she wore over her ripped jeans) who had refused to let Hugh out of her sight. Trevor dubbed her the giggler. God help him, he was going to go mad.

There had to be someone on this cruise ship younger than fifty and older than twenty who he could hang out with. Preferably female. Preferably cute.

His gaze latched on to a woman at the far end of the lobby with shoulder-length blond hair. She wore tight black pants and brown boots that came up to her knees. Her coat was open to reveal a long, red sweater. It matched her lipstick. Red. Perfect. The woman next to her, a brunette, was pretty hot, too, but Trevor spied a ring on her finger. Taken. So, were these two friends, sisters? Married? Oh, please, no.

The hottie gave her hair a flip with her left hand. No ring. Naked finger.

Naked. Man, it had been too long.

Trevor had to find out who they were. He started to swim through the crowd of people still waiting to check in to meet them. Harriet could say what she wanted about propinquity accomplishing the same thing as seeing a beautiful woman from across a crowded room. He'd endured Harriet's propinquity for nine hours and fifty-five minutes, actually more, counting the bus ride to the dock. Now he saw a beautiful woman and he knew which worked for him.

A salmon swimming upstream had it easier. There were simply too many people milling around and Kurt was calling him, ready for them to finally check into their room. He frowned as he watched the two women disappear down the hall on the stern end.

Well, it was a small ship. He'd find Miss Red Lipstick.

He swam back to where Kurt stood and took his key card for their room.

A voice at his elbow said, "I guess I'll see you in the lounge."

Harriet. He didn't want to be mean to the kid, but he didn't want to encourage her, either.

Too late, he chided himself. He'd already done that when he gave her the chocolate bar. Unfortunately for him, her mother had never taught her not to take candy from strangers.

He dredged up half a smile and said, "Yeah, maybe."

It was, indeed, a small ship. He hoped he wouldn't have to spend all his time on board hiding in the stateroom.

Not that it would be a bad room to hide in. It was about the size of the room he and Kurt had shared growing up. Except no one had gotten the memo about changing a queen to two singles.

"I'm not spooning with you," he cracked.

"If they don't get this fixed you're on the floor," Kurt

joked back. "I'll stop at the desk on our way out and tell 'em to fix it."

"On our way out? We just got in."

"And we've time to check out the city before the ship leaves. Come on. There's a shop I want you to see."

"In the red-light district? What would Mom say?"

"Don't get all excited We're not going there. That won't get busy until tonight."

"Yeah? How do you know?"

"I heard."

"So where are we headed?" Trevor asked as they walked back over the gangplank and off the ship. "The Rijksmuseum?"

"Not enough time to do it justice. But you are gonna see art."

The entire city was a work of art if you asked Trevor—tree-lined canals, tall, gabled brick houses and proud old buildings such as the stock exchange, which was completed in 1903.

Bicycles were everywhere in the shopping areas. "These guys have got it figured out," Trevor said as he looked at a bike parking area. He'd never seen so many bikes parked in one place in his entire life.

"Yeah, they do. You'd like living here. People ride their bikes everywhere."

Trevor sure loved riding his. He enjoyed his car, but when it came to getting back and forth to work he and his bike were one. A Saturday morning ride was always good for an endorphin high.

The city center was a pulsing anthill of people getting around, not just by bike but also on foot. It was all a little too crowded for his taste.

Soon after they turned onto Haarlemmerdijk he spotted

the attraction his brother had wanted him to see. Oh, yes, this was art.

"Wow," he said as they stopped in front of the window.

"Thought you'd like it," Kurt said.

Jordino Chocolateria was a veritable museum of edible art, and Trevor ogled the creations the way a man would ogle the girls on display in that famous red-light district. Small, chocolate treat boxes shaped like colored vases held tiny treats, an elaborately carved chocolate frame held a miniature Dutch Masters painting, gold boxes held chocolate men's shirts of varying colors. But what he loved the best were the high heels—blue, pink, green, red, lavender, orange. The tiny colored-candy sprinkles densely coated the underlying chocolate, giving them texture and pizzazz, and each sported a red, chocolate rose on the top of the pump. The dark chocolate stiletto heels reminded you of the artist's medium.

He snapped a picture with his phone.

"Maybe you need to expand your product line," Kurt said.

"Maybe," Trevor agreed.

"Think their stuff is as good as yours?"

"Let's find out."

Inside, Trevor bought them both a chocolate truffle and he bought a red high heel.

"You hoping to find Cinderella?" Kurt teased.

"Market research. Those shoes are amazing." He'd seen high heel pumps made from chocolate before, but nothing like these. The truffles were spectacular, too.

Kurt popped his in his mouth, chewed and nodded. "As good as yours, bro. Maybe even better."

"As good as, not better," Trevor said with a grin.

They left the chocolate shop and made their way back to

the ship, via the Anne Frank House so Trevor could at least see the outside.

"Thought I'd get some takers for this but none of the kids wanted to spend the extra money."

"I'd have gone," Trevor said.

"Misty and I have both toured it. By the time I knew you were coming it was too late to get tickets. You usually have to buy them two months in advance."

"Good to see it's still such an attraction," said Trevor. "People can't be allowed to forget what happened over here." He turned thoughtful. "Do you think people are basically good?"

Kurt shrugged. "I think they want to be. Most people," he amended.

"Yeah," Trevor said. "Not counting Dad."

"Not counting Dad," Kurt agreed.

Trevor thought of the chocolate shoe he was carrying, boxed and bagged with the care due such treasure. "Mom would have loved that chocolate shop."

"Yeah, she would've."

"You know, Misty kind of reminds me of her."

"She's got a lot of Mom's good qualities," Kurt said.

"You gonna make it permanent?"

"Yeah, so don't get any ideas."

Trevor was sure his brother had gotten the last good woman out there.

Kurt and Misty had met online. Maybe Trevor needed to try that. He sure hadn't done so well on his own. There had to be someone somewhere who had both a big smile and a big heart. *Are you out there, Cinderella?*

He thought of the woman he'd seen on the ship. What was she like? Did she already have a Prince Charming?

If she didn't, would he qualify? He was just an average guy

who liked to watch football and play poker with his buddies, go for a bike ride in the summer, make a batch of lasagna and have friends over. He gave money to environmental charities and cancer research (in honor of Mom). But he was also stubborn and tended to hold a grudge, even though he knew better. And he snored. Not very princely.

But Kurt wasn't all that princely, either, and he'd found somebody. You never knew.

The face of the cutie on the boat danced in front of him. He did have a shoe.

Even Denise, who had twice the energy of Catherine, agreed that a little rest would be good before going to the lounge. The two women stretched out on their beds and within minutes Denise was snoring. Catherine found she was simply too wound up to sleep in spite of her jet lag.

She was actually here, in Europe, taking a cruise. It had been on her bucket list for years, and was something she'd lobbied for doing once Bill retired. They'd done their share of camping when the kids were small—nothing Catherine had enjoyed but she'd been a sport. They'd finally bought an RV, something Bill had always wanted, and had taken a couple of short trips in it. Those trips had been fun but she'd still had to cook and clean. The idea of taking a vacation where she didn't have to do anything but enjoy the scenery had appealed strongly to her.

"We'll take a cruise as soon as I retire," he'd promised after she'd showed him yet another cruise brochure, and they'd gotten passports.

But then, two years before he could retire, he'd had a massive heart attack and died, and she'd abandoned the idea of taking that cruise. In fact, she'd abandoned the idea of doing much of anything.

Now here she was, with the dream coming true. Bill would have loved this. They should never have waited. Life, she was coming to realize, had to be lived in the now because you could head for the future only to discover when you got there you didn't have the one you'd planned on.

She certainly hadn't planned on losing Bill, who'd always been so healthy, and she'd never dreamed she'd be facing what lay ahead of her. Somehow, she'd gotten it into her head that by sixty-one she'd dodged the cancer bullet. But when it came to cancer there was no cutoff date, no safe zone.

Denise finally awoke with a snort. She saw Catherine next to her, wide-awake, and stretched and smiled. "Did I snore?"

"Only a little. Very delicate."

"Did you sleep at all?"

"I guess I'm too excited," Catherine said.

"Well, then, let's get up and check out the rest of the ship. We can grab a bite and relax until the welcome program at six."

They freshened up, then went down the narrow hallway, back through the lobby and up the few stairs to the next level where their map of the ship showed the lounge to be.

"I'm going to be in heaven," Denise predicted, checking out the coffee station. "We can make everything from lattes to cappuccinos. Ooh, and cookies. I will definitely splurge tomorrow."

"I will definitely splurge today," Catherine said, and helped herself to one. "Delicious," she reported.

The glass doors in front of them slid open, leading them into a huge area that was bigger than any lounge Catherine had ever been in. Windows ran along both sides of it, offering two different views of the city. The bar was centered so you passed it no matter which side of the ship you entered from, and it boasted almost more bottles than a liquor store. The rest of the lounge was filled with groupings of upholstered chairs and sofas and coffee tables. At the bow end, a long table displayed an elaborate gingerbread town, coated with frosting snow and sparkling with all manner of candies. Beyond that was a glass-enclosed space set up for casual dining with more tables and chairs and a buffet-style serving station.

The women went there first, helping themselves to crusty rolls, soup, cold cuts and salad, then circled back to the lounge, where several of their fellow cruisers had already staked out conversation areas.

Catherine caught sight of the woman who had sat next to her on the plane. The woman smiled and waved.

Catherine waved back. "Uh-uh," she said to Denise, trying not to move her mouth.

"For sure uh-uh. Let's start our own party," Denise suggested, and headed for a grouping in the middle of the room.

Party. Catherine liked the sound of that.

They were barely seated before a server wearing a white jacket was in front of them, asking what they'd like to drink.

"Dirty martini," said Denise. "Extra olives, please."

Catherine wasn't much of a drinker and she hesitated.

"Give her a rum and Coke," said Denise. "You can pretend you're back in college," she told Catherine with a grin.

"That sounds good," Catherine said. "And extra cherries, please."

"Of course," he murmured.

Denise sat back in her chair and surveyed the room. "This is the life. I think, instead of going into a nursing home when I'm older, I'll live on a cruise ship. No cooking, no cleaning, someone to wait on me every day, and laundry service. Plus beautiful scenery."

"But you'd only have the friends you made until the cruise ended. Then they'd leave and you'd be alone," Catherine said. That felt too transient after having lost a husband. She wanted something more permanent.

As if anything was permanent. Who was she kidding?

"Then you'd make new friends," Denise said as the man returned with their drinks. "Or, better yet, you get a bunch of your friends to go along with you and you all book rooms next to each other. You'd be planning your own floating retirement community."

Catherine smiled. "Now, there's an idea." *Except you'd never see your children.*

She decided to keep that thought to herself. Denise would be sure to make some snide comment in light of her kids' poor holiday behavior.

"There's someone I'd invite to the neighborhood."

Catherine was in the middle of reaching for her drink and made the mistake of looking to see who her friend had spotted. And there it went, tipping over on the little table, splashing her in the process.

"Oh, no," she said, brushing at her slacks. "I can't believe I just did that."

"Thank you, girlfriend. That was like a psychic signal. He's coming our way."

Catherine was embarrassed, then flustered, as a tall man with tanned skin, salt-and-pepper hair and a finely chiseled face approached them. He had a younger woman in tow, somewhere in her forties, perhaps, with dark hair and pretty eyes. Wife or daughter? He was fit enough looking, probably in his sixties but one of those super agers, so it could be either.

"What a shame," he said as their server mopped up the spill. "Let's get you another drink What are you having?"

What she was having didn't seem very impressive. Catherine should have been drinking champagne or a martini like Denise. "Just a rum and Coke. I'm not much of a drinker," she told the stranger.

"No champagne?" he suggested.

"A little too sour for my taste," she admitted. Plebian her.

"Not all of it," he said. "Let me introduce you to something I think you'll like."

Food was included in the price of the cruise. So was any wine or beer passengers drank with their meals. Drinks in the bar were a different story.

"Oh, I couldn't," Catherine protested. Judging from the expression on her face, the young woman with the stranger agreed.

"I could," said Denise.

He smiled at Catherine. The man had a beautiful smile. "Looks like you're outvoted," he said, and spoke to their server.

"Really, you shouldn't have," Catherine protested as their server left.

"I think I should," he said easily. "Do you ladies mind if we join you?"

"Not at all," said Denise. She was practically purring.

The man sat down in a chair opposite Catherine and crossed his legs. His slacks were expensive. So were his shoes. He leaned back in his chair, ready for a nice, long visit. The woman, also well dressed in black leggings, stylish half boots and a black cashmere sweater, took a chair and perched on the end of it, ready to leave as soon as it was socially acceptable.

Which she would have to do soon if she wanted to find another place to sit. The lounge was starting to fill up, people staking out seats and munching on sandwiches, ordering drinks, getting acquainted. Another half an hour and it would be very hard to find a place to sit.

"I'm Rudy Nichols," he said. "This is my daughter, Athena."

"Nice to meet you," Denise said. "I'm Denise and this is my friend Catherine. We're doing a girlfriend trip," she added, and lifted a hand to slip a lock of hair behind her ear. The left hand with the bare ring finger. Oh, brother.

"Do you ladies cruise very much?" Rudy asked.

"I've done the Mediterranean, both sides of the Caribbean and the Hawaiian Islands. This is my first river cruise," Denise told him.

He nodded, smiled, then turned expectantly to Catherine.

"This is my first cruise ever," she confessed. "My husband and I had talked about taking one, but..." She could feel her throat closing up and her eyes starting to sting with tears. "He died." She probably sounded pathetic. But losing your mate was pathetic.

Rudy's easy smile turned sober. "I'm so sorry. It's hard to lose someone you love. I lost my wife six years ago. I still miss her."

"Oh, I am sorry," Catherine said, seeing the pain in his eyes.

Thankfully, their server arrived with a bottle of champagne and several glasses on a tray.

"Shall we toast to better times ahead?" Rudy suggested once their flutes were filled with sparkling bubbles.

Catherine nodded and tried not to think about what was waiting for her in January. "To better times."

They'd just taken their first sip when two women approached. Catherine remembered seeing them in the milling crowd down below, both slender and attractive, one with light brown hair cut in a shaggy bob, the other with longer blond hair.

"Are these seats taken?" asked the brunette, pointing to two empty seats.

"No, by all means, join us," Catherine said as Rudy stood to greet them.

"Thank you," said the brunette, speaking for both of them. "It's getting crowded in here." The blonde settled in the seat opposite Rudy and she took the other. "I'm Sierra Johnson and this is my sister, Sophie Miles."

"Rudy Nichols, my daughter, Athena," said Rudy.

Athena gave the newcomers a steely look. Catherine remembered that Athena was the goddess of war. This woman could probably live up to her name.

"And Catherine," he continued, "and… Denise, right?"

Denise nodded, smiled like they were already best friends, then took a sip of her champagne.

"Nice to meet you all," said Sophie. "I'm looking forward to this cruise. I hope no one gets sick, though," she added, which struck Catherine as odd. Of all the topics to bring up when first meeting fellow travelers.

"It looks like they have plenty of hand sanitizers on board," Rudy said easily.

"That's good," Sophie said. "I brought my own, but it's good to have extras on hand."

"Where are you girls from?" Catherine asked. A much better topic than germs, which made her think of illness, which made her think of her own precarious health.

"Washington state," Sierra told her.

"Us, too," Catherine said.

"We're from California," Rudy volunteered. "I hope you won't hold that against us."

"We won't. As long as you don't move to Washington," Denise said with a teasing smile.

He nodded, getting the joke.

There had been a time when Washingtonians resented the influx of Californians into their state, raising the price of houses and changing the political landscape. Californicating, they'd called it. But those days were gone. Everybody was moving to Washington now, and not just from California.

"Tell me, Sierra, what do you girls do when you're not traveling?" Denise asked.

"I'm afraid my job isn't very exciting," Sierra said. "I work in admissions at a hospital in Seattle. My sister's the one with the cool job."

"Oh? What do you do?" Denise asked her.

"I'm a professional shopper," Sophie said.

"Aren't we all?" said Athena. It sounded like a sneer.

"No, really, I do it for a living," Sophie said. "I purchase gifts and giveaways for event planners and corporate executives, shop for companies needing help with employee gifts. That sort of thing."

"Now, there's a creative way to make a living," Rudy said. "How did you settle on that?"

"It happened gradually. I helped a couple of friends who were getting married find bridesmaid gifts. Someone else was giving a baby shower and wanted ideas for party favors. More people started coming to me and then one of my mom's friends, who's a writer, wanted to do some giveaways. She paid me and pretty soon I was in business."

"Never knew there was such a thing," said Denise. "It sounds fun."

"It is. I love my work. What about you?" Sophie asked her.

"Me? I was just a boring Realtor."

Who'd been the top seller in her office. "There's nothing boring about you," Catherine said to her.

"How about you, Catherine?" Rudy asked.

She was the boring one of the group. A stay-at-home mom for years—cookie baker, Camp Fire Girl volunteer, PTA secretary. She'd never had her own business or made a killing in real estate. She'd always thought it would be fun to write a book but she never had. Never learned to ski, never took up painting. Never even entered a recipe contest, although all her friends had urged her to. She knitted, but who would care about that?

"I'm afraid I didn't do much at all," she said, feeling suddenly inadequate. "I was an elementary school secretary. I do like children," she added.

"Do you have children?" Rudy asked her.

"Two. A son and a daughter." *Who are both too busy to be with me.* She forced the corners of her lips to stay up. *Hold that pose.* "You obviously have a lovely daughter," she said to him. Or she would be if she smiled.

"I do," Rudy said. "I'm a lucky man."

"Are you retired?" Catherine asked.

"Getting ready to in another year," said Rudy. "I'm a doctor."

"A doctor?" Sophie repeated, and looked at him as if he'd just said, *I'm a god.*

"What kind of doctor?" her sister asked.

"Just a lowly GP."

"A general practitioner. They treat everything," Sophie said. "You're so lucky to have a father who's a doctor," she told Athena.

"I'm lucky to have a father who's such a good man," Athena corrected her.

Sophie didn't appear to be listening. She was too busy smiling at Rudy.

She gave that lovely, shoulder-length hair a flip, crossed those slim, probably varicose-vein-free legs and leaned forward. "What's the most interesting case you ever had?" she asked him.

Oh, brother, Catherine thought in disgust. She wasn't interested in remarrying or even in having a shipboard romance, not with what she had waiting for her after the holidays. So, really, she shouldn't have been bothered by the conversation getting snatched from her. She'd certainly never thought of herself as insecure or the jealous type. But watching this young interloper in action, she felt both. Honestly, the girl was way too young for Rudy. Who'd invited these two to the party, anyway? Oh, yes, her.

Athena's eyes narrowed as she listened while Sophie the shopper grilled her father about his medical career. Next she'd be wanting to know about his 401(k) and his California real estate investments.

Athena was sure she could get rid of Sophie easily enough by pointing out the age difference between her and Daddy. He'd learned his lesson with that misalliance. And this woman was even younger than Nicole had been, for heaven's sake.

But the two older women were another matter. Denise was obviously on the hunt. Athena could tell by the way she'd looked at Daddy when they first entered the lounge. She was in great shape for someone her age, but that red hair. Really? Obviously dyed. Still, Athena had to admit, it looked good on her. It was thick and she wore it short and sassy. Daddy wasn't that into redheads, though, thank God.

Catherine was a little on the plump side but she had one of

those sweet faces that made you think she'd be a good neighbor, the kind who watched your house when you were gone and brought over freshly baked banana bread. Yes, she was a stealth hunter, good at disguise. She wasn't dressed to kill, just wearing a red turtleneck top and boring black slacks to send out the signal that flashy clothes weren't important. She was keeping her agenda well hidden, pretending to be only mildly interested in Daddy. Her hair was chin length and slightly curly. And blond. Fading and shot with silver, but blond, nonetheless. Daddy had a thing for blondes, and this one was the right age for him. Ugh.

She'd made sure Daddy knew she was a widow. Yes, very clever, very sneaky. She was the one Athena would have to watch out for. She was looking for a second husband with a fat wallet.

She could look all she wanted but she couldn't touch. Athena would make sure of it. Her father had suffered enough heartbreak and no way was she going to let that happen to him again.

Well, damn. The hottie Trevor had spotted when he first came on the boat was already surrounded by people. And here he was all aftershaved and spiffed up and ready to make a good impression.

Who was that old dude she was talking to? No, not talking to. Flirting with. He watched as she flipped her hair and smiled at the guy. Okay, Trevor had to admit that he looked good for somebody who had to be at least sixty—George Clooney hair, good physical condition—but still the man was old enough to be her father. Trevor noticed that the woman sitting on the other side of him didn't look happy. Worried about competition, maybe.

"There you are."

He turned to see Harriet approaching.

He felt as if he'd swallowed a rock and it was sitting there in his gut. Was this how an animal felt when it was cornered?

"Hey, Harriet," he said, trying for a tone that was polite yet discouraging.

"We're all sitting over there." She pointed across the lounge to a group of chairs along one of the windows, by the grand piano. Hugh was slouched in one, and there was his tagalong, the giggler, along with two other guys. Kurt was nowhere to be seen. And now, Trevor was going to be nowhere to be seen.

"Okay, catch you later," he said, then turned and went back the way he'd come. When it came time for dinner he was going to make sure he was seated nowhere near the tables of the German 201 class. Kurt was on his own because Trevor was determined to talk to the hot mystery woman.

4

BY SIX O'CLOCK THE LOUNGE WAS PACKED WITH happy cruisers, all styled for winter in long pants and sweaters, many celebrating the season, wearing red or green. One man wore a Santa hat.

With the exception of a group of college students, most ev-eryone appeared to be forty or older, which made Sophie and Sierra two of the younger passengers on board. That didn't bother Sophie. She liked older people. Her parents were in their sixties and they were great. So was her grandpa, who was eighty-four and still the life of every holiday party with his light-up bow tie and his repertoire of silly jokes.

She especially liked older people who were doctors. Rudy Nichols was so handsome. Considerate. And easy to talk to.

A doctor! She'd already met a doctor and they hadn't even left the dock yet. Oh, yes, this cruise was meant to be.

"We are going to have a ball," Denise was saying.

Yes, they were. Sophie looked to catch her sister's eye and share a smile, but Sierra was busy checking her cell phone in hopes of finding a text from her husband. He'd said he couldn't come on the cruise, but what was stopping him from sending her a message—broken fingers? If he ruined this trip for Sierra, Sophie was going to throttle him.

No, no, she wasn't going to let Mark do that. She was going to make sure Sierra had a good time.

The ship's cruise director appeared, a round-faced cheerleader type with light brown hair cut in a short bob, dressed in a jaunty uniform of slacks and a dark blue jacket over a white blouse. She wore a red scarf tied around her neck in a jaunty bow. She looked about Sophie's age, and she was bubbling over with enthusiasm. She introduced herself as Elsa.

"We have many wonderful excursions planned for you," she told everyone. "And, of course, we know you will enjoy visiting the Christmas markets in the various towns we visit. Every evening we will tell you about the next day's adventures so you can plan what you would like to do."

What you would like to do. Sophie would like to get to know the good doctor better.

"And we, your crew here on the *Heart of the Rhine*, are going to make sure you enjoy your time on board with us. We have our fabulous chef, Bruno, who will be making many German specialties for you along the way. Say hello, Bruno," she called to the man wearing a white jacket and a chef's toque who stood by the entrance to the buffet in the stern. Bruno waved and everyone acknowledged him with polite applause. "And Peter here in the lounge will make sure you enjoy all manner of wonderful drinks. You will want to try his candy cane cocktail."

"That sounds good, doesn't it?" Sophie said to Rudy.

"Indeed, it does," he said, smiling at her.

"You'll have to try one," his daughter said to him, not even looking Sophie's direction. Not very friendly. Sophie wasn't sure she liked Athena.

Next Elsa pointed out a stocky man in a black suit, seated at the baby grand piano. "And we have Jacques here at the piano to entertain you with your favorite songs. We have some fun activities lined up and a music trivia game. Maybe your team will win a prize."

"That would be us," Denise said to the group.

"And now," Elsa said, "I would like to introduce you to our captain, Captain Hans Ritter, who will lead us in our toast to our voyage."

As she spoke, servers had been circulating through the lounge, passing out glasses of champagne. "Free champagne. Pretty cool, huh?" Sophie said to her sister.

Sierra nodded and smiled. Sophie could tell it was a forced smile.

Thank you, Mark, for not even bothering to text your wife and see if she landed okay. She was barely gone and already forgotten.

Mark had taken them to the airport and said all the right things. Such a shitty deal he had to work. He was sorry he was going to miss seeing all those cool places, but he knew the sisters would have a good time together. Maybe he'd been trying to make the best of things, but it seemed to Sophie that he hadn't had to try all that hard. He'd seemed almost chipper as he said bon voyage to his wife. Glad to have her gone for a week? Sophie hoped not.

She also hoped her sister would be able to enjoy herself. Between "I'm going" and "We're now boarding" Sierra's moods had bounced from excited to depressed and back again. In the end Mark had managed to find just the right blend of regret and encouragement to get her to pack her bags and go, all the while reminding her it would have been a sad waste of money not to. Though now Sophie was thinking that if Sierra didn't have any fun it would still be just as sad a waste of money.

Once everyone had their champagne, the captain made his toast. "We welcome you all aboard," he said. "Here is to making good friends and good memories."

"I like that," Sophie said, and gave her sister a shoulder bump. Sierra smiled at her, a good sign, and that made Sophie smile, too.

She shared it with Rudy and he smiled back. His daughter, the sour lemon, frowned. What was her problem, anyway? Maybe she needed a nap.

Oh, well. Everyone else was nice. "Catherine reminds me of Grandma Wilson," Sophie said as the sisters left the lounge after the toasting ceremony.

Grandma Wilson had been their favorite grandma. She'd never come to visit without bringing goodies from her little garden or homemade divinity, and she'd taught the girls how to play canasta. She'd been a soft-spoken woman with a ready smile and a listening ear. They'd lost her three years earlier and Sophie still missed her. Grandma Wilson had been her buddy.

"She does," Sierra agreed. "And I like her friend Denise. I want to look like her when I get old."

Denise did know how to rock that whole aging-lady thing. *Frumpy* was obviously not a word in her vocabulary. Her white blouse had been simple but expensive. Yet not as expensive as the designer jeans she'd been wearing or the heels under them. Or the emerald ring on her right hand. The scarf, Sophie was sure, was Hermès.

"Do we want to try and sit with them at dinner?" Sierra asked as they stopped at the hand sanitizer station on their way back to their room.

"For sure. And Rudy," Sophie added as she stepped into the bathroom to check her makeup.

Sierra followed her and stood in the doorway. "Rudy. The man old enough to be your father? That Rudy?"

Sophie didn't have to look her way to see the disapproving frown. She knew it was there. "What does age matter if you're soul mates?" She dug some mascara out of her makeup bag.

"You are not soul mates," Sierra said firmly.

"How do you know?" Sophie shot back. Sierra's marriage didn't exactly indicate she was an expert on soul mates. Saying that out loud would have been unkind, but that didn't mean Sophie couldn't think it.

Sierra made an exasperated sound. "Just because he's a doctor."

"'A doctor would be the perfect husband for you,'" Sophie quoted. "Isn't that what you told me when you first invited me on this cruise?"

"I didn't mean an old doctor."

"He's not that old, and he's very attractive."

"I don't care how attractive he is, he's too old for you."

"Women get together with older men all the time, you know," Sophie said. "Anyway, I like Rudy. He's friendly and a good conversationalist. And there's something to be said for older men. They're mature and responsible. Half the men our age are nothing more than little boys in big bodies—all about having fun and running away from commitment." Like her last boyfriend. "They don't think of anything but themselves." *Rather like Mark.* She kept that thought to herself also.

"Tell all that to his daughter. I'm sure his daughter will be delighted to see you getting together with her dad."

Sophie put away her mascara and turned to her sister. "What's with her, anyway? She ought to be wearing a T-shirt that says Grinch Girl."

"I don't know. Maybe she doesn't like women younger than her hitting on her dad."

"I wasn't hitting," Sophie insisted. "I was just visiting with him."

"You were hitting," Sierra said, trying to imitate Sophie's hair flip.

"Your hair's not long enough to make that work," Sophie teased.

"Lady Godiva wouldn't have enough hair to get this man. His daughter is going to make sure of that."

"We'll see," Sophie said.

"You'd better watch yourself. Athena's liable to push you right off the ship."

"Don't even say things like that," Sophie said, horrified. "If I fell in the river this time of year I'd catch pneumonia."

Due to the size of the ship there was only one dining room and one dinner seating time and that was at seven. The dining room offered open seating, and an array of tables fanned out before Athena and Rudy, all of them elegant with white linen tablecloths, fine china and silver and wine goblets sparkling in the light of the candles on the tables.

A feeling of foreboding crept over Athena when her father led her to a table for six not far from the restaurant entrance and seated them facing the door. As if it had all been rehearsed,

Catherine and Denise, the two older women they'd met in the lounge, entered, looking around.

Denise was the first to spot them, said something to her friend and waved, and Daddy motioned them over. Oh, boy. Was this how it was going to be for the whole cruise?

Of course it was. This was exactly what Athena had suspected would happen, which was why she'd come along in the first place.

And not only Catherine and Denise, but here came the sisters, as well. "Do you have room for two more?" asked the one called Sophie.

Hard to say no since there were still two seats left.

"Certainly," Daddy said. "Join us, please."

Oh, boy. What to do?

Subtlety was required. Her father wouldn't be pleased if Athena rebuffed their new acquaintances. He'd want to know why. And she didn't dare tell him. He would pull father rank on her and inform her that he was well able to take care of his own social life and certainly didn't need his daughter running interference. She'd once heard a radio finance guru call it powdered-butt syndrome. Parents, the ones who changed your diapers and raised you, often didn't take kindly to a role reversal and weren't prone to taking advice. She'd have to find ways of discouraging fortune hunters without her father ever realizing she was doing it.

She smiled politely. She could, after all, be polite. Polite but discouraging.

So now they were six: Sophie and her sister, Catherine sitting on Daddy's other side and Denise. A regular harem.

The waiter handed Athena a menu. Suddenly nothing looked good.

"Everything sounds so delicious I don't know how I'll choose," Catherine said.

"You don't have to," Daddy told her. "If you want two appetizers or two main courses you may request both."

"How about two desserts?" asked Sierra. "I don't think I can choose between almond cake and chocolate mousse."

"Have two desserts," Denise advised her. "Life's uncertain, eat dessert first and make it worth your while."

Sierra smiled at that, and Sophie said, "Do what makes you happy, Sissy."

The two were obviously close and Athena envied that. Being an only child, she'd never enjoyed the camaraderie of a sibling. She'd settled for girlfriends, but she and her best friend, Mel, had been friends since third grade. Practically sisters.

Mel had wholeheartedly approved of Athena's plan to go on the cruise as her father's bodyguard. "Men are too trusting," she'd said. "I read about one retired doctor who found someone online and wound up paying for a house for her. Then, when it was time to meet in person, he bought her a plane ticket to France and they planned to meet at the Eiffel Tower but she never showed up. He had a limo and champagne and everything."

Athena could picture her own generous, trusting father doing the very same thing. Daddy was a romantic at heart. He'd never forgotten an anniversary, often brought home flowers for Mom for no reason and, once they became empty nesters, frequently drove her to beachside towns on the California coast for weekend getaways. He'd spoiled Athena, too, buying her jewelry for her birthdays—everything from birthstone rings to pearls—taking pictures of her in all her finery before every high school dance. Getting all teary-eyed when he walked her down the aisle. Getting teary-eyed again when she got divorced and insisting on sending her and her friend Mel to Hawaii to help Athena heal her broken heart. Her mother had confided that he'd hoped she'd meet someone while walking on the beach. As if meeting someone, on the beach or otherwise, was a good idea when she was newly divorced.

He'd been just as happy to spoil Nicole, indulging her every whim. A new car? Sure. Blue to match her eyes. She did have spectacular eyes. Botox? She didn't need it but if it would make her feel better, okay. Trips to Tahiti and Fiji, a cruise in the Greek isles. A Caribbean cruise, which included getting some expensive new jewelry in Grand Cayman. It was only money. Money that was quickly evaporating.

Not that Athena minded seeing her father spend money. She just minded seeing him spend it on someone who didn't love him and was only using him.

And then, along came the heart surgeon with the summer house in the San Juans, the boat and the ski lodge in Schweitzer. She'd divorced Daddy faster than you could say *more money*, leaving him hurt and broken. Her poor, innocent father. He'd been so naive and trusting. Didn't see the writing on the wall from the beginning of their relationship: *The End, Coming Soon.*

Now here was a whole table full of potential *The Ends.* Athena had her work cut out for her.

Conversation over dinner was congenial, the kind of easy talk you had with people you were getting to know. The older ones compared the ages of their grandchildren while the younger ones shared more about what they liked to do for fun. They all bantered over which state was the best to live in. And, of course, they had to ask each other about the various dishes they were enjoying.

Catherine licked up every bite of her pork stuffed with dried plums. "I'm going to have to see if I can duplicate this when I get home," she said to no one in particular.

"You like to cook, then?" Rudy asked.

"I enjoy being in the kitchen," she said.

"There's an understatement," said Denise. "She can name you every show on the Food Network. One of the highlights of Christmas is getting a jar of her raspberry jelly."

"That sounds yummy," said Sophie. "My grandma used to make jam. I always helped her."

She looked wistful and Catherine took that to mean that her grandmother was no longer around. Rather than ask, though, she simply said, "She sounds like a wonderful woman."

"She was," said Sophie. "You remind me of her."

"I'll take that as a compliment."

"Good. It was meant as one. I sure miss her. She left a big hole in our hearts when she died."

Rudy wasn't smiling anymore. "I can understand that."

"My mother left a big hole in ours," said Athena. "She was irreplaceable."

A compliment to her mother and maybe a warning to any woman who might be trying to do just that, thought Catherine. Athena had hardly looked happy to see her and Denise approaching their table for dinner.

She supposed she couldn't blame Athena for feeling the way she did. The loss of her mother probably made her father doubly precious. It stood to reason she'd be reluctant to share, fearful of losing his affection.

"How long ago did she die?" asked Sierra.

"Six years," Athena said, and looked almost ready to cry. "I still miss her so much. She was my best friend."

Catherine couldn't help feeling sorry for her. "Life's not the same after you lose someone you love," she said.

Her life hadn't been. She'd felt so lost without Bill. Thank God she had such good friends.

"But I do believe it makes the people left in your life all the more precious," she continued, hoping to put everyone back in a happy frame of mind.

Rudy smiled at his daughter. "Yes, it does," he said, and she smiled back. It was plain to see how much they loved each other.

"I always say, you should appreciate both what you had and what you still have," said Denise. "My husband, Carlisle, was a good man and we had a happy life together, but after a year and a half of mourning I decided enough was enough. Those of us who are still here can't spend the rest of our lives living in the past. That's the worst kind of ingratitude, if you ask me. Life's for living and if we're still here we should be living it to the fullest."

"Well," Catherine said, "no one can accuse you of not doing that."

"I should hope not," said Denise. "I'm going to milk every bit of joy I can out of every minute of every day." She pointed a finger at Catherine. "And so are you."

Catherine could feel her cheeks warming. Was everyone at the table wondering what kind of pathetic loser she was?

"I am," she said. "I'm here with you, aren't I?"

Denise smiled. "Yes, you are. And so you should be. Bill wouldn't want you to stop living your life. You have to make the most of what you have now."

"Find something good in every day, right?" put in Sophie, looking at her sister.

This was a good place to end such a serious conversation with people they'd just met. "Speaking of good, doesn't this Bûche de Noël look delicious?" Catherine said as their waiter set one down in front of her.

Athena wasn't ready to switch topics. She ignored Catherine's comment, frowned at Denise and said, "But you can't just go skipping off and forgetting the people you've loved. I certainly can't forget my mother."

"I didn't say you should." Denise's tone of voice bordered on scolding. "But do you honestly think those who have crossed over before us are insulted if we enjoy our lives? They're on to other things themselves, not placing bets with each other to see whose family can stay miserable the longest. Life goes on and we have to, as well."

Athena looked frankly disapproving. "That seems so...disloyal."

In a way it did, and Catherine felt suddenly guilty for being on a cruise, enjoying herself. Enjoying visiting with a handsome man.

"All right, let me ask you this," Denise said, settling in for a good debate. "Did your mother love you?"

Athena's brows lowered and her mouth dipped down at the corners. "Of course she did."

"And she loved your father?"

"Absolutely. And he loved her."

"Goes without saying," Rudy murmured.

"Did it make her happy when your life wasn't going well?"

"Of course not," Athena replied in disgust.

"Did she enjoy making your father miserable?"

Athena looked ready to beat Denise with a dinner plate. "No!"

"Then why would she want to see either of you miserable now?" Athena didn't have anything to say to that and Denise continued. "No one wants that for the people they love. I know my husband didn't want that for me, and I sure don't want that for my daughter. I've already told her when I'm gone I expect her to have a wake—invite all my friends and family to tell funny stories about me and drink and laugh. And I expect my daughter to take some of the money I plan to leave her and buy a fancy car and take a road trip with one of her girlfriends. I'll be smiling down on her the whole time, bugging the angels to sweep aside the rain clouds and give her sunny skies the whole way."

"Well said," Rudy approved. He raised his wineglass. "Here's to sunny skies ahead for all of us."

"I'll drink to that," Catherine said, and raised her glass, as well.

"Me, too," said Denise.

"And me," said Sophie, and her sister smiled politely and lifted her glass, as well.

Athena struck Catherine as the kind of woman who didn't like to lose an argument. She wasn't smiling when she raised her glass and she said nothing.

In the hopes of ensuring she and Denise didn't go another round, Catherine said, "I must confess, I am looking forward to this cruise."

"Good," said Denise. "Bill would have been happy to see you fitting in something nice before..."

Catherine cleared her throat loudly and gave her friend a pointed look. "Before anything could come up to stop you," Denise amended.

"You have to do something nice for yourself once in a while," Sophie added, looking at her sister. "Even if other people let you down."

Sierra bit her lower lip and nodded. She pushed away her dessert plate, leaving her cake untouched. Who had let her down? What was her story?

"Yes, you should," agreed Denise. "A cruise is one of the nicest things you can do."

"You sure meet great people," Sophie said, looking at Rudy. "And you never know, I've heard of people finding their soul mates on a cruise."

"I've heard of people getting taken in by con artists," put in Athena, which made Sophie blink in surprise. "You never know about strangers."

"Well, I like to think the best of people," Sophie said.

"A good philosophy," Rudy agreed, and she beamed at him.

Denise pointed out the dining room window. "Look, everyone. We're moving."

Sure enough, the lights of the city were slipping by. They were on their way.

"Oh, my," Sophie said weakly.

It had been a big, delicious dinner. Too much of a big, delicious dinner, and Sophie was feeling uncomfortably full. Now, with the boat moving, she was suddenly feeling more than full. She was beginning to feel queasy.

"I think I'm getting seasick," she announced.

"You can't get seasick," her sister assured her. "There are no waves on a river."

"I don't know," Sophie said uncertainly. She was sure she was getting sick.

"You're imagining things," Sierra told her.

Sophie shook her head. "I don't think so."

"You were fine until Denise said we're moving," Sierra whispered. "It's all in your head."

Not all of it. Some of it was in her stomach.

"Rudy, what's the best thing for seasickness? Is it too late to take Dramamine?" Sophie asked him.

"It's best to take it ahead of time," he said. "Maybe all you need is some fresh air."

The good doctor didn't offer to accompany her to the upper deck for some of that restorative fresh air. Maybe it was just as well. Barfing was something a woman should do without witnesses. And yes, she was sure she was going to be sick.

"You do look a little green," Athena said. "You might want to go lie down."

She wanted to go, all right. Time to hang over the railing. She excused herself and bolted out of the room.

Trevor had seen the two women enter the dining room and had been following them in, determined to get a seat at the same table, when Harriet and the giggler found him.

"We saved you a seat," Harriet said, taking him by the arm and hauling him toward two tables, each filled with students.

"Actually, I was going to…" he began.

"We had a bet," Harriet interrupted him. "Hugh said you'd ditch us as soon as you could. I told him you were here to be with your brother and you weren't that big of a jerk."

Yeah, he was.

"Harriet, you guys are my brother's responsibility, not mine."

Her eyes got big. "Don't you want to spend time with your brother?"

"I'll have plenty of time to spend with my brother."

"Hugh was right," the giggler said in disgust.

"I'm not part of your tour, guys," Trevor explained.

"You don't want to sit with us at all?"

Great, now Harriet looked about ready to cry. Well, shit.

"Sure, I do," Trevor said. "But I want to mingle a little, too." Except the sisters had found a table for six and taken the last two seats. Too late to mingle. "But I'll sit with you guys tonight," he said to Harriet. "I don't want you to lose your bet with Hugh."

Harriet smiled. She wasn't a bad kid, really. Just annoying. Even so, he vowed to make this the last night he sat with the German 201 class.

"What did you wager, by the way?" he asked as the girls towed him toward the table where his brother was holding a conversation with the class in German.

Harriet's face turned red. "One of your chocolate bars. I was going to pay you," she hurried to add.

"That's good to know."

"Um, are you going to be giving away some more of them?"

"I'll give you a bar at breakfast," he promised.

"Awesome," she breathed. Then, to the giggler, "I told you he was nice."

Most of the kids were nineteen and twenty and were excited at the prospect of getting to drink legally. Many of them already had beer and a couple of the guys were well on their way toward fueling their high spirits, laughing loudly and drawing irritated looks from the senior citizens seated at a nearby table.

"Ruhe, bitte," Kurt said to them as Trevor settled himself on a chair between Harriet and the giggler.

Yeah, like that would shut them up. He felt a little like he used to feel at big extended family Thanksgiving meals when he and Kurt were relegated to the kids' table. *No room at the grown-up table. You kids are all sitting here. And don't throw olives at each other.*

Hugh was seated on the other side of the giggler and Harriet leaned across her and said, "I told you he'd come. You owe me a refrigerator magnet."

Hugh made a face and took a drink of his beer.

"Make a bet with her tomorrow night," Trevor said. "I guarantee you'll win." That made Harriet scowl and the giggler giggle.

Trevor looked longingly at the other tables where everyone was enjoying adult conversation. At his table one of the boys was demonstrating how to make a spoon stick to his nose. Another was breaking the sound barrier with his belch.

It was a long dinner.

"Bûche de Noël," Harriet was saying when dessert arrived. "Do you know what that translates into?"

Trevor saw the elusive blonde at the other table get up and suddenly leave. To heck with Bûche de Noël.

"I bet Hugh doesn't know," he said, getting up. "Excuse me."

"Where are you going?" Harriet called after him.

Wherever that woman is going. He gave Harriet and company a farewell wave and hurried out of the dining room. It was a small ship. He'd find her.

5

THE TOP OF THE SHIP HAD A WALKING TRACK AND miniature golf course, lounge chairs and the requisite shuffleboard, all in demand in nice weather. But on this nippy night no one was up there watching the city of Amsterdam slip away into the darkness except Sophie, and her pleasure in that was tainted, both by the cold and her upset stomach. She could very well freeze to death before she even managed to hurl. And hurl she was going to, she just knew it.

She leaned on the railing and groaned. Maybe she shouldn't have come on this cruise, after all. She hated the idea of being sick the whole time. She hated throwing up. It was such a nasty experience.

Dramamine tomorrow, she vowed. She'd take one first thing in the morning. If she survived until morning.

"You're not going to jump, are you?"

She turned at the sound of the male voice behind her and saw a tall, beautiful specimen of manhood walking up to her. He wore jeans and a trendy-looking sport jacket with a maroon-colored sweater underneath it. He looked like he should be getting ready to pose for the cover of GQ.

In her current state of misery all she could think was, *Who cares who he is?*

She waved him away with a hand. "I'm seasick."

He didn't go away. Instead, he came and stood next to her. "Wow, you must get motion sickness just watching car chase scenes in movies."

Actually, she had once. She held her head in her hands and shut her eyes so she couldn't see the water swooshing alongside the boat. "I think I ate too much."

"Easy to do. All that great food. Lucky for you, I happen to have the cure for seasickness with me."

She turned and looked at him hopefully. "Dramamine?"

"Something better." He took a small chocolate bar from his jacket pocket and tore off the outer wrapping.

"Chocolate?" At a time like this?

"Chocolate with candied ginger. Ginger is great for an upset stomach. And you know how good dark chocolate is for you. All those flavanols and polyphenols." He unfolded the white inside paper around the bar, then held it out to her. "Try a bite. It will help." When she hesitated, he added, "I promise."

She did love chocolate. And she knew ginger was good for an upset stomach. When she was a little girl her mom used to make her ginger tea whenever her tummy was upset.

She took it, broke off a piece and put it in her mouth. The chocolate was smooth and sophisticated and the ginger added a sharp bite and brought back memories of herself stretched out on the living room sofa with a blanket and a pillow stuffed into one of her mother's fancy embroidered pillowcases, her mom leaning over her with a pretty china mug.

"That is good," she said to the man, and took another bite. To make sure she got enough ginger in her stomach. "Do you always carry chocolate bars with you?"

"You never know when someone may be having a chocolate emergency," he said. He leaned against the railing and smiled at her. He had the kind of smile that could drop a woman's panties at ten paces.

She took another bite. "This is really good."

"Thanks. I'm pretty proud of that flavor."

She studied him. "Wait a minute. Is this… Are you a chocolatier?"

"As a matter of fact, I am. My name's Trevor March and I own a chocolate company."

"That is seriously impressive," she said, and took another bite.

She offered the last third to him and he shook his head. "You need it more than I do. Is it working?"

She didn't feel so sick. "It appears so." Chocolate wasn't a cure for freezing to death, though. She should go below where it was warm.

She stayed put and tried not to shiver.

"Good," he said.

"What's the name of your chocolate company?" she asked.

"Cupid's Chocolates."

"Cupid's Chocolates? Seriously? I just opened an account with your company. Sophie's Helping Hand. We shop so you won't drop."

She gave up on the not-shivering thing. She really needed to get back inside before she caught pneumonia, but she hated to end her conversation with Trevor March. It wasn't every day a woman met a great-looking guy who owned a chocolate company. If only he was a doctor.

"I think I saw an order come through from you a couple of weeks ago," he said as he took off his jacket.

She nodded. "For a nonprofit fundraiser dinner dance. We placed your little truffle gift bags at each plate as party favors."

"So you're Sophie of the Helping Hand, then?" He draped his coat over her.

"Thanks. Yes, I'm Sophie Miles." Now she was a little warmer but he was going to freeze. "We should get back down below before you catch pneumonia."

"I never get sick. I get plenty of vitamin C."

"Oh, that is good for you. I take one every day."

"I mean the other vitamin C."

There was another she didn't know about?

"Chocolate," he said. "Chocolate cures everything."

She snickered. "What a bunch of baloney."

"You feel better, right?"

She did. "That's probably because of the ginger." Or pheromones.

"Let me buy you a drink to warm you up, a brandy or something," he offered.

"Oh, I have people waiting for me." Her sister would be. And if she didn't get to the lounge and stake a claim on Dr. Rudy one of the older women would for sure. Trevor March was a treat, but he wasn't a doctor.

"I'll go down with you," he said. "Who all are you here with?"

"My sister. And some other friends."

He nodded as they walked toward the stairway. "Old friends?"

"New ones."

"So you and your sister are doing some kind of girl trip?"

"Her husband was supposed to come. But at the last minute he couldn't so she called me. I'd never done a cruise before and she convinced me it would be fun. How about you?"

"My brother suckered me into this. He got the bright idea that if he brought his German class he could get a discount on the cruise. Not sure the discount was worth it."

"I saw that group," Sophie told him. "It looks like they're having fun."

"They are, and they're nice enough kids. But I'm not into babysitting."

"Not into kids?" she half teased. A lot of men didn't like children. She had no intention of getting together with someone like that.

"Not a dozen at a time," Trevor said.

Did Dr. Rudy like kids? He was a little old to be starting a family. But lots of men married younger women and did exactly that. A woman would never have to worry when her children got sick if she was married to a doctor.

"So, your sister's married. Anyone special in your life?" he asked. Getting right to the point.

How to answer that? "Um."

"*Um* means not yet, right?" he said, and smiled.

"Well." That smile was what every girl wanted for Christmas. Trevor March himself was what every girl wanted for Christmas. Every girl who wasn't prone to illness.

That wasn't her. She had to stay focused. Anyway, Dr. Rudy had a great smile, too.

They were below again in the main part of the ship and on their way to the lounge.

"Anyway, if this other guy is only an 'um,' you want to stay open to other possibilities, right?" he argued.

"How do you know I won't turn out to be an 'um'?" she argued, handing back his sport coat.

"I don't. But I have a sneaking suspicion you won't. I already know you have good taste. You like my chocolate."

That made her chuckle. "Almost every woman likes chocolate."

"But not every woman has such a pretty smile."

Trevor March had a way with words.

They reached the lounge and she looked to where she and her sister had sat the night before. There was Sierra and the two older women, Catherine and Denise. And Rudy and his daughter. Crudballs. An older man, short and stocky, wearing a Santa hat, was joining them, taking the seat Sierra should have been saving for Sophie. *Thanks, sis.*

"Do you see your friends?" Trevor asked.

She frowned. "I do, but it looks like somebody took my seat."

"That sucks," Trevor said, wearing the same smile. "I see two seats over here. How about joining me for a while and catching up with your sister later?"

There was no place to sit over by Dr. Rudy unless she plopped in his lap. "All right," she said. She sure didn't want to go back to her room now that her tummy was feeling better.

"We can talk some more and find out if either of us is an 'um,'" he said.

Sophie strongly suspected there was little about Trevor March that qualified as an "um." He was the kind of man who could easily pull a woman off course. Darn Sierra, anyway. She should have saved her sis a seat.

★ ★ ★

Catherine noticed that Sierra hadn't said anything about the seat next to her when a short husky man took the seat between her and Denise. "Do you think your sister plans to try and join us?" she asked.

"I doubt it," Sierra said as she took the drink the server had brought her.

"I'm sorry she's not feeling well."

"It happens a lot."

"Poor girl."

"My sister is a bit of a hypochondriac," Sierra said. "She had asthma as a child. She outgrew it, but she still worries a lot about her health."

It was hard to imagine someone so young and seemingly healthy always being focused on illness.

All she could think to say was, "Poor girl. I do hope she'll feel better by tomorrow."

Sierra looked across the lounge. "I guess she's fine now." She held up both hands in a helpless gesture and shrugged.

Catherine followed her gaze and saw her sister entering the room with a man somewhere in his thirties. She frowned across the lounge at Sierra.

"It's too bad we didn't save her a seat," Catherine said.

"She's not suffering any obviously."

Judging from the looks of the man she was with she certainly shouldn't have been. He was fit looking with dark hair, and as handsome as she was cute. Together they made a very attractive couple.

The man who had taken Sophie's seat introduced himself as Charlie. He quickly proved himself a nice addition to the group, keeping everyone—especially Denise—entertained with his quips and jokes. Charlie lived in Bellevue, a high-end Seattle suburb. He owned several rental properties around the city, and with Denise being in real estate, they had plenty to talk about. It was plain to see she'd been his main target when he joined them. But he wasn't above sharing jokes with the others.

"You know why Santa never goes on a diet?" he was saying to Rudy. "He has to keep his figure. His contract has a Santa clause."

Everyone groaned and Charlie said, "Okay, that one's not ready for prime time yet. But I'll keep trying. Laughter's the best medicine, right, Doc?"

"It definitely is good medicine," Rudy agreed.

"Where do you practice?" Charlie asked.

Rudy told him and that started a conversation going between the two men.

"And what do you do, Athena?" Catherine asked.

"I'm an executive assistant for a film agent in Los Angeles."

"Now, that sounds glam," Denise said, encouraging Athena to share more.

"It's work, like any other," Athena said, and turned her head toward Charlie. Conversation over.

Catherine and Denise exchanged looks. *Every party has a pooper, that's why we invited you.*

Catherine returned her attention to Sierra. "It's nice to be doing a trip with your sister."

Sierra's smile faltered and she stared at her drink. "She took my husband's place. He couldn't get away from work. This was supposed to be a surprise but it didn't work out."

From the expression on the woman's face Catherine wondered if more than just the trip wasn't working out. "That's too bad."

Sierra took a sip of her drink. "Oh, well. Sophie and I will have a good time."

And here came their cruise director, Elsa, to tell them all about the good time that was planned for them the next day. "I hope you all enjoyed your first dinner on the *Heart of the Rhine*," she said. This produced appreciative applause and she continued. "Chef Bruno has many more wonderful treats planned for you as we make our journey down the Rhine. And now, tomorrow, we have planned for you several shore excursions to enjoy. We know many of you will want to visit the Kinderdijk windmills. This is a unique and historic UNESCO World Heritage Site and you will be able to tour a working windmill."

"That sounds like fun," Catherine said to Denise.

"Are you ladies doing that one?" Rudy asked.

"I want to," Catherine said.

"Me, too," said Denise.

"I do, too," Rudy said, and smiled at Catherine.

"So do I," put in his daughter.

"Count me in," Charlie said.

"And we will also make a brief stop in Rotterdam where those of you who have already signed up will disembark the ship to join our Dutch cheese maker tour."

"No cutting the cheese for us, eh?" quipped Charlie, producing a collective groan from the others.

"Then tomorrow afternoon at three, right here in the lounge, Chef Bruno will show you how to make Appelflappen, a traditional Dutch treat."

"I bet they'll have free samples," said Charlie.

"I'll be there then," said Denise.

So would Catherine, if her energy level held up. "It sounds like we have a full day ahead of us tomorrow," she observed.

"I'm looking forward to it," Rudy said, and smiled at her.

His daughter didn't say anything.

"Feeling like the kid who didn't get invited to the party?" Trevor asked Sophie as the cruise director set aside her mike and the pianist began playing a jazzy medley of Christmas songs.

Sophie had been stealing a lot of glances at the chatting group in the middle of the lounge, wishing she was there. Not that Trevor March wasn't *wunderbar,* but a girl who was prone to health problems didn't need *wunderbar.* She needed a doctor. And how was Sophie supposed to make a connection with that doctor from the opposite side of the lounge?

Still, she'd thought she was being discreet. "Is it that obvious?" she asked.

"No, I'm just that observant," Trevor said. "It's one of my many good qualities."

"It sounds like you've got a lot of good qualities," she teased.

He grinned. "I do."

"What are your other good qualities?"

"I'm entertaining, generous, I can cook."

"A man who cooks, that's impressive."

"Can you?"

"Of course I can. No one makes a better French silk pie than me."

"A pretty big brag to make to a guy who owns a chocolate company."

"I'm that confident."

He nodded. "I'm impressed. Most of the women I've dated wouldn't even know what a French silk pie was, let alone how to make one. Nobody likes to cook anymore," he finished sadly.

"I do. It's one of *my* good qualities."

"I bet you've got a ton."

"Oh, I don't know," she said.

Right now being magnanimous sure wasn't one of them. She shot another glance over to where her sister, the traitor, sat with Dr. Rudy and company. He and Catherine seemed to really be hitting it off. Or maybe he was just being polite. It looked like Denise had already found someone, so that took her out of the running. Catherine was another story. She was still on her own, and frustratingly, irritatingly nice. Hard to compete with nice, especially from across the room.

Sophie suddenly felt cranky. And tired.

But Catherine had to be tired, too. Sophie was younger. She could outwait her.

"Would you like another glass of white wine?" Trevor asked.

"I'd better not," she said. "Wine always makes me sleepy."

And she had to stay awake. Had to outwait Catherine. Had…to…

The sound of someone snoring jerked Sophie awake. Who was that? Her. And here she was on the fake leather sofa with her head on Trevor March's shoulder.

She pulled away, mortified. "Oh, gosh, I'm sorry. Please tell me I didn't drool on your jacket."

"Okay, I won't," he said. "Looks like the jet lag has hit."

She glanced to where her sister and the rest of her dinner companions had been sitting. There was no one there. In fact, there were a lot of empty seats in the lounge.

"Your sister stopped by," Trevor said. "I told her I'd walk you to your room after you woke up."

"What if I hadn't woken up?"

"I have no problem spending the night in the lounge with a beautiful woman's head on my shoulder."

"Someone you don't even know." Good Lord, and here she was using him for a pillow.

"Someone I'm getting to know."

"Drooling on your jacket."

"What's a little drool between friends? Anyway, I didn't notice. I was too busy admiring how thick your eyelashes are. And real, too. You don't see that very much anymore."

"You are sure good with the flattery thing," she said, standing up. She was going to give Sierra an earful when she got back to their room.

"Another one of my fine qualities."

"You sound practically perfect."

"Oh, I am," he said, and stood up also. "Except that I'm a slob and I lose my temper in traffic and yell at people a lot."

"That could get you killed."

"Not as long as I keep my car windows rolled up. Come on, I'll walk you back to your room."

"I'm probably pretty safe walking there all by myself," she said as they left the lounge.

He looked at her, shocked. "You haven't heard of the cruise ship ghost?"

"Cruise ship ghost?"

"Oh, yeah. One of the earlier captains of this ship. He died on it. He ran it aground."

Sophie raised her eyebrows. "Can you run a ship aground in a river?"

"This guy did. He'd been drinking too much schnapps and wasn't paying attention. He knew there'd be a big scandal and he'd lose his job so he went into this very lounge, drank one last shot of schnapps and then broke the bottle and slit his wrists with it."

"Eeew."

"They say he walks the halls every night at..." Trevor checked his watch. "Eleven-thirty. Every cruise he's on the lookout for a woman."

"Lonely, huh?"

"No, he just figures he'll get more sympathy from a woman than a man and he needs someone to bandage his wrists."

"Okay, that was the stupidest ghost story I ever heard," Sophie said, shaking her head at him.

"I guess storyteller doesn't go down as one of my talents."

"And I guess I don't need an escort."

"Let me walk with you, anyway," he said.

"You're hard to say no to."

"I hope so," he said with a grin.

It didn't take them long to get to her stateroom, which was probably just as well. Trevor March was a very tempting distraction. If Sophie hadn't met Dr. Rudy first she'd have been very happy hanging out with Trevor. But she *had* met Rudy. She'd made up her mind, knew what she wanted, and she was going to make sure she got it. Or rather, him.

"Thanks for protecting me from the ghost," she said as they stood in front of her stateroom door.

"Ghost protection is one of my specialties."

"I'll remember that," she said. She brushed at the wet spot on his jacket. "And sorry about the drool."

"Anytime you need a shoulder to sleep on."

Oh, no. There would be no more of that. Before he could mention the next day's activities and try to make any plans, she unlocked her door, murmured, "Good night," and slipped into the room.

She found Sierra in a sleep tee, stretched out on the bed with her phone.

"You sexting? Want me to leave the room?"

"Right." Sierra tossed her phone aside. "I was checking Facebook."

"So you haven't heard from Mark?"

"No, and honestly, I don't expect to."

Sophie plopped onto her side of the bed. "I'm sorry, Sissy."

Sierra shrugged. "He's busy at work." Then she changed the subject. "Who was that gorgeous man you were talking to?"

"His name's Trevor March. I met him when I went up to the top deck to get some air."

"You sure got more than air."

"He's not a doctor." That said it all.

"Who cares? Just looking at him is bound to cure whatever's wrong with you. What does he do?"

"He owns Cupid's Chocolates."

"Does it get any better than that?"

"Never mind him. How come you didn't save me a seat?"

"Because you said you were sick. I figured you'd go back to the room and take a bunch of medicine and go to sleep."

"Well, I didn't," Sophie said irritably, her earlier sympathy for her sister temporarily shelved.

"Then you weren't sick?"

"I was sick. Trevor just happened to have something with him that made me feel better."

"Oh, motion sickness meds?"

"No, chocolate with ginger."

Sierra gave a snort. "Chocolate, the new cure for motion sickness."

"Everyone knows ginger helps with an upset stomach," Sohie said, frowning at her.

"And everyone knows you can't get sick on a river cruise."

"Well, I did," Sophie insisted. "I do get sick a lot, and that's why I should be with a man who's a doctor."

"Used to get sick," Sierra corrected her. "You're perfectly healthy now."

Her sister didn't get it. Things could come on you suddenly, out of the blue. One minute you could be running on the soccer field, the next you could be collapsed on the sidelines, gasping for air, your mother calling 911.

Sierra's expression softened. "Okay, so it would be great if your perfect man turned out to be a doctor. But it's not Rudy. He's way too old for you."

"He is not."

"Come on, he's Dad's age. If you slept with him it would be like having sex with your father."

Sophie scowled at her. "Thanks for sticking that image in my brain."

"It should be in your brain. Anyway, I think he's interested in Catherine."

"Thanks to my own sister not saving me a seat. All he had to talk to was Catherine."

"I think all he wanted to talk to was Catherine. Give up, Soph."

"No way. What's she got that I haven't got in better condition?"

"It's not gonna happen," Sierra predicted.

"Oh, yes, it is. I have a whole week. Men have fallen in love with me in less time than that."

"And fallen out of love in less time than that, too."

"Oh, ha ha."

Sierra yawned. "You can work on proving me wrong tomorrow. Right now I need to go to sleep."

So did Sophie. Her head was buzzing. Jet leg was about to take her down for the count. She brushed her teeth, put on her plaid flannel jammies and climbed under the covers. Moments later she was as soundly asleep as her sister.

Then came the wee hours of the morning when she dreamed herself into an emergency room. She had a terrible fever. Pneumonia? West Nile virus? Yes, that was it, because she'd just come off a cruise down the Amazon and a mosquito the size of a bird had bitten her.

"I need Dr. Nichols," she told the nurse who was taking her blood pressure. The nurse looked a lot like Elsa.

"Oh, yes, you need to get well right away, because we have such a wonderful outing planned for you tomorrow," the woman said. "One hundred and three fever. I think the doctor will want to bleed you. I'll get the leeches."

"Leeches?" Sophie whispered. "I don't want leeches. I want Dr. Nichols."

The curtain around her bed parted, and there stood, not Rudy, but Trevor March. He was wearing a stethoscope and a white lab coat over jeans. The coat hung open to reveal a beautifully sculpted bare chest.

"What seems to be the problem?" he asked.

"I'm dying. I have West Nile virus. Or maybe bubonic plague," she informed him.

"Let's listen to your heart," he said. Instead of using his stethoscope he pressed an ear to her left breast. "A rapid heartbeat." He pulled away and looked into her eyes. "Your pupils are dilated and you're flushed."

"What have I got, Doctor?"

"Nothing that can't be cured by a night with me." He pulled out two chocolate bars and said, "Take these and call me in the morning. I make house calls. Or better yet, you can make the house call." Then he kissed her on the cheek, winked at her and left her sitting on the bed, holding a chocolate bar in each hand.

The nurse returned to the room and handed her a piece of paper. It was pink and shaped like a heart.

"What's this?" she asked. "A prescription?"

"Dr. March's address," said the nurse, who suddenly looked like Athena.

"What happened to Dr. Nichols?" Sophie asked.

"He's not available. And why do you want Dr. Nichols? He's old enough to be your father."

"Um," said Sophie.

Nurse Athena glared at her, pulled out a hypodermic needle the size of a hunting knife and snarled, "Get out of here before I have to use this on you."

Sophie got out of there and the next thing she knew she was standing in front of a two-story house made entirely of chocolate. The front door opened and there in the doorway stood Trevor March. He'd changed out of his white coat and jeans and was now wearing nothing but red underwear with little candy canes on them.

"Come on in," he called. "What are you waiting for?"

She went up the front path—made of white chocolate slabs—and stepped onto the chocolate porch.

"How are you feeling now?" he asked, and slipped an arm around her.

"Not so bad," she said.

"Come on back to my bedroom. I'll make you feel even better," he said, and kissed her neck. "Here, let me take your coat. Let me take your everything."

He took his time taking and Sophie was only down to her bra and panties (red with little candy canes—they matched!)

when she awoke with her heart beating, her hair damp and her throat dry. She was sure she was flushed. Was her subconscious trying to tell her something?

She frowned. Her subconscious needed to shut up. Trevor March the chocolate man seemed like a pretty great guy. But she didn't need a great guy. She needed a doctor.

6

"HOW MUCH YOU WANT TO BET A CERTAIN DOCtor will be looking for you this morning?" Denise said to Catherine as they entered the dining room for breakfast.

"That would be nice, but really, I'm not interested," Catherine said. "I'm in no shape to be thinking about a relationship."

"Shipboard romances aren't relationships. They're a fun diversion," Denise argued. "I can tell you right now, I intend to enjoy flirting with Charlie. You should enjoy yourself, too. You never know. Sometimes those diversions can lead to something serious," she added.

"I doubt it," Catherine said.

"Who says you can't fall in love more than once in a lifetime?"

"Someone who's not sure she'll have a lifetime ahead of

her." There was a depressing thought. Her chances of surviving this were good, but sometimes that dark road beckoned and she couldn't help but go down it.

"Don't say things like that," Denise scolded. "You're going to be fine. You should live like you believe that."

"I don't know if I do," Catherine said with a sigh. "There are no guarantees."

"Okay, then," Denise said, "all the more reason to live life to the fullest right now. Will you look at this spread?" she said as they approached the breakfast buffet.

It was, indeed, a spread. Set up in the middle of the dining room, it offered every imaginable breakfast food—pastries, cheeses and cold cuts, a variety of breads, fruit, yogurt, cereals, coffee, tea, milk, juices and fruit. And an omelet station with a chef standing ready that drew Catherine like a magnet.

What would she like in her omelet?

Cheese, bacon, tomatoes, peppers and onion.

No problem.

She watched as the chef poured in premeasured egg, swirling it in the pan to make sure it reached the edges, adding ingredients, expertly folding it all and then sliding a perfect, golden-brown omelet onto Catherine's plate.

When was the last time anyone had made breakfast for her? She thought it was when the kids were in fourth and sixth grade. They'd brought her cereal on a tray for Mother's Day. Now she got a card from her daughter and chocolate-dipped strawberries delivered from her son. Would it be tacky to ask them to come over the next Mother's Day and bring her cereal in bed?

If she had a next Mother's Day.

Denise had already helped herself to some yogurt and fruit

and scoped out a table for them. A waiter showed up with coffee just as Catherine sat down, asking if they'd like some.

"Yes, please," she said to him. "It's such a luxury to have someone wait on you," she told Denise. "I think I could get used to being pampered."

"I think you should. When was the last time that happened?"

Hard to remember. Catherine was always the one taking care of others—starting with when she was a teenager taking on cooking for her two younger brothers and her father after her mother died. She'd been seventeen. After two years of college, she'd married, and in another few years she was taking care of her own family. Eventually, her father had moved in with them and she took care of him before he died. Then it had been Bill's parents who needed help. It seemed she'd always been watching over someone. But now, who was watching over her?

Her friends, she reminded herself. Thank God for them.

"Feel free to join us," Denise offered as Rudy approached, his daughter trailing him like a shadow. He held a plate with cold cuts, cheese and a crusty roll in one hand and a small glass container of yogurt in the other.

Athena was carrying only a bowl with hot cereal. Like Denise, not a big eater, which explained the fact that she was equally as svelte. Catherine looked down at her own breakfast. In addition to her omelet she'd gotten a pastry, yogurt, some cheese and cold cuts. Oink.

Well, it was a cruise. And hadn't Denise just advised her to live life to the fullest?

"This is quite the breakfast, isn't it?" Rudy said to Catherine as he slipped into the seat on the other side of her.

She'd just stuffed a chunk of pastry in her mouth so all

she could do was chew and nod. What a sparkling conversationalist.

"We were just saying how nice it is to be waited on," Denise said, speaking for both of them. "It's a real treat for Catherine, who's always doing for everyone but herself," she added, singing Catherine's praises like a true best friend.

Rudy smiled at Catherine. "Everyone deserves to be waited on once in a while."

"How did you sleep?" Denise asked him.

"Great," he said. "And you?"

"I was out like a light," Denise said. "So were you," she told Catherine.

"I was tired," Catherine confessed.

"Adjusting to the time difference can be tough," said Rudy.

"Yes, but you know what they say about that," Denise said. "When the going gets tough…"

He nodded. "The tough get going."

"No, the other 'you know what they say'—the tough go shopping. I'm going to do that when we hit Cologne. I read it's got one of the world's biggest Christmas markets."

"We'll have to check that out, won't we?" Rudy said to his daughter. "Some blown glass, perhaps? Or some Christmas decorations for your tree."

"I want to buy a cuckoo clock when we get to the Black Forest," said Denise.

"Me, too," said Catherine. "I always wanted a cuckoo clock." Maybe she'd have to get herself one. Merry Christmas to her from her. "But that's jumping pretty far ahead. I think I'll just concentrate on enjoying today." To the fullest, like Denise advised. If she concentrated hard enough on today, maybe she could dodge the shadow of an uncertain tomorrow.

"I'm sure we will," Rudy said, and the smile he gave her made her heart do the jingle bell rock.

Shipboard romance, what would that be like? Outside of a movie or a book she hadn't enjoyed much romance since the night Bill proposed.

They'd left Seattle and driven out into the country, far from city lights where they could find clear skies and stargaze. He'd taken her to a park on the edge of a lake, laid out a blanket and produced a bottle of champagne and two plastic cups. Then he'd told her she was the most important thing in his world and promised to love her for the rest of his life.

He'd kept his promise. And if his idea of love was mowing the lawn and keeping her car running, so what? He'd never remembered their anniversary (she'd always been the one to make the plans) but he'd never forgotten her birthday. The gifts weren't wildly romantic—a Crock-Pot, then, when she hadn't been overly thrilled with his practical present, cash. Later on, when they got popular, it was gift cards. But they always came with a birthday card signed, *Love, Bill*. It would have been nice if he'd brought her flowers or chocolates once in a while, but then she'd never asked. So whose fault was it, then, that she never got any?

Really, most men weren't romantic. Not like in books and movies. Anyway, there was more to life than romance. Like someone making you an omelet, getting to choose from a variety of delicious pastries, cruising on a beautiful ship and watching the world go by. And getting to see a windmill close-up.

"I'm looking forward to seeing the windmills," she said. "I always thought it would be fun to go in one. I never thought I'd get to, though."

"Yeah, but who's going to blow on the paddles and make them turn?" joked Charlie, who'd stopped by the table to visit.

Catherine looked out the window. "It looks like there's a bit of a breeze now."

"It'll be a cold one," Charlie predicted. "Better stick close to me," he said to Denise. "Body warmth and all that," he added, waggling his eyebrows at her, and she gave him a flirty grin in return.

Good, thought Athena, watching Denise and Charlie. One down, one to go. Technically speaking, two to go, if you counted Sophie. At this point, though, Athena wasn't. Daddy wasn't showing any interest in her.

Catherine, though…Athena had seen the way he looked at her—as if they were on a Valentine's Day dinner date. And Catherine was eating it up, all shy smiles and downward glances.

And all that talk of shopping! If he started spending money it would be like hanging a sign around his neck that said Sugar Daddy. She hoped she could convince him to keep his wallet out of sight.

Breakfast over, everyone dispersed to their rooms to brush teeth and fetch jackets. "I sure do like Catherine and Denise," Daddy said as they made their way to their staterooms. "Don't you?"

Okay, this had to be handled with finesse. She couldn't diss the women or he'd get defensive, demanding to know what she thought was wrong with them? Not that he cared what she thought of Denise. Denise was the smoke screen.

"They seem nice," she said cautiously.

"Catherine reminds me a little of your mother."

Catherine wasn't anything like Athena's mother. Athena's

mother had been slender and well-dressed. Vivacious. Classy. Catherine was…unremarkable.

"How does she remind you of Mom?" Athena asked.

"It's her smile. You can tell she's kindhearted."

"Just from her smile?"

"Doesn't she strike you as kindhearted?" Daddy asked.

"I don't know her well enough." *And neither do you.*

People did that all the time, read into other people the kind of character they wanted to see. Athena had done it when she got married.

So had her father on his second time around.

"Daddy, promise me you won't rush into anything," she pleaded.

He frowned at her. "Athena."

It was the beginning of a scold, she could tell. "I don't want to see you get hurt."

"I don't want to see me get hurt, either." He put an arm around her and hugged her. "Don't worry, honey. I learned my lesson."

Athena wasn't so sure. If you asked her, her father needed a tutor.

Sophie had overslept and Sierra had been moping around the room, moving slowly. As a result they got to the dining room at the tail end of breakfast and there was no sign of their new friends. Crudballs.

"We'll see them when the tour starts," Sierra said with a shrug, and headed for the buffet.

Sophie frowned. She was willing to bet Catherine and Denise had gotten to the dining room in plenty of time to see Dr. Rudy and his daughter. They'd probably bonded over pastries. She found a plate and helped herself to a Danish. No guilt. It was only one and this was a cruise, after all.

Surprisingly, her sister, who normally avoided carbs, took one, too. Then she grabbed a doughnut, as well.

"Pastry?" Sophie asked, surprised.

"Hey, it's a cruise, and I'm eating for two—me and Mark." Sierra frowned and took a big bite out of her Danish.

"I'm sure you'll hear from him today," Sophie said as they made their way toward a table. "He probably hasn't figured out the time difference."

They sat down at the table and Sierra stared at her plate. "I should have stayed home."

"No, Mark should have come," Sophie said firmly.

"If I'd known he wouldn't have been able to get away, I'd never have booked this. I still don't get it. I thought he could take the time off. In fact, I'm sure I remember him saying back in October that he had some days he needed to take off before the end of the year or he'd lose them."

Even though Mark had tried to explain his job to Sophie once, she still didn't really know what he did. He was some kind of something that had to do with claims at an insurance company. Was he so important he couldn't take some time away? Surely his boss could have let him take a week's vacation, especially after assuring Sierra it would be no problem.

"Maybe you were right, maybe you guys do need some time apart," Sophie offered, echoing her sister's weak excuse when she'd first called Sophie with the news Mark wasn't going.

"I just need to hear from him." Sierra took a vicious bite of her pastry. Then she shoved aside her plate and stood. "I'm going to the room. I'll see you there."

She was probably off to text Mark. For the third time since they'd boarded the ship. Well, there was the time difference.

Except the night before would have meant morning for him. Even accounting for meetings or whatever, he should have had time for a one-sentence reply. The fact that he hadn't said a lot. Poor Sierra. Hopefully, she and Mark would be able to resolve their issues.

Of course they would. This was only a bump in the road. Meanwhile, though, Sophie was going to do her best to distract her sister from that bump and make sure she enjoyed the German scenery.

She was seated by herself at the table, finishing her coffee, when the German class walked past, a giant amoeba with twenty-four legs. Except amoebas didn't have legs. They were just blobs. And there with the…whatever…was Trevor March's brother. She didn't see any sign of Trevor, though. Maybe he'd overslept, too.

Just as well. Sophie needed to concentrate on Dr. Rudy.

She lingered over her coffee another twenty minutes, wanting to give her sister some alone time, then went to the room to get ready for the morning tour. She found Sierra sitting on the edge of the bed, staring out their French balcony window.

"I guess we should start getting ready," Sophie said. "The tour starts in half an hour."

"You go. I think I'll stay on the ship and read."

"You paid a lot of money for this," Sophie reminded her. "You should at least try and enjoy some of it."

"I am," Sierra insisted.

"How?"

"I'm eating."

Yeah, pastry. "Which means you've got some calories to burn. And what better way to burn them than looking at old windmills." Sierra didn't say anything, so Sophie went into sales pitch mode. "That is a once in a lifetime experience, something you might never get to do again." Still no reply. "Mom will want to see pictures of us having fun together."

"Send her a picture of you having fun. She'll be fine with that."

"It will be interesting," Sophie promised. "And you can just as easily wait for a text walking around sightseeing as you can sitting in the room. Anyway, there's nothing you can do about Mark. He's in Washington and you're here. Whatever is going to happen is going to happen."

Wrong thing to say. Sierra looked like she was going to cry.

Sophie rushed on. "But you don't know what that is, so why spoil something you paid for and were looking forward to by worrying?"

"I can't help it," Sierra said miserably.

"Don't let Mark be the Grinch and steal this trip from you. You've been excited about it for months."

"I was excited about doing it with him." Sierra's cheeks turned pink. "Sorry, Soph. You know what I mean."

"I do. And I'm sorry he's not here. But he wanted you to go have fun so let's try to have some fun. Let's make some nice memories, you and me. What do you say?"

Sierra pursed her lips and sighed. "I say you're right. Let's go look at windmills."

A large group of people had opted for touring the windmills and were gathered around a woman in dark slacks and a bright red windbreaker, huddled inside their own jackets and trying to ignore the drizzle and wind. Sophie caught sight of Dr. Rudy and his daughter, who were standing with Denise and Catherine and the same short guy she'd seen sitting with them the night before. Catherine was wearing jeans, tennis shoes and a bright red coat with a hood that made her easy to spot while her friend Denise was looking stylish in a black raincoat, cinched tightly to show off her skinny waist, worn over leopard-print leggings and knee-high boots. When Sophie was old she wanted to be Denise.

"Welcome to Kinderdijk," their tour guide said to everyone. "We are the largest concentration of old windmills in the Netherlands. We are below sea level so we have claimed this land from the sea. To do that you must build a dike around the water. Then the water is pumped out, leaving us land to work. This land is called a polder."

"Interesting," Sierra murmured.

Sophie didn't care about the whys and hows. She just wanted to see inside a windmill.

"You may be wondering why this name," said their tour guide. "I will tell you. This means 'children dike.' And that is because of the baby that was found back in 1421. During the Saint Elizabeth's flood the Grote Hollandse Waard flooded," she continued with a sweep of her hand. "When the storm subsided, a villager went to the dike between these two areas to see what could be salvaged and in the distance he saw a wooden cradle floating on the water. As he came nearer he saw a cat was on it, trying to keep its balance by jumping back and forth. This was making the cradle rock. When he got closer he saw there was a baby inside. The cat had kept it safe. That story has been published in English as *The Cat and the Cradle.* Now, come with me and I will show you our windmills."

The group fell in line, like so many ducklings. There were sure a lot of them. "Let's move closer," Sophie said to her sister, then took Sierra's hand and swam up toward the front of the line in the hopes of latching on to the good doctor.

"Hi, everyone," she said brightly to the group. "Did you all sleep well last night?"

"Like a rock," said Denise.

The man next to her said, "Me, too. Call me Rocky."

"Rocky," Sophie repeated.

"Actually, my name's Charlie," he said. "I have a sick obsession with word play. And you, oh flower of youth, are…?"

"Sophie," she said with a smile. "And this is my sister, Sierra," she added, pulling Sierra closer.

"Names as lovely as the women who bear them," Charlie said. He reminded Sophie a little of one of her uncles, good-natured and full of flattery. Wouldn't he like to get together with Catherine?

"Are you feeling better?" Catherine asked her.

She wished it had been Dr. Rudy asking, but she smiled and said that she was. "The fresh air did the trick. Thanks to your advice," she said to him.

"Good," he said. "It's no fun to be sick when you're traveling."

"No, it isn't. And I do want to travel more," Sophie said. "You like to travel, don't you, Doctor?"

"Please call me Rudy," he said. A good beginning.

"Rudy," she said, and smiled at him.

"Yes, I do. You always meet the nicest people," he added, and smiled. At Catherine.

Athena frowned. So did Sophie. This was going to be an uphill battle.

Following their tour guide, they strolled along a paved walk, picturesque with plots of green and ancient windmills laid out between canals, reeds of some sort clinging to the banks. "I grew up swimming in this canal," said their tour guide. "In winter we skated on it."

"Like Hans Brinker," murmured Catherine.

"Ah, yes," said Rudy.

Who the heck was Hans Brinker?

"Here in Kinderdijk the Lek and Noord rivers meet," their guide continued. "Our battle with the sea became more and more of a problem as time went on, and in the thirteenth century canals were dug to get rid of the excess water. After a few centuries a new way was thought of to keep the polders dry. Our fathers decided to build a series of windmills to pump water into a reservoir. The water could be let out into the river through locks whenever the river level was low enough. This way we kept our land for farming. We will be going into a windmill now so you can see how the families lived."

Finally. "Going inside a windmill," Sophie said eagerly to her sister. "How many people ever get to say they did that?"

Sierra smiled. This was a genuine, happy one, and Sophie hoped she'd see more of those as the trip went on.

The windmill looked massive until you got inside it. "The family who lived in this had thirteen children," said their tour guide.

"Childbirth thirteen times?" Sophie said weakly. "That poor woman."

"Because of the high fatality rate of children, a miller needed a large family to make sure there would be enough labor to work the mill and the surrounding farms," the guide continued.

"Think of having fifteen people squished together inside this living space," Sierra said, looking around.

It was, indeed, small, and everything was set up around the giant wheel at the center that turned the windmill blades. The ground floor had a kitchen of sorts with a small, white enamel stove. Shelves held pots and bowls. A tiny bed that looked more like a train berth was tucked into a cupboard on one wall, with a curtain hung for privacy. A small table sat by a window and it held an old-fashioned sewing machine. Sophie wondered how people managed to live together in such a small space as she walked around with the rest of the tour group.

"I feel like a sardine looking for a place to lie down in the can," she said to her sister.

"I think I'd get claustrophobia," said Sierra.

Sophie eyed the steep stairs with their narrow treads that led to the next level. "I wonder if those fatalities she mentioned were from kids falling down the stairs."

More people were coming in and Sophie caught sight of a couple of the college students. The next wave. Was Trevor March with them? Not that it mattered.

She heard Rudy's laugh coming down from the next level up and turned to see the newcomer, Charlie, climbing upstairs, right behind Denise. The good doctor and Catherine had to already be up there. She who hesitated was lost. Sophie hurried to join them.

"You're wasting your time," her sister said behind her.

"I'm just going up to see what the next level looks like."

A frail-looking grandma type wearing a long coat and snow boots was coming down the stairs as Sophie was about to go up, so Sophie waited. The woman was almost down when she lost her footing. Sophie saw it and rushed to steady her.

"Thank you," the woman said, looking at her like she was a superhero. "I'd have hated to fall and break something, especially at the beginning of my cruise."

"You sure would," Sophie said in agreement as she helped the woman down. "Enjoy the rest of the cruise," she said in farewell, and hurried up the stairs to the next level, where she found Rudy and company.

It looked as cramped as the ground-floor level, with more beds stuffed into cupboards.

"Can you imagine living such a simple life?" Catherine said to Sophie as she came to stand next to her.

She would have stood on the other side of Rudy, but his daughter was firmly in place there.

"A little too simple for me," Sophie said. Where were the closets? Where did people put their clothes? "And I thought my apartment was small. Yikes."

"Well, a person doesn't need a lot to be happy," Catherine said.

"Do you really believe that?" Athena asked, sounding almost skeptical.

"Yes, I do. It's not about what you have but who you're with."

Sierra had joined them in time to hear that and the smile she'd been wearing vanished like a leaf on the wind. If only Mark would check in. Then maybe her sister could enjoy herself.

"I'll second that," Charlie said, grinning at Denise. "Who you're with makes all the difference."

"Yes, it does," Sophie said to Sierra. "Come on, let's take a selfie for Mom."

Sierra went along with the picture taking, then eventually followed Sophie to the top level of the windmill. Here they could see the wheel that turned the blades close-up. It was an enormous, impressive thing, moving slowly, a reminder that once upon a time life moved at a slower pace.

Sophie was disappointed that no one from their party had joined her other than her sister.

"Catherine's nervous about the stairs," Sierra reported. "She decided she'd gone far enough."

"She missed out," Sophie said. "This is the most impressive part of the windmill."

But when it came time to go back down she found herself wishing she hadn't climbed to the top level. Those stairs were sooo steep, and the treads way too narrow. A person could fall, break a leg. Or a back.

"Why did they have to make these so steep?" she said to her sister, who was going down in front of her. "They're a regular accident trap."

"Don't worry, I'll cushion your fall."

"Who's gonna cushion yours?" Sophie retorted.

She made it to the last set of stairs just fine, though. Okay, no problemo. Sierra was already on the ground level.

And there went Rudy and Catherine out the door. How was it they always managed to get so far ahead of her? Sophie picked up her pace.

And missed a step.

Suddenly it was anything but quiet inside the windmill.

7

DOWN THE STAIRS SOPHIE WENT, LIKE A PUPPET cut loose from its strings. Thump, thump, screech, screech. She sent two women scuttling for safety before she hit the floor and bounced over onto her side. There she lay like a landed fish with a sprained fin. A sea of concerned faces suddenly loomed over her—the two women who'd dodged a collision, the tour guide, her sister, several of the German students.

This was embarrassing. And painful. Her ankle, which she'd twisted on the way down, was screaming at her. *Look what you did to me!* Had she broken it? What if she'd broken it? Would she have to go to a hospital? Where was Dr. Rudy when you needed him?

"Are you all right?" asked Sierra.

"Can you move?" the tour guide asked, probably worried about lawsuits.

"Let me see," said a male voice. It wasn't Rudy's. Instead, here was Trevor March, pushing through the crowd and bending next to her. "Where does it hurt?"

"My ankle," she whimpered. "I think I broke it."

"Maybe not." He unzipped her ankle boot and removed it and started feeling around.

"Ow!" she protested.

"I bet she broke it," said a brown-haired girl, one of the students. She looked dispassionately at Sophie, as if studying an interesting specimen. "She won't be able to do anything now."

Trevor shook his head. "I don't think anything's broken," he said to Sophie.

She frowned at him. "How can you know?"

"I took a first aid course in college. Here, people," he said, "let's give her some room."

Several people took a step back. With the show over, the college kids drifted away, all except for the one girl, who was taking a rather ghoulish interest in Sophie's injury.

"Let's see if you can stand up." Trevor took one of Sophie's hands and pulled her to her feet.

She winced at the thought of him pulling up her dead weight. It probably felt like pulling up a baby elephant.

"I don't think you should put any weight on that foot," he said, handing her back her boot. Then, before she could protest, he scooped her up into his arms.

"She can probably walk just fine," said the girl, contradicting herself.

"You can't carry me all the way back to the ship," Sophie protested. "I can hop back. My sister will help me."

"It's a long way to hop," he said, and started for the door. "Go ahead, put your arms around my neck."

She did need to hang on so she did. And really, it was a long way to hop. But darn, she felt so stupid. Where was Dr. Rudy? She needed a diagnosis.

"I'll go find Rudy," Sierra said, as if reading her mind.

Trevor didn't wait. He started off down the path toward where the ship was docked.

"You're going to get a hernia," the girl called after him.

"She's right," Sophie fretted.

"Don't listen to Harriet. What does she know?"

"Everybody knows you can get hernias from lifting heavy things."

"You're not heavy, so don't worry about it."

"I'm sorry you're having to carry me all this way," Sophie said. Although it didn't seem to be fazing him. The man wasn't even winded.

"I'm not," he replied, and smiled.

He had an awfully nice smile. She caught a whiff of his aftershave, something satisfyingly spicy. She could feel the hardness of his chest against her. Okay, maybe she wasn't so sorry, either.

If only she hadn't made such a public spectacle of herself.

"That was so embarrassing." She would now be pointed out on the ship as the klutz who fell down the stairs in the mill.

"Those stairs were tricky. I bet you're not the first person who's fallen on them."

"I wish that made me feel better."

"I've got something in my room that will make you feel better."

"Ice?"

"I can get that, too," he said.

They were met with plenty of concerned staff as they came up the gangplank and someone was dispatched immediately to fetch ice for Sophie's ankle, while another staff member put in a call for the doctor in port to come to the ship. Yet another staff member accompanied Trevor and Sophie down the hall, then used Sophie's key card and opened the door so Trevor could take her into the room. He barely had her settled before a steward appeared with ice in a plastic bag wrapped in a towel, along with reassurances that the doctor had been summoned.

Trevor slipped pillows under her foot and then laid the ice on it. "You need to elevate it. Do you have any ibuprofen?"

Of course she did because you never knew. "There's a bottle in the bathroom."

He nodded, found the bottle and shook out a pill, then brought it to her, along with a glass of water.

"I don't do this all the time," she said.

"What, climb around on steep stairs in windmills?"

"Fall." The little old lady she'd helped had been a warning from the travel fairies. Too bad she hadn't paid attention to that warning and watched where she was going.

"It happens," he said just as Sierra arrived with Rudy, and Catherine, Athena close behind.

Even Denise and Charlie had come, and squeezed in the room behind the others. Standing all clumped together they looked like carolers getting ready to serenade her. Instead of carols, they offered commiseration.

"You poor kid," Denise said.

"I'm so sorry," Catherine added.

This was seriously embarrassing. "Thank you," Sophie murmured. "I feel like an idiot." This was why she needed to marry a doctor. Things happened. To her. A lot.

"It's always the pride that hurts the worst," Denise said.

That was for sure.

"Those stairs were treacherous," Catherine said.

Athena said nothing. Why was she there, anyway?

"Let's see what we have here," Rudy said. He sat down on the bed and examined Sophie's wounded ankle. "Not too much swelling. No deformity. Nothing appears to be broken, but let's keep an eye on it. For the meantime, keep on doing what you're doing, Sophie—ice and elevate. Do you have some ibuprofen?"

"Already gave her one," said Trevor, and Rudy nodded his approval.

The shore doctor finally arrived, along with Elsa the cruise director, who was looking concerned. He, too, examined the foot and came to the same conclusion. "Only a mild sprain," the doctor assured Sophie.

Mild? It didn't feel mild.

"You don't have much swelling," he continued. "I am sure you'll be fine in a few days."

"But what if I'm not?" she fretted.

"Don't worry," Elsa said to her. "We have doctors in every port, and if you need something done we will make sure to get you to a hospital."

"Hospital?" Sophie echoed weakly.

"In case they need to cut off your foot," Trevor teased, then slipped out of the room before she could inform him that he was not funny.

"I'm sure you'll be fine," Rudy said, patting her shoulder. "Stay off your foot the rest of the day. Ice every couple of hours for twenty minutes, no longer. Keep taking the ibuprofen." Another pat on the arm and then he was off the bed, and saying to the others, "Let's let her get some rest, shall we?"

Everyone trooped out of the room, and Sophie noticed as

Rudy left he put a guiding hand to Catherine's back. Great. Sophie was down for the rest of the day and Catherine had Rudy all to herself.

The other doctor left her with a bandage to wrap her ankle once she was up and around and then he, too, was gone, leaving her and her sister alone in the room.

"I'm glad it's only a sprain," Sierra said, perching on the other side of the bed.

Sophie scowled. "Only a sprain? I'm stuck here and missing out on everything."

There was a knock on the door and Sierra went to answer it. Sophie heard Trevor's voice.

"Brought something for the patient," he said.

"She could use some sweetening up," said Sierra the sympathetic.

She ushered Trevor back into the room. "Vitamin C," he said to Sophie, and held out a chocolate bar. "Dark chocolate, nuts, Rainier cherries."

"Wow," breathed Sierra.

He handed Sophie hers, then reached into his coat pocket and brought one out for Sierra, too.

"Thanks," she said, sounding like he'd just offered her gold. Almost as good, that was for sure.

"That's really sweet of you," Sophie said to him. "Thanks. And thanks for carrying me back. I hope you didn't get a hernia."

"Nah. I'm buff."

Yes, he was.

"I guess you're down for the count, huh?" he said to her.

She sighed. "Yes. What a poopy way to spend my first day of the cruise."

He reached into another pocket and produced a deck of playing cards. "You girls play cards?"

"As a matter of fact, we do," Sophie said.

"Gin rummy?" he asked.

"You guys go ahead and play. I'll see if I can find some food," Sierra offered, and slipped out of the room.

The ice was working. The painkiller would be soon, as well. She suddenly didn't feel quite so bad. "Sounds good," she said, unwrapping her candy bar. So did the prospect of playing cards with Trevor.

"Shall we enjoy a light lunch in the lounge?" Rudy suggested as the group made their way back down the hall.

"Yes, let's. I'm ready to relax," Catherine said, and the others fell in with them.

They'd just made their way to the casual dining area when she spotted Sierra coming toward them. "Did you get your sister all settled?" Catherine asked her.

"Yes, Trevor's with her and they're about to start a card game. I'm going to bring them some food a little later."

"Maybe you'd like to join us for lunch," Catherine offered.

"That would be nice actually. I think right now I'd be a third wheel back in our room."

"It's a shame your husband couldn't join you," Catherine said as they got into the food line. "It's nice to be able to make these memories together." Sierra's face dropped. Oh, dear. Clearly that was a sore subject. "My husband and I had talked about taking a cruise after he retired," she hurried on, rushing past the awkward moment.

"You didn't get to?" Sierra prompted.

Catherine shook her head. "He died before we could." She sighed. "I'm afraid we never did much of anything exciting.

We were too busy when the kids were younger. You know, work, sporting events, school projects. Even after they moved out there was always something—caring for our aging parents, a surgery or two." She shrugged. "It seemed like time for us always got put on the back burner. We'd just gotten passports and were starting to make plans when he died."

"That's awful," Sierra said.

"It was," Catherine said. "I was looking forward to doing things together."

"So were my wife and I," put in Rudy.

Catherine had been so busy talking with Sierra she'd momentarily forgotten he was next to her, hearing all about her less than stellar life. She could feel a warmth stealing over her face.

"How did your wife die?" Sierra asked. "If you don't mind my asking."

"I don't. Melanoma. I wish I'd caught it. She was a California girl, spent lots of time in the sun. I'd sent her to a dermatologist for regular skin checks, but then one year..." He shook his head. "By the time we caught it, it was too late."

Now his daughter jumped into the conversation. "You can't blame yourself, Daddy. You were a wonderful husband. My mother meant everything to him."

"Lucky her," Sierra said wistfully. Then, to Rudy, "I hope you'll find someone else wonderful one day."

Athena didn't look happy at the idea of that. "I think Daddy knows there'll never be anyone like my mother."

She was looking at Catherine when she said it. It was hard not to take the hint.

That was okay, though. Catherine wasn't looking. But if she was, Rudy would be perfect.

They got their food and settled in the little dining area at the bow of the ship. Rudy managed to position himself and Catherine a few seats away from Athena.

"My daughter means well," he said to Catherine in a low voice.

"Of course she does. She's a good daughter." Catherine wondered if her own daughter would look out for her as scrupulously.

He shook his head, looked a little embarrassed. "Sometimes she thinks she's my mother."

"I think it's sweet that she's watching out for you."

"I guess I can't blame her. She's afraid I'll do something stupid. But I've got to say, booking this cruise was one of my smarter ideas. It sure beats sitting home, looking at four walls and being lonely."

"Yes, it does," Catherine agreed. Bill may not have been the most perfect man in the world but he'd been her man. She missed eating dinner in front of the TV together, watching a mystery or lying side by side in bed at night, each of them with a book. Missed those good-night kisses. Missed having someone in the house with her. Sometimes it felt like she was rattling around in a giant mausoleum.

"I don't think anyone should have to be alone if they don't want to be," Rudy said emphatically.

"I agree," Catherine said, then saw the hopeful expression on his face. "But sometimes circumstances prevent you from doing what you really want."

He shook his head. "I don't buy that."

He would if he knew her circumstances.

"You know, I'm feeling a little tired," she said. "I think I'll go to my room and rest."

He looked confused, probably wondering if what he'd said was chasing her away.

"I need to charge my batteries," she added.

"Of course," he said. She got up and he, too, stood, like a gentleman. "I hope I'll see you later."

"I'm sure you will." It was a small ship. They, of course, would see each other. What if they continued to see each other, spent more time together? What could come of that?

Nothing, most likely. He'd already lost a wife to cancer, had suffered right alongside her. Catherine doubted he'd want to endure that kind of battle again with another woman. She shouldn't encourage him any more.

It was awfully hard to be noble when you were with a man who was such good company. Catherine hadn't felt this happy in a year and a half.

She went to the room, stretched out on her bed and tried not to waste time imagining how pleasant life would be if she was stretched out in a bed every night with Rudy Nichols next to her. She failed.

Sophie Miles was more intoxicating than fine whiskey, and carrying her to the cruise ship had been a sweeter treat than any chocolate concoction Trevor could create.

Sierra had brought them rolls and cold cuts from the buffet, then disappeared again, and they'd sat there munching and playing progressive gin rummy for hours, though he was finding it hard to concentrate on what card was wild. Her hair kept falling in front of her face, and he wanted so badly to tuck it behind her ear for her. And that smile was irresistible.

He watched as she tapped her lips with a finger while she inspected her card hand. How soon before she'd let him kiss her?

Good Lord, he had it bad. But who wouldn't? She was pretty and sweet and her laugh was like champagne bubbles.

She rearranged her cards, grinned and then laid them down. "I'm out," she chortled, discarding.

He frowned and looked at the mess in his hand. "You're killing me."

"I'm sorry," she said, not the least repentant.

"Yeah, I can tell." He finished his play, then tallied up the points she'd caught him with and groaned. "You caught me with fifty points, for crying out loud. Where'd you learn to play cards like this?"

"It's a gift." She picked up the piece of cruise line stationery and added fifty more points to his column.

"I should take you to Vegas."

He could picture them in Las Vegas, eating at one of those high-end restaurants, watching the fountain show at the Bellagio. Staying at the Bellagio. Playing craps in the casino, her blowing on the dice for luck with those kissable lips.

"I've never been to Vegas," she said.

"Me, neither. Let's go and I'll stake you at the poker table."

She cocked an eyebrow. "Yeah? Are you a gambler?"

"Total high roller. I play poker with my brother and a couple friends once a month for some pretty high stakes. Quarters."

She snickered. "You *are* a high roller."

"I know, right? I guess when it comes down to it I don't like to risk losing my hard-earned money."

"Me, neither," she said, and began shuffling the deck. "Except wasn't starting your own business a gamble?"

"In a way I guess it was. But I'd done my research, worked hard. I felt like it was a pretty sure thing. You started your own business, too, so it looks like you did some gambling."

"Not really," she said. "I didn't have to invest a lot of money in my business other than business cards. And I was still working at a paying job."

"Oh, yeah? What did you do?"

"I was a waitress. It was good money. I worked nights and made pretty good tips. It got me through two years of community college. But all that being on my feet. I didn't want my arches to fall."

She'd been worried about falling arches?

She must have read his expression because she frowned and said, "You have to take care of yourself."

There was that. "And, might I say, after seeing your foot, that you're doing a very good job keeping those arches in tip-top shape?"

"Now you're making fun of me," she said, shaking her head at him.

He half smiled. "Maybe just a little."

"Anyway, I was able to make my business a success. I get to work with some really nice people and I get to shop to my heart's content without spending any of my savings. I'd say that makes what I do an ideal job. I enjoy going to work each day. I bet you feel the same way about what you do," she added.

"You're right, I do. Hard to balance work and life sometimes, though."

"But there's more to life than work," she said.

Which was a perfect lead-in for the question he wanted to ask. "Like fun, friends…boyfriends. Why aren't you on this cruise with a boyfriend?"

"I could ask you the same question," she said.

"I like girls."

"So where's yours?" She focused on shuffling the cards.

"Before this cruise I'd have said I haven't found her yet."

Her cheeks turned pink and she kept her eyes on the cards

as she dealt them. "Okay, up to thirteen and kings are wild. This is your last chance."

"I hope not."

That sent the blush all the way down her neck. He knew she was attracted to him. He could feel the electricity thrumming between them.

But he could also tell she wasn't ready to plug into it yet. Okay, he could be patient.

Being patient sucked, he decided later as he wrapped her ankle so they could go to the lounge before dinner. He wanted Sophie Miles, and he was beginning to suspect that he might even want her for keeps.

8

BY SUNDAY EVENING SOPHIE'S ANKLE WAS FEELing better and, with it wrapped, she was sure she could manage to walk to the lounge after dinner for the promised evening music trivia game. By the time she'd taken more ibuprofen and limped into the lounge, leaning on Trevor's arm, Sierra following behind, the seats around Rudy were taken. His daughter was on one side and Catherine sat on the other. Denise was there with her friend Charlie and another man. Even the neighboring seats were occupied by two couples. Denise saw them and waved.

Frustrating. Was the universe trying to tell Sophie something? They found three seats around a coffee table and Trevor was quick to prop her foot on the table with a sofa pillow under it. He was sweet and considerate. Why, oh, why couldn't he have been a doctor? That would have made him perfect.

There was one seat free in their conversation area, and the man with glasses who'd been shepherding the students around slid in and took it. He looked a lot like Trevor.

No wonder. "This is my brother, Kurt," Trevor said, and introduced Sophie and Sierra. "You okay to leave the children for a while?" he asked Kurt.

"Yep. They're all stuffed from dinner and happy."

Kurt looked over to where the students sat in two groups, spread along the windows on the opposite side of the lounge. Sophie followed his gaze and saw that the girl who'd been on hand to make unwanted comments when she'd fallen was looking in their direction and frowning. Prime seats in the lounge were, obviously, hard to find.

"Harriet was asking where you were at dinner," Kurt said to his brother.

Trevor kept his gaze averted from the other side of the lounge. "That's nice."

"You're breaking her heart," Kurt teased.

"For five minutes. She'll recover."

Kurt chuckled. Then he said to the sisters, "So, ladies, tell me a little about yourselves."

"Not much to tell," Sierra said. "We're from Seattle."

"Love Seattle, especially Fremont," said Kurt. "The troll under the Aurora Bridge is the best."

"Portland's pretty cool, too, though," put in Trevor. "We've got Voodoo Doughnut and Powell's, best bookstore in the country."

"We've been to Powell's," Sophie told him. "It is incredible. I've never been to Voodoo Doughnut, though."

"Come down and I'll take you," Trevor promised.

"Lots of stuff to do in Portland," Kurt said. "I even hear there's a chocolate company there you can tour. What the heck's the name of that place?" He grinned at Trevor. It was plain to see he was proud of his brother's accomplishment.

"I bet we can guess," Sophie said, and held up the latest chocolate offering from Trevor.

"Is he bribing you to hang out with him?" joked Kurt.

"No bribes necessary," Sophie said. Trevor was ridiculously easy to like.

Elsa had a mike in hand now and was filling them in on the next day's activities. "Tomorrow we will be offering you all shore excursions to Cologne, where you will find many lovely Christmas markets to shop in. We offer you an optional excursion that will take you to the top of Cologne's astonishing cathedral with a local guide. Or you may wish to join the buses that will give you a tour of the city. You may visit the Old Town with all its attractions. Then, later tomorrow afternoon, we will have a guest lecturer here in the lounge who will discuss the daily life of a modern German citizen and share with you information about the culture. Of course, before you return, I most highly recommend you visit the market at the Dom, which is in front of the cathedral. You will certainly find some lovely Christmas gifts there, and I know you will want to sample some Glühwein, which is our favorite drink this time of year when we are meeting friends and shopping. It is a spiced hot wine and it is delicious."

Sophie sighed. "It sounds so fun. I hope I'll be able to walk by tomorrow."

"You probably shouldn't risk it," said Sierra.

Sierra was always trying to talk Sophie out of her various illnesses, so seeing that even her sister was taking this injury seriously felt somehow vindicating. But it was also disheartening. Sophie didn't want to miss out on all the Christmas market fun.

"Well," Trevor said thoughtfully, "we're getting bused there so you'll be off your feet for part of the time."

"Maybe we can find some crutches somewhere," said Sierra.

"Or you can lean on me," Trevor offered. "We could always shop a little and then find a place to sit and eat until the next bus back to the ship arrives. Ice up as soon as you get back on board."

"I like that idea," Sophie said. "Except if you want to go do stuff don't let me hold you back."

"I want to do stuff," he said. "With you."

Trevor March was the kind of man you wanted to do things with. And there'd sure been nothing wrong with his bedside manner. She had to be practical, though.

So far that wasn't exactly working out. Honestly, life shouldn't be so complicated.

"And now," Elsa said, "it is time for our trivia contest. We have some questions for you, and Jacques will be helping us out at the piano. So form your teams and then I need someone from each team to come get a form."

"Are we a team, ladies?" Kurt asked.

"Why not?" Sierra said with a smile, and Sophie was glad to see her sister enjoying herself in spite of the fact that she still hadn't heard from her husband.

Teams were formed and the fun began, starting with picking a name. "Let's be the Chocoholics," Sierra suggested. "I think Trevor's turning my sister into one."

"Nothing wrong with that kind of addiction," Trevor said, clearly happy with the name choice.

"Here is our first song," said Elsa. "Can you name it and tell me what group sang it?"

Jacques began to rock out at the piano. Kurt leaned forward and said to Sierra, who was in charge of writing down their answers, "'Smells Like Teen Spirit,' Nirvana. Loved that group."

"Me, too," Sierra said, and wrote it down.

"All right. Everyone ready for our next song?" asked Elsa. "Take it away, Jacques."

It was another song both Kurt and Sierra knew, M.C. Hammer's "U Can't Touch This," and they both began dancing in their seats.

"Now, we'll go a little further back in time. Who can guess this song?" Elsa said, and Jacques began to play a soft, soulful piece.

"Beats me," said Trevor.

"We know that one," Sierra said. "It's our mom's favorite. 'Bridge Over Troubled Water' by Simon and Garfunkel. I love the message in that song. He's promising to be there for the other person like—"

"A bridge over troubled water," Sophie supplied.

"Good message," Kurt approved, and Sophie suspected that both he and his brother were the type of men who would put the lyrics of that song into practice.

"Now we have a song you'll all know. Until he could come up with the right lyrics, Paul McCartney walked around singing 'scrambled eggs,'" Elsa said.

The four looked at each other. "Scrambled eggs?" said Trevor.

The pianist began to play and Sierra gleefully wrote down the answer. "'Yesterday' by The Beatles."

"Jacques now has another song for you from the 1960s," Elsa said.

"Uh-oh," Kurt said.

"Uh-oh is right," echoed Trevor.

Sure enough, it wasn't a song any of them knew. Something jazzy.

"I guess that wasn't one of your mom's favorites," said Trevor.

"Afraid not," said Sierra.

The competition continued with songs clear back to the forties and stretching into 2020. They all knew the newer songs, and thanks to Sophie and Sierra's parents and grandparents the women knew a lot of the older ones. One they were sure was an Elvis song but nobody could think of the title. Sierra wrote down Elvis, figuring a half point was better than no points. Everyone in the room knew "Mamma Mia" and started singing along with Jacques as he played, including the sisters, who swayed back and forth in sync, singing together.

At last the questions were over and teams had to exchange papers to grade. Sierra was checking answers for a group of women who'd labeled themselves the Silver Foxes. The Silver Foxes were getting almost every answer right, even the newer songs.

"We've gotten most of them, too," said Sophie, confident of a win.

"And this song?" Elsa asked after Jacques had played it again.

"'All Shook Up,'" called several people. "Elvis."

"That's one we missed," Sierra said. "Darn."

Finally the list had been gone through and the totals tallied, papers exchanged again. The Chocoholics tied with the Silver Foxes and cheers rose up from both tables when they were each awarded a bottle of champagne.

"We're awesome," Trevor said as the brothers and sisters each knuckle-bumped each other.

Several of Kurt's students stopped by to congratulate them, led by Trevor's number one fan.

"I knew all but the really old ones," she bragged.

"How many can you translate into German, Harriet?" Kurt asked.

"Most of them."

"I tell you what. You guys form teams and have a competition to see who can put the most song titles into German and I'll have a prize for the winning team."

"Champagne?" Harriet asked eagerly.

"No. Chocolate," said Kurt.

She pointed to Trevor. "His?"

"Sure."

"Even better," she said, and dashed off to organize the competition.

"There goes the rest of my chocolate," Trevor said.

"I doubt it. I don't think Harriet will get many takers."

"She certainly seems fond of you," Sierra said to Trevor. "It was sweet that she came over."

"That kid has been tailing me since we met at the airport. I wish she'd glom on to someone her own age already," said Trevor.

"That's my bro," Kurt said. "He's irresistible to women."

Sophie was beginning to think so.

"Oh, well, we almost won," said Denise's new pal Charlie.

"Those new songs threw me," said the newest member of their little group, a tall, blondish man named Arnold, who seemed to be in competition with Charlie for Denise's attention. "Who on earth is Lizzo?"

"The person who sang that song we didn't get," Charlie cracked.

"There's always tomorrow," Denise said, and downed the last of her martini.

If Catherine was going to have any energy for tomorrow she knew she'd have to get some sleep tonight. She'd been covering her yawns for the last half hour.

"Speaking of tomorrow, I think I'll turn in and get rested up for Cologne," she said, standing.

"A good idea," Athena approved. Probably not because she really cared about Catherine leaving to rest up. She was simply happy about her leaving.

"We'll see you in the morning," Rudy said, standing, as well, and the other two men followed suit.

Denise was showing no sign of moving. Why should she? She still had plenty of energy and two men interested in her.

"I'll see you a little later," she said to Catherine. "If you're awake."

She went to the room, got ready for bed and then slipped in between the covers. She was asleep within minutes and never heard Denise come in.

She awoke the next morning feeling refreshed but still tired. "I think maybe I won't do the city tour, after all," she said to Denise as they got dressed.

"Tired?"

"A little."

"You looked pretty beat last night. You probably should take it easy. But I hate to see you miss the fun."

"I'll be fine. It's lovely here on the ship and I did bring a book to read. Anyway, I've already had a lot more fun than I would have if I'd stayed home."

"It's not over yet," Denise said. "But you're smart to pace yourself."

"Anyway, I know you won't be lonely. Although you might get tired juggling two men," Catherine teased.

"It is a terrible problem to have," Denise said, straight-faced. "This is so much fun, isn't it?"

"It is. I'm really glad you talked me into coming."

"I'm glad you came. Come on, let's go get some breakfast."

The dining room was starting to fill up, but they managed to find an empty table with four settings where they were soon joined by Charlie. Arnold came in right on his heels, looking suave in jeans and a black sweater worn over a white shirt with a crisp collar. Charlie, on the other hand, wore slacks, a Nordic print green sweater that made no attempt to hide his girth and a Santa hat. Everything about Charlie said party while Arnold's attire and demeanor said sophistication. Two different men. How would Denise ever choose? Knowing Denise, she'd find a way to keep them both.

"You girls ready to spend money and drink Glühwein?" Charlie asked as Arnold slid into the last seat.

"I am," Denise said. "I think Catherine's leaning toward staying on the boat."

"Not feeling well?" Charlie asked Catherine.

"Just a little tired," she said.

"Would you like me to drink your share of Glühwein?" he asked with a wink.

"I think you should," she told him.

Glühwein, shopping, seeing the cathedral. It would have been fun, she thought wistfully. But the day would be too long and she'd be done in. She gave herself permission to pace herself. There would be more good times ahead. Better to take the adventure in small bites that she could digest.

She caught sight of Rudy entering the room with his daughter and experienced a moment of longing even though she knew nothing could happen between them. There was no room at their table for anyone else. Just as well, she supposed, and sighed.

Athena and her father had entered the dining room to find it nearly full. And, oh, look. What a shame. The two predators already had people sitting with them.

"It looks like Catherine and Denise have found some new friends," she observed. Oh, happy day. Now she could quit worrying about Daddy.

He frowned. "I'll find us a table if you want to go get something."

She did indeed. She celebrated this new turn of events with an omelet.

The celebration was short-lived. After her omelet she returned to the buffet to splurge on a doughnut, making the mistake of leaving her father alone at their table. Well, not exactly alone. There were two other couples there, and he'd seemed to be enjoying visiting with them as he finished his coffee and cereal.

But she returned to the table to find him gone.

"Your father said he'd be right back," one of the women at the table said to her. "He went to say hi to someone."

It wasn't hard to guess who that someone was. Athena abandoned her doughnut and hurried to where her father sat, visiting with Catherine. The other three who'd been with her had left and it was just the two of them at the table. Ugh.

She got there in time to hear her father saying, "I don't think I want to do the city tour, either. What would you say to a quick peek at one of the Christmas markets? There's one right next to the cathedral so we could see that, too."

"I must admit, I would love to at least see the cathedral. And I'd like to maybe do a little bit of shopping."

Shopping, it had been Nicole's favorite pastime. Déjà vu all over again, thought Athena bitterly. She donned a smile and slipped into the vacant seat next to her father.

"Daddy, I was wondering where you went. Are you ready to go?" *Do the tour with your daughter like you'd planned?*

"Honey, I think I'm going to let you do the tour without me," Daddy said.

"I was looking forward to us doing that together," Athena said. It sounded a little like whining. But they'd made plans and now he was ditching her.

"If you already had plans with your daughter please don't let me upset that," said Catherine.

Very gracious of her.

But was she being gracious or strategic?

"Of course you're welcome to join us old folks," Daddy said, reaching out and giving her shoulder a squeeze. "I thought you really wanted to do the tour."

"Only because I thought you wanted to do it," Athena told him. "I just wanted to be together."

"Well, then," Daddy said with a nod. "That settles it. Shall we all meet in the lobby in twenty minutes?"

Catherine nodded and excused herself, leaving father and daughter seated at the table, father looking at daughter suspiciously. Athena felt suddenly uncomfortable under that fatherly gaze.

She didn't want to rain on his holiday parade, really, but she remembered how things had gone with Nicole and her once the woman entered their lives. It had started with, "I hope we can be friends. I really do love your dad." She'd known it wasn't true, but Daddy hadn't tuned into that. Then they'd gotten married and it had gone to, "It's none of your business how much money I spend. He can't take it with him. Or are you worried there won't be anything left for you?" As if Athena was as mercenary as her.

Anyone could have seen what Nicole was up to, but her father was living proof that love is blind. He'd married the woman in spite of the red flags waving all around him and he'd stayed blind right up until she ripped out his heart and left a substantial dent in his savings.

Athena had struggled to keep her mouth shut, gritting her teeth through family gatherings, pretending she hadn't heard when she caught her aunts gossiping in the kitchen about the new wife when Daddy brought her to the family Thanksgiving gathering. She'd hoped against hope that maybe Nicole would turn out not to be as shallow and grasping as she'd appeared. The hopes had been in vain.

Daddy's sisters hadn't hesitated to say, "I told you so," when Nicole dumped him, but as far as Athena had been concerned there'd been no point in pouring salt in the wound. She'd kept her mouth shut and vowed to never let him get hurt again.

"Athena, what are you up to?" he asked now. "You were looking forward to that tour. I heard you talking about it with Denise last night, and now you're not doing it."

She had been looking forward to taking the tour. But if she had to do guard duty instead, so be it.

"I'm not up to anything," she insisted. She could feel the warmth of a blush stealing onto her cheeks and felt like she was fourteen all over again, trying to convince her parents that she hadn't sneaked off to meet a boy instead of going to her best friend's house like she'd said.

He cocked an eyebrow. "I hope you're not thinking I need a chaperone at this age."

"No, of course not."

"Are you sure?"

Okay, guilty as charged, and maybe there was nothing wrong with Catherine Pine. Maybe Athena was being paranoid. But she'd rather be paranoid than see her father hurt again.

"I just want to spend time with you," she protested. That much was true. She did. "I thought we were going to do it together."

"I'm sorry, darling. That was thoughtless of me."

"It was," Athena said, and realized her feelings were hurt. "I mean, you've barely met this woman. You don't know anything about her."

Daddy's penitent expression disappeared. "Really, Athena, I'm a grown man and I don't need a babysitter."

Oh, yes, he did. But he wasn't going to admit it. Much easier to scold her than admit his own weakness.

A good defense was a good offense. "Fine. If you don't want me along," she said, using her best huffy voice.

He softened. "Of course I do. If you're joining us to be friendly and have a good time. But you need to let me handle picking my own friends. I know you worry, but your old man's okay now. I can take care of myself."

The man who had fallen into such a trap telling her he could take care of himself? It was the equivalent of a child saying, "I can cross the freeway by myself."

"I understand," she said. It was a good, neutral comment. No promises made.

Though she knew he took it as a promise that she wouldn't interfere. "All right, then. In that case, let's go get our coats."

She nodded, and they left the dining room together, her father happy that he had things settled and her determined to have a little talk with Catherine Pine the moment she could get her alone.

If she ever could.

They found Catherine waiting for them by the gangplank, wearing her red coat and a knitted hat. "Are you sure I'm not spoiling your father-daughter time?" she asked.

At that point, what were they to say? Yes, go away?

"Not at all," said Daddy, looking at Athena.

She managed a weak smile.

"It's awfully kind of you to share your father with me for a little while," Catherine said to her.

Yes, a little while. Not the whole cruise.

"Daddy's never met a stranger," Athena said.

"I'm sure he hasn't," Catherine said, smiling at him. "There's a gift not all of us have."

Athena didn't. It seemed as she'd gotten older she'd gotten less trusting. Her divorce and Daddy's fortune hunter had done that to her, she supposed.

Was Catherine a fortune hunter, looking for a man to take care of her? She did seem like a nice woman, Athena would give her that.

But people weren't always what they seemed. When they were first together Athena's husband, with his big smile and his big laugh, had looked to her like a man who would be happy to hang in there for the long haul. He hadn't been. He'd gotten tired of house repairs and mowing the lawn and having to come home after work on Fridays instead of being able to go out for drinks with his pals and flirt with twenty-year-olds whose bra sizes were bigger than their brains. He'd been almost as big a heart crusher as Nicole. Although nothing topped her.

Catherine's smile looked genuine. Was it? Only time and close observation would tell. And whether Daddy liked it or not, Athena was going to be observing very carefully.

9

TREVOR WAS ON THE SAME TOUR BUS AS THE SISters, and he slipped into a seat right behind them. And Harriet made sure she beat his brother to the empty seat next to Trevor. Oh, joy.

Her butt was barely in the seat before she started in. "Did you know this is a two-thousand-year-old city?"

"No, but I bet our guide is going to tell us that," he said.

Harriet shrugged as if to say, *What does he know?*

The last thing Trevor wanted was a history of Cologne from Harriet. He changed the subject. "How was your song-translating contest?"

She frowned. "Nobody wanted to do it. They're all lazy brains."

"Maybe they just wanted to party."

"That *would* have been partying."

For a moment, Trevor felt sorry for the kid. Being smart was a gift, but sometimes that gift went unappreciated by others.

"Most of the class just came here to drink and spend money, but I'm here for more than souvenirs. I'm here to learn and expand my horizons. Education is the key to success."

"Can't argue with that," Trevor said.

"I had a scholarship to Western."

And here she was at a community college. "How come you're not there?"

"Money. The scholarship wasn't enough. And I had no intention of being saddled with a student loan."

Not enough money to make up the difference of the scholarship but here she was on this trip. Interesting.

"I only got to come on this trip because I saved my tip money from my barista job and did a bunch of housesitting last summer."

"Good for you." An ambitious kid. She'd go far.

"I'm getting my AA and then transferring. My parents said if I did that they'd help me pay for two years at Western so I can get my BA. After that I'm going to get my master's and then a doctorate. I want to be a history professor."

Harriet had her whole life mapped out. Good for her.

"I'm not going to get married, though. Commingling money is a bad idea."

"Sounds like you've got your life pretty well planned," he said.

"I do. All that's missing is the right man. I want someone mature and successful."

Here she paused to give him a coy smile. Oh, boy.

"Someone who wants a woman who's smart. You're a businessman. I bet you want a smart woman."

Now he was feeling squirmy.

Giggles danced back to him from where the sisters were sitting. Yeah, easy for them to laugh. They weren't stuck sitting next to Miss *Big Bang.*

"I think I'm a little too old for you, Harriet," he said.

"Age is just a number," she informed him.

The bus doors shut and their guide picked up his microphone. Thank God.

"Welcome to beautiful Cologne," said the guide as the bus started moving. "Or, as we call it, Köln. I am Karl, and it will be my pleasure to tell you all about our wonderful city. Cologne is two thousand years old."

"Told you," Harriet whispered.

"It spans the Rhine River and is the fourth largest city in Germany. We are famous for our medieval cathedral with its twin towers. Cologne is one of the key inland ports of Europe and remains a banking center as it was in the Middle Ages."

"I knew all that," Harriet said in disgust.

"He's just warming up. I'm sure he'll eventually tell you something you don't know," Trevor said, feeling a little disgusted himself. Harriet knew a lot of stuff, but somebody needed to make her take a class in social interaction.

"The city was heavily bombed during World War II, and our cathedral was badly damaged, but it survived the bombing," said the guide.

"I read that the towers were used as an easily recognizable navigational landmark by Allied aircraft," Harriet said to Trevor. She shook her head. "Poor Germany. It has such a dark history, doesn't it?"

"I think most of the people here would as soon try and forget it," Trevor said.

"Some things you shouldn't forget, though. You know that

saying, if you don't learn from history you're bound to repeat it."

Trevor was familiar with the saying but he was surprised she knew it. "I don't think anyone's planning on repeating that particular history," he said.

"No. And Germany isn't the only country with a dark past."

Oh, no. Was she going to start listing them?

Thank God their guide was speaking again. "We have many Christmas markets here in Cologne for you to enjoy. The oldest is the Angel Market in our city center with over one hundred and fifty wooden booths selling merchandise and good things to eat. But you will also find good shopping in the Alter Market in front of our town hall and the Cathedral Market in front of the cathedral."

The guide continued, telling them about points of interest as they passed, showing them the various Christmas markets. Harriet kept up her own running commentary, as well. The minute the bus let them off, Trevor grabbed his brother's arm and hissed, "Help."

Kurt took pity on him and called Harriet over to join the rest of the group for some last-minute reminders about meeting times. Trevor breathed a sigh of relief and wove through the crowd to the sisters.

"Would you ladies like a Christmas present pack mule?"

"A good idea," said Sierra. "I know Sophie's going to go crazy."

"I am not," Sophie said. Then admitted, "Well, maybe a little." She looked around her, taking in the galaxy of twinkle lights and myriad booths offering everything from soaps and candles to candy, meats and, of course, Glühwein, the popular spiced wine drink. "I don't know where to start."

"Let's start over here," said her sister, pointing to a booth selling a selection of painted glass candleholders.

"Ooh, those are beautiful," Sophie said.

Trevor had to admit, they were pretty cool. Blues, reds and greens, with colorful winter city scenes painted on them.

"I think I want to get some of these small ones for Mom for Christmas," Sophie said. "Oh, and maybe for Carla and Marina."

"I thought you already had something for them," said Sierra.

"I do, but you can never buy too many presents for your friends."

Trevor decided that was a good idea, and bought some for his mom and his business manager.

Every booth held something fascinating—incense burners shaped like little cottages, nutcrackers, ornaments, scarves and Lebkuchen, the favorite German cookie. The sisters couldn't seem to pass a booth without buying something. Actually, neither could Trevor, and it wasn't long before he was not only helping them carry their purchases, but had several of his own, as well.

He had just bought them all Lebkuchen hearts when Sophie sneezed. "Oh, no," she fretted. "I think I'm coming down with a cold."

"You're downwind from that booth selling incense," said her sister. "That's enough to make anyone sneeze."

"I don't know," Sophie said dubiously, and shivered.

"You need something to ward off the cold," Trevor said. "There's a booth selling Glühwein. I think that would help you feel better. Wine has a lot of healing properties in it."

"You could be right," Sophie said, and her sister rolled her eyes.

"Come on, ladies, let me buy you something to drink."

"You don't have to do that," Sierra protested.

"I know, but I want to."

The wine came in special collectible mugs. "These are adorable," Sophie said. "I'd like to collect a whole set."

"With all the Christmas markets we'll be hitting I bet you'll be able to," Trevor said to her, and vowed to buy her one at each stop.

Part of their excursion included lunch and they arrived at the specified restaurant to find the German class already at tables and enjoying bratwurst and sauerkraut and, of course, beer. Trevor steered the ladies to a table as far away as he could get.

His brother did stop by to say hi and see how their shopping had gone. "Looks like you got into the holiday spirit," he observed, pointing to the pile of bags on the chair next to Trevor.

"We found so many treasures," Sophie informed him happily. "We're really going to be spoiling our family and friends this year."

"I hope you spoil yourselves, as well," Kurt said.

"I did buy myself a nutcracker," Sophie told him. "I love those."

Trevor saw her reaching down to rub her ankle. "Is it hurting?" he asked.

"A little," she said.

He snagged a chair from a nearby table. "Here, let's prop it up." He helped her prop up her leg, then signaled for their waiter. "I'll see if we can get some ice for it."

"Good luck with that," Kurt said. "Europeans aren't into ice."

"It's okay," Sophie said. "I brought some ibuprofen."

"Let's ask, anyway," Trevor said.

This particular restaurant did cater to tourists, though, and fortunately, the waiter was able to return with some ice in a glass.

"Not exactly a lot," Trevor said as Sophie wound a napkin around the tiny pile.

"I'm surprised you got any," Kurt said.

"This is kind of tacky taking off my boot in a restaurant," Sophie said, looking around at their fellow diners.

"Everybody's too into their food to pay any attention to us," Trevor assured her. "Better to be tacky than miserable. You don't want it to swell."

She took her boot off.

Harriet had spotted them and was making her way to the table. "Be right back," Trevor said. Then, to his brother, "Where's the can?"

"I'll go with you," Kurt offered, and fell in step with him. "So, how much money have you blown trying to impress Sophie?" he teased as they made their way to the restroom.

"Not nearly enough. I've just begun to impress."

"She seems pretty nice."

"She is." She was more than nice, though. She was enthusiastic, obviously generous and fun to be around. He could see this going somewhere.

Harriet was still stationed next to the seat Trevor had vacated when he returned, visiting with the sisters. More like pumping them actually, asking where all they'd been.

"Mind if I join you after lunch?" she asked.

"Sure," Sierra said. "The more, the merrier."

For who?

Harriet happily turned her back on her professor and her fellow students and practically glued herself to Trevor when they left the restaurant.

"You probably shouldn't be walking so much on that ankle,"

she said to Sophie. "It's gonna swell up. You should go back to the ship."

"Maybe I should," Sophie said.

Trevor was aware of Harriet next to him, oozing hope that Sophie would do a vanishing act. "Does it hurt? Want me to take you back?" he offered, and Harriet frowned.

"Do you want to go back?" asked her sister.

"Not really," Sophie said. She looked in the general direction of where their ship was docked and bit her lip, considering.

"You did just ice it and take a pill. And your ankle is wrapped."

Sophie looked down at her ankle. "I think I'll be fine a little longer."

"You'll be sorry. It's gonna swell," Harriet predicted. Then she pulled on Trevor's arm. "Hey, look. Chocolate stuff. Let's go check it out."

"Okay, ladies, it looks like we're checking out the chocolates," he said as Harriet started towing him away. The girl was surprisingly strong. He looked over his shoulder to make sure the sisters were following. *Please don't desert me.*

One minute they were behind him and the next they'd stopped at the booth selling scarves. Harriet steered him on mercilessly, right up to the counter of the chocolate booth.

"Look at these awesome chocolate Santas," she said.

"Yeah, cool." Trevor watched as Sophie held up a scarf to her sister. Sierra shook her head. Sophie nodded, and dug into her purse.

"Oh, and a reindeer," Harriet enthused.

Sophie bought the scarf and handed it to her sister. Then they started strolling toward Trevor and Harriet. Sophie glanced in the direction of the cathedral and her eyes lit up. She said something to her sister and pointed.

Trevor looked to see where she was pointing. There came Rudy and his daughter and Catherine.

Sophie took off in that direction, her sister following.

Trevor watched them, feeling suddenly sour. Of all the Christmas markets in town. *Bah, frickin' humbug.*

Awkward was the one word that kept coming to mind as Catherine, Rudy and Athena strolled between the different booths, admiring the artisans' wares. Still, she hadn't let the awkwardness diminish her enjoyment of Cologne.

She had been awed by the beautiful Gothic cathedral with its twin towers. And those gorgeous stained-glass windows had left her breathless. She took a picture of one and sent it to both Lila and William. Just in case they were wondering if she was having a good time.

The market was a sweet finish, dessert for the soul. "I'm so glad you convinced me to leave the ship," she said to Rudy as the three of them turned into the maze of booths, her on one side of him and his daughter on the other.

"I'm glad you could join me," he said.

"Us," Athena corrected.

"Both of you," Catherine said diplomatically.

Although, really, *glad* wasn't the word that came to mind when she thought of Athena's presence. The woman was like some mythological creature, standing guard over her father.

It was a little mystifying. Catherine could understand Athena's love for her mother and could appreciate her missing her mom. But this guardian at the gate thing seemed extreme. Her father probably had many years left. Surely his daughter would want him to be happy.

"I think we need sustenance," Rudy said. "How about some Glühwein?"

"That would be lovely," Catherine said.

"Yes, it would," Athena agreed.

He offered an arm to each of them and they walked as a threesome to a booth decorated with fir boughs and red ribbons that was doing a brisk business selling the seasonal drink. It was pleasant to walk arm in arm with a man, Catherine thought. She missed that kind of comforting closeness.

Mugs of spiced wine in hand, they began to stroll down one of the many aisles of booths offering holiday goods. Catherine was drawn to one with some beautiful Christmas ornaments, and she bought royal blue and silver bell-shaped ones for both her daughter and her daughter-in-law.

"I know they'll both love these," she said to Rudy.

"You should buy one for yourself, too," he said.

"I have plenty of ornaments. There comes a time in life when you have to stop filling up your house with things. And I do want to watch my budget."

But she was tempted to forget everything she'd just said when they stopped at the booth selling German pyramids, the charming table decorations where little candles turned the paddles and base. Catherine found herself entranced by a three-tiered one that offered varying Nativity scenes.

"These remind me of the one Mom always put out every year," said Athena.

"I remember my mother had one when I was a child," Catherine said. "I have no idea what happened to it."

"I don't know what happened to ours, either. Things get lost when people remarry," Athena said, her voice tinged with bitterness, and Catherine was aware of Rudy stiffening next to her.

Ah, so was there more to Rudy's story than simply losing his wife?

Another booth was selling jewelry, including silver charms. "Oh, Daddy, look, charms," Athena said to her father, walking him toward the counter.

"Come on, Catherine," he said, making sure to include her. "Let's see what they have. Whenever we traveled I always bought Athena a charm," he explained. "She's got quite a collection on her bracelet."

"What a lovely idea," Catherine said. She stepped up to the counter and looked at the bracelets and various charms. One of the cathedral caught her eye.

She was suddenly aware of Rudy at her elbow. "Would you like that?"

"It's sweet, but I don't even have a bracelet."

"That can easily be fixed," he said, picking one up.

"I couldn't let you," she protested. They barely knew each other. It wouldn't be right. Anyway, she could afford to buy her own charm. And the bracelet.

Before she could say anything more, though, he'd picked up both, saying, "Just to get you started."

"I really can't accept," she protested.

"Sure you can." He turned to his daughter, who was observing their interaction with a frown. "It's only a charm, Athena. Don't worry."

What on earth did that mean?

"Did you find one you like?" he asked Athena.

Still frowning, she handed one over, murmuring her thanks, and he paid the seller.

"Always nice to have a memento," he said, handing Catherine hers.

"Thank you. That was very kind of you," she said.

But she felt uncomfortable. What was happening between her and Rudy had all the makings of a whirlwind romance, but Athena's reaction to her father's generosity was an indication that nothing good would come of the wind that was kicking up. This wasn't going to go anywhere. Living in the moment was one thing, but leading someone on to expect a future was quite another.

She should say something, tell Rudy that she wasn't looking for a man, let him know what was waiting for her in the future. But the idea of sharing all that with a new friend felt like the equivalent of going on a first date and blurting everything bad about yourself before the main course had even arrived.

If she were being honest she'd have to admit that her dilemma went beyond awkwardness. This was a lovely ride she was on and she hated to get off. Surely the ride would end soon enough as it was.

"Rudy!" called a voice.

Catherine turned to see Sophie Miles hurrying toward them. She wore a black parka that was short enough to show off her slim legs. The skinny jeans didn't hurt, either. Her gloves were also black, but she had a red knitted hat on her head. Looking at her, Catherine thought of a young Christie Brinkley. Top that with a bubbly personality and she was the whole package. Merry Christmas to Rudy.

She wasn't limping so it appeared her ankle was better. As she got closer Catherine saw the bandage rising up from inside her sneakers. Still wounded but not badly enough to affect her. The young healed so swiftly. Catherine could remember when nothing hurt. Stiff knees and a stiff back went with the territory once you got older.

Her sister was with her, as well, shaking her head, and trailing behind them came Trevor and one of the German students.

Like Sophie, he was smiling, but his wasn't quite so enthusiastic. It wasn't hard to see he was smitten with Sophie—that had been clear from the moment he carried her from the windmill back to the boat. She, however, seemed determined to make a connection with Rudy.

Honestly, she looked younger than his daughter. Catherine couldn't imagine him taking her seriously. Admittedly, she didn't want to imagine him taking Sophie seriously. If only she wasn't facing the health challenges she was. She'd give the girl a run for her money.

The thought of what lay ahead rolled in like a dark cloud and she kicked herself mentally for letting it invade the adventure she was having. *Don't go there*, she scolded herself, and stepped a little closer to Rudy. *You're still on the ride. You don't have to get off yet.*

"I see you found the Glühwein," Sophie said, beaming at first him, then Catherine. For Athena the beam went from bright to low. "It's delicious, isn't it? And wine has lots of antioxidants, doesn't it, Rudy?"

"It does have resveratrol," Rudy said, "but you'd have to drink a lot more wine than this to receive any benefit."

"Then we'd better get drinking," joked Trevor, who had joined them in time to hear.

"Chocolate's better," said the student, "and it's got antioxidants in it." She dug out the chocolate Santa she'd purchased. "It's probably not as good as yours, though," she said to Trevor, eyeing him like he was a giant chocolate delight.

It was plain to see he wasn't thrilled to have her along, but he still managed a smile for her and a "Thanks." Trevor March had a good heart.

"What all have you bought?" Sophie asked Catherine.

"Not much yet. I'm pacing myself." Speaking of pacing,

she was beginning to feel tired. How soon before she could suggest going back to the ship?

"Me, too," Sophie said.

"At a fast pace," Trevor joked, and held up several bags.

"You have to spread the wealth around," Sophie said.

Catherine noticed that everyone seemed to find that amusing but Athena. There was something in her that was at war with the general joviality of the rest of them, the human equivalent of a bad smell in a house that one could never quite locate the source of.

"Speaking of spreading the wealth, shall we look a little more?" Rudy asked Catherine.

She'd have liked to, but she was beginning to feel tired. "You know, I think I'd as soon go back to the ship. But if you'd like to stay longer, please don't let me stop you," she added. "There's still so much to see."

"I think I'm ready to go back and relax with some hot chocolate laced with schnapps," said Rudy, looking at Catherine.

"Me, too," said Athena.

Enjoying hot chocolate sounded great to Catherine, too. So did a nap. Hot chocolate first and then a nap.

"All right," said Sierra. "We'll see you all back on the ship."

"If you two want to stay longer, please don't let me spoil your fun," Catherine said as the three of them started for the pickup spot where the buses were running.

"I'm good," Rudy said. He turned to his daughter. "You didn't want to stay longer and shop with Sophie and Sierra?"

"No. There will be lots more chances to shop," Athena said. "Anyway, I'm here to spend time with you."

It wasn't hard to see what was going on. Rudy wanted to be free to enjoy himself and his daughter was determined he wouldn't have so much as one moment of freedom.

In a way Catherine found that sweet and couldn't help feeling just the slightest bit jealous of how very much his daughter adored him. Of course, Catherine's children loved her. But not with this level of devotion. She was part of their lives, but she was something they took for granted as much as they did the air they breathed. They sucked it in every day without noticing.

"You are so lucky to have a daughter who truly enjoys your company," she said to him as the three of them left the busy market.

"Yes, I am," Rudy said, looking fondly at his daughter. "But then I imagine your children enjoy your company, too."

They certainly hadn't last Christmas, and they wouldn't be this one, either. "They do," she said, and left it at that.

Back on the ship she shed her coat and made her way to the lounge, where Rudy had already gotten drinks for them. It felt good to simply sit and look out the window at the houses perched along the bank of the Rhine.

"It's so pretty over here," she said. "I almost feel like I'm in a fairy tale." It felt like one—charming Christmas markets with festive lights and decorations everywhere, their beautiful ship. A handsome prince.

Guarded by a dragon.

"I never tire of coming to Europe," Rudy said.

"What's your favorite country?" Catherine asked him.

"Hard to pick. They all have their own special flavor."

"Where all have you been?" she asked.

"Oh, let's see. I've seen Italy, cruised the Mediterranean."

"You and Mom did that for your thirtieth anniversary," put in Athena.

"We did. It's a very romantic country. But then, so is France. Ever been to France, Catherine?"

Only in my dreams. "I'd like to go someday. I'd also like to take one of those cruises down to Mexico. I've never been." There were so many places she'd never been.

"That's a good one," he said.

"Maybe I'll have to try that next," she said.

Once she was done with chemo she'd treat herself to a cruise, she decided, and felt pleased with herself for thinking so positively. How could you not think positive when you were living a fairy tale?

"How about you, Athena?" Catherine asked, determined to draw her into the conversation.

She shrugged. "Oh, I don't know."

"What do you mean you don't know?" her father chided. "How about that trip to London?"

Her face brightened. "That was special. Daddy had a patient who owned a second house just outside of London. He let us have it for a week and Mom and Daddy took me there for my twenty-first birthday." She looked at her father, adoration in her eyes.

"We used to go to Hawaii a lot when she was growing up. She's done a fair bit of traveling since."

"After my divorce," Athena said with a scowl, "I don't care if I ever see Paris again."

"Maybe someday you'll see it with someone wonderful and that will take the bad taste out of your mouth," Catherine suggested.

"Maybe," Athena said with a shrug. Then added, "I would like to visit Greece."

"So would I," Catherine said. So many places she still wanted to see, so many things she wanted to do. Was she going to get a chance to do them?

"Let's toast to more adventures in the future," Rudy said, and raised his glass mug to her.

"To more adventures," she said, and she, too, raised hers.

"To adventure," Athena said a little less enthusiastically.

Catherine found herself feeling sorry for the woman. Apparently, all had not gone as planned in her life.

But then, things often didn't go as planned, and if there was one thing Catherine was coming to realize it was that you had to make new plans. There was no point in sitting around moping over what hadn't gone right, no point wishing things could be different. She couldn't bring back her husband, she couldn't reraise her children. Life was what it was and you had to grab on to those good moments and enjoy them while you could.

"You know," she said, "I think I'll go sample some of those cookies. Would you two like me to bring you back some?"

"Sure," Rudy said happily.

Cookies and hot chocolate and a pretty view from aboard a river cruise ship, and a nice man to enjoy it with—this was a good moment.

"The Lindt chocolate museum isn't far from where we're docked," Sierra said as she and Sophie and Trevor rode back to the ship. "I was really hoping to see it. How's your ankle holding up?"

Sierra had actually been having a good time and Sophie was willing to do anything to keep that happy vibe going, even though she was beginning to worry about her ankle.

"I can handle another hour on it. Trevor, do you want to check out your competition's home base?"

"Sure," he said. "Anyway, I'm sure you two will have more bags you'll need help carrying."

The Lindt store attached to the museum was a veritable chocolate treasure chest, and they did, indeed, make more purchases. Sierra bought some chocolate for Mark, and Sophie bought some chocolate truffles for Trevor as a thank-you for his chivalry. She also took pictures for Instagram and some selfies of the three of them to post on Facebook. But by the time they were done with their visit her ankle was starting to hurt.

"I think I'd better get back on board and ice up," she finally said.

"Want me to carry you?" Trevor offered.

"I think you've got enough to carry," she said, pointing to the extra bags. They might have gotten a little carried away with the shopping.

"Thanks for helping us out," Sierra said to him as they left the store.

"Happy to."

Sierra smiled as they started to walk along the riverbank. "This has been a good day."

Her sister's words were music to Sophie's ears. "Yes, it has," she agreed. But boy, was she ready to put her foot up.

"I'll second that," said Trevor. "Or should I say third it?"

They strolled along the bank past trees decorated with white lights perched in their branches like shimmering fairies. On the water several river cruise ships were lined up, all uniquely decorated with strings of lights and wreaths. People walked past them, bundled up in coats, hats and scarves, all chatting and laughing. It felt a little like being inside a travel brochure come to life.

Their own ship, clad in lights, was glimmering in the late-afternoon dark, and Sophie could see lights on in the dining room and staterooms, which made it look like one long, elegant houseboat. In a way it was—a festive escape and home away from home for holiday travelers. As they walked up the gangplank, members of the crew were on hand to greet them with trays of hot chocolate.

"I could get used to this," Sophie said as the sisters made their way to their stateroom, Trevor by their side.

"Me, too," said Sierra.

She looked happy and relaxed. The day had been a success.

"You gonna have room in your luggage for all this stuff?" Trevor asked once they were inside and he'd set the sisters' bags on their bed.

"Oh, yes," Sophie assured him. "We each brought extra luggage just for our goodies." She looked at the collection of bags, filled with scarves, candleholders, ornaments and nutcrackers. "I am going to enjoy displaying that nutcracker and making my friends jealous."

"They're going to be jealous when they see all those selfies you took with Trevor," Sierra said after he left.

"He is gorgeous, isn't he?"

"He's more than that. He's really sweet. If you're smart, you'll give up on Rudy and pay attention to Trevor. Anyway, Rudy's not interested."

"Maybe he doesn't realize that I'm interested," Sophie said, ducking into the bathroom to wash down another ibuprofen. "Maybe he just thinks I'm being friendly."

"And maybe he's too busy looking at Catherine to see you. If he does at all he probably sees you as a kid," Sierra said as Sophie came back out to get the ice bucket.

"Well, he shouldn't. I'd make a great trophy wife."

Sierra gave a snort. "Yes, just what every woman aspires to be. Honestly, you don't need to marry a doctor. All you need is good insurance and someone who doesn't mind driving you to the emergency room every other week and keeping you off WebMD."

"Ha ha," Sophie said.

There was nothing wrong with being practical when looking for a life partner, she thought as she went to fetch ice for her ankle. A doctor would understand her health concerns.

She returned just as Sierra's phone pinged with a text from her husband. "Finally," Sierra said, and Sophie could hear the relief in her voice. But reading his message stole her smile. She dropped onto the side of the bed, staring at her phone screen. "'Glad you're having a good time,'" she read to Sophie. "No 'I miss you' or 'Wish I was there.' I could fall off the ship and he wouldn't care."

Very underwhelming. "At least he texted," Sophie said. It was better than nothing. But not much.

"Only because he got tired of me blowing up his phone. He doesn't even miss me."

"You shouldn't jump to conclusions," Sophie told her. "Maybe he was so busy working..." Right. Even Sophie wouldn't buy that.

"What husband doesn't tell his wife he misses her or say he loves her?"

Okay, yes, Sierra should jump.

The pain in her sister's eyes was heartbreaking. Sophie set aside the ice bucket and sat next to Sierra and put an arm around her shoulders.

"He doesn't deserve you," she said.

"I shouldn't have gone." Sierra pressed her lips tightly together. It wasn't enough to keep the tears from spilling.

"Maybe you shouldn't have stayed," Sophie said softly. Sierra didn't owe forever to a man who didn't deserve it. "Maybe it's time to—"

"Don't say it," her sister said sharply.

Sophie sighed and shut up. Instead, she sat there, hugging Sierra while the tears flowed down her cheeks. Men were pigs.

But not all men. And not doctors. They were just clueless turkeys.

10

CATHERINE'S BODY FINALLY INSISTED SHE GO LIE down, and she excused herself and went to the room to rest. She was still napping when Denise came in.

"Don't tell me you've been in here all afternoon," Denise said, dumping her purchases on her bed.

"No. I wound up seeing the cathedral and spending a little time in one of the Christmas markets."

"By yourself? I'll wager not."

"No, I went with Rudy and Athena."

Denise made a face. "That girl. Such a sourpuss."

"I think she's got trust issues."

"Haven't we all?"

"Looks like you spent a fair amount of time in the market," Catherine said, pointing to the bags.

"Oh, yes." Denise pulled out a red wool scarf from one. "Charlie bought me this. Isn't it pretty?"

"Yes, and it matches his Santa hat," Catherine teased. "What did your other admirer get you?"

"Glühwein."

"I can tell who's the most determined. Does this put Charlie in the lead?"

Denise chuckled. "They're both nice men, but I'm not interested in anything permanent. I rather like being on my own. You, on the other hand," she said, pointing at Catherine, "are meant for marriage."

"What's that supposed to mean?" Catherine demanded. "Are you saying I can't make it on my own?"

"Not in the least. I'm saying you're not wired to be selfish. You need someone to do things for. I like being in charge of my own schedule, doing what I want when I want. You like taking care of people. Which," she added, "is why your kids take such advantage of you. And that is why you can't stay a widow. The little bloodsuckers will suck you dry."

Catherine frowned. "My children are not bloodsuckers."

"You need a life of your own," Denise said, unrepentant. Then, before Catherine could get properly insulted over her friend's assessment of her life, she grinned and said, "I'm glad you came on this trip. You really do deserve to have a special holiday. I hope you milk every moment for all it's worth."

How could you stay irritated with such a good friend? "Thanks for getting me to come. I am making some great memories."

"And we've barely begun. Come on, it's almost time for that predinner talk from our social director. Let's go find out what's on the schedule for tomorrow."

They made their way to the lounge, stopping to grab a

cookie from the cookie bin. "I won't need a car to get home from the airport," Denise said as she bit into one. "With everything I'm eating I'll be able to roll myself home."

"Me, too," Catherine said.

But who knew if or when she'd ever be able to do something like this again? She grabbed one last cookie and a latte from the fancy coffee machine before following Denise through the automatic sliding door into the lounge.

"There's the gang," Denise said, pointing to where Rudy and his daughter and one of the sisters sat, along with Trevor. "Looks like they saved us seats. Shall we join them?"

"Might as well," Catherine said, although she was sure Athena would be none too happy to see her.

On their way they passed some of the students who had staked out seats by a window. One girl in ripped jeans and a faux leather jacket over a low-cut snug-fitting top was typing away on her phone with dark purple fingernails. A blue-haired, chunky boy in jeans, boots and an old, beat-up leather jacket was idly checking out something on his phone and sneaking looks at the girl seated across from them, the same little, plain-faced girl who kept popping up on the fringes of their group. It wasn't a bad face, Catherine thought, but one that could have benefitted from some embellishment.

Unaware of the boy across from her, she was staring across the room at Trevor as he passed out chocolate to the sisters and Athena. She watched with the intensity of a dog sitting next to the dinner table, hoping for a treat. Catherine couldn't help feeling sorry for her. Youth so often specialized in aiming love the wrong direction.

The lounge was already three-quarters full, but the group had claimed their same section of the lounge, draping sweaters and jackets over the chairs. All were happy to welcome

Denise and Catherine. Even Athena was smiling, although it looked a little forced.

Catherine would have liked to ask her, "Is there a particular reason you seem to wish I'd fall off the ship?" But manners forbid such directness.

Denise, on the other hand, wouldn't have worried about such a fine point. But then she had one of those large personalities that bravely went where lesser women never dared to go.

Catherine didn't like confrontation, much preferred diplomacy and a soft word. Looking at Rudy's kind face, she wanted to spend more time with him, simply for the pleasure of it, nothing more. She'd have to find a way to convince his daughter that she wasn't out to steal away her father. How could she when they barely knew each other?

And yet he'd already stolen Catherine's heart. She was going to hate to see this cruise come to an end. If only she didn't have such uncertainty waiting for her in the new year.

She wished she didn't have so many treatments looming. Sadly, she'd waited too long to make that appointment with her gynecologist. She'd seen the tiny spots of blood but they'd been so rare. She'd concluded she had a kidney stone. Blood in the urine was a sign. Surely that was all it could be at her age.

It hadn't been. If only she'd realized what was happening sooner. The doctors could have simply removed her damaged uterus and that would have been that. By the time her cancer was diagnosed the alien baby had chewed its way half through the uterine wall and her oncologist had worries that some cells might have escaped to do damage elsewhere. So it would be on to six rounds of chemo followed by radiation. She wasn't looking forward to losing her hair, she wasn't looking forward to dealing with possible side effects of the chemotherapy. She wasn't looking forward to the new year at all.

At least she'd have the wonderful memory of this trip to look back on. And the memory of Rudy Nichols's smile.

"May I order you a drink?" he asked her.

She could almost feel Athena stiffening on his other side. Drinks, charms…what next?

"No—" she smiled as their waiter approached "—but I can order something for myself. Can your bartender make me something festive and sweet?" she asked the man.

"I think he can," the server said.

"Tell him to surprise me," Catherine said.

"Does this mean you're not going to let me buy you any more drinks?" Rudy joked as the man left.

"It means I'm not about to take advantage of you," she replied.

Athena looked surprised and then suspicious. Was her father a soft touch? He was obviously generous, and sometimes generous people got taken advantage of.

The server soon returned with a white drink in a martini glass that had been sugared around the edges. "This is called a Winter Wonderland," he said to Catherine.

"What's in it?" she asked.

"Cream, white chocolate liqueur, crème de cacao."

She took a sip. It was the tastiest thing she'd had in some time.

"Tell him it's delicious," she said to the server.

"I think I want one of those," Denise said, and then Sophie decided she did, too.

Sierra hadn't joined them yet but Catherine assumed she'd be along soon. "Should we order one for your sister?" she asked Sophie.

Worry skittered across Sophie's face. "No. She won't be coming. She's not feeling too good."

Her sister had seemed fine earlier. There was not feeling good and life not being good. Catherine wondered if, in Sierra's case it was the latter. She'd taken a liking to the sisters, and hated to think of such a once in a lifetime experience being marred for either of them by something bad.

Charlie joined them just as the waiter was serving their cocktails. "I see we survived another day in the fatherland," he observed. "I'll take a drink," he said to the waiter. "Not that, though. Scotch, rocks." To the others he said, "I need something stronger. Denise shopped till I dropped. My feet are killing me."

"Poor man," she said, patting his arm.

"But I don't mind," he added, seeing her other conquest sauntering their way.

Soon everyone had a festive drink and their table had a fresh bowl of bar munchies.

"Did everyone have fun today?" Denise asked.

"Oh, yes," Rudy said easily.

His daughter opted to sip her drink rather than speak.

"How about you?" Denise asked Sophie. "Did you find anything special in the market?"

"All kinds of things," Sophie said, and proceeded to list them, finishing with, "And I got a gorgeous scarf for my sister." At the mention of her sister, her enthusiasm faded a little.

Denise wisely moved on. "You never did tell me what you got," she said to Catherine.

"I found some beautiful ornaments for my daughter and daughter-in-law," Catherine said. "They're shaped like bells."

"I hope you got something for yourself," Denise said sternly.

Catherine would have liked to mention the charm and bracelet Rudy bought her. She didn't want to appear ungrateful. But since his daughter hadn't exactly been happy about the purchase she decided to keep her mouth shut about it. No sense bringing up a sore subject.

"This trip is what I gave myself," she said.

Their cruise director had arrived on the scene, and taken the mike. Her greeting to the travelers spared Catherine from having to say anything more. She decided she would be sure to thank Rudy again later for his kindness.

Meanwhile, their server had returned with more drinks and Elsa was asking everyone if they had enjoyed Cologne.

"Tomorrow," she said, "we will be stopping in the village of Braubach. Many of you have signed up for the excursion to Koblenz, where you will enjoy a walking tour of this beautiful Roman city. And we also, in the morning, have the excursion to tour Marksburg Castle, the seven-hundred-year-old fortress that is the only Rhine castle never to have been conquered. It will provide you with excellent views."

"That sounds good," said Arnold, who had joined them and claimed the empty seat on the other side of Denise.

"At the end of our morning tours we will be casting off at 11:45 and will enjoy scenic sailing on the Rhine during which I will be offering commentary for you," Elsa said. "Then at 3:45, I know you won't want to miss Chef Bruno's demonstration of how to make Rüdesheim coffee. We will be serving that and tea on the terrace along with a variety of German pastries."

"Best pastries in the world," Charlie informed the rest of the group.

"Tomorrow at approximately five in the afternoon we will be docking in Rüdesheim, famous for their wine, especially Riesling. There you may enjoy walking about the town to shop at the Christmas market or join us for an excursion to the Eberbach Monastery estate for a dinner of German specialties. I know you will want to be back on the boat at nine for a demonstration by a traditional glassblower right here in our lounge where he will create for you a work of art from industrial glass."

"Decisions, decisions," quipped Denise after Elsa had finished her spiel.

"What's everyone going to do?" Sophie asked, looking at Rudy.

Rudy looked at Catherine.

"I think the castle sounds intriguing," she said. "You can't come to Germany and not see a castle." *And find a prince.*

"I'm up for the castle," said Rudy.

"Me, too," Sophie said with a determined nod.

"What did you want to see, Athena?" Catherine asked.

"Actually, I had signed up for touring the castle," she said.

Catherine strongly suspected that if she and Rudy had opted for the walking tour of Koblenz, then Athena would have switched to that.

"Who knows? We might find a prince," Denise quipped.

"I was thinking you already had," Charlie said to her.

"Same here," put in Trevor. He turned to Sophie. "You may call me your highness."

"You can call me anything," said Charlie. "Just don't call me late for dinner."

Judging from his round belly it looked like no one ever had.

The cocktail hour ended and the group of friends made their way to the dining room where Charlie and Trevor and Arnold all found seats at a table near the original six. Catherine noticed that the girl who had been so intently watching Trevor had managed to beat an older woman to a seat next to him. She caught the pained look on his face, quickly covered by polite indulgence. Yes, a very nice man.

Catherine hoped Sophie Miles would wake up to the fact. Why on earth she was so fixated on Rudy was a mystery.

It wasn't such a great mystery why the college girl kept trailing poor Trevor. He was attractive enough to catch any woman's eye, young or old. But it was so plain he wasn't interested. Longing for someone who wasn't interested was a strange and inexplicable phenomenon.

The next morning Catherine found herself in the omelet line with Trevor's young admirer and introduced herself.

"I'm Harriet," the young woman said. "I'm here with my German class."

"How fun to be traveling with friends in your class," Catherine said.

"It's okay," Harriet said, damning her traveling companions with faint praise.

"I saw you last night in the lounge after dinner. That was quite an interesting-looking man sitting next to you," Catherine ventured. Trevor had been sure to make himself scarce until Harriet had gotten settled, luring Sophie to a table with some chocolate.

Harriet rolled her eyes. "Hugh? He's such a child. I prefer older men."

Ah, so little Harriet was suffering from a superiority complex. "When it comes down to it they're all children, no matter what their age," Catherine said. "But the fact that this—Hugh, was it?—is taking such a difficult language, just as you are, says something, doesn't it? So does the fact that he wanted to come on this tour."

"He just came for the beer," Harriet scoffed.

"I can't blame him. I came for the food," Catherine joked. *And to get away from my pathetic life.*

Harriet's plate was already piled with pastries. "The food is good."

"Are you going to see the castle?" Catherine asked.

"Oh, yeah. Everyone is."

"Even your beer-drinking friend?"

"Yeah."

"Sounds like he's interested in something besides beer," Catherine said.

"He's got to do something."

"Interesting that he chose the castle. A man with an interest in seeing the world, now there's a treasure. I bet he'll give some woman an exciting life."

She saw Harriet cast a speculative glance to where the boy sat with some of the other students. Maybe she'd planted a seed.

Rudy and Athena had found Catherine and Denise's table as had Sierra and Sophie. Trevor had stopped by to visit and, though Sophie was talking to him, it was plain to see from the looks she cast across the table that Rudy was still her primary interest.

"Funny how people often can't see what's right under their noses," she remarked to Denise when it was time to embark and they were walking to their room to brush teeth and get their coats.

"Like you're one to talk. Can't you see how smitten Rudy is?"

"Of course I can. I can also see how unsmitten his daughter is."

"That girl definitely has issues."

"Yes, and I'm one of them."

"She'll come to love you. We all do."

"You're so full of frijoles," Catherine said, embarrassed by her friend's praise.

"I speak only the truth. What's not to like?"

What indeed? There was certainly something Athena didn't like. It had to be the threat of another woman, because Athena didn't appear to be any more fond of Sophie than she was Catherine. Sophie's sister had opted to stay on the ship, so Sophie attached herself to Catherine during the tour, which meant she was also attached to Rudy.

"Sierra's still not feeling well?" Catherine asked her as they all entered the impressive old fortress high above the river.

"She'll be fine."

"I'm sorry she's missing so much," Catherine said.

"She'll join us later." Sophie's tone of voice added, *I'm going to make sure of that.*

She was also going to make sure she got next to Rudy. As they walked the castle, taking in its massive stone walls, the rooms with their cavernous hearths, the old cannons and suits of armor, it was almost comical watching as Sophie maneuvered to stand near Rudy and make snippets of conversation while Trevor hovered at her elbow. Then there was Athena, never leaving Rudy's other side and dividing her frowns between Catherine and Sophie. At least she was an equal opportunity antagonist.

"You all looked like you were hooked together with invisible rope," Denise teased once they were back in their room on the ship. "At this rate your shipboard romance is going to wither on the vine."

"That's okay," Catherine assured her. "I'm having a great time, anyway." She sat on her bed and sighed.

"You look pooped," Denise observed.

"I am a little tired."

"Want to stretch out for a while? I can bring you something from the lunch buffet," Denise offered.

Catherine stretched out and snuggled down against the pillows. "That would be great. But if I fall asleep wake me up in time for the coffee demonstration."

"Will do," Denise said, and started for the door.

"And, Denise."

She turned.

"Thanks for being such a good friend."

Denise smiled. "That goes both ways. Pleasant dreams."

No need to wish her that. Catherine was already living one.

Athena was both surprised and relieved to see Denise entering the lounge alone with no Catherine in tow. Daddy had already staked out a table in the small dining area at the bow of the boat not far from the buffet and was enjoying a prelunch cup of coffee. Maybe, for once, it would be just the two of them and they could enjoy some worry-free father-daughter time.

"Your friend isn't joining us?" she asked as Denise stepped behind her in the buffet line and helped herself to a crusty roll.

"She's a little tired. She decided to rest a while."

Athena nodded, taking that in. Catherine Pine sure was out of shape. Another reason she was no match for Daddy, who worked out at the gym and played tennis three times a week. He needed someone who could keep up with him.

What was she saying? After what he'd gone through with Nicole he didn't need anyone. Period.

Catherine awoke in time to go watch Chef Bruno demonstrate how to make Rüdesheim coffee, a tasty drink made with strong coffee, sugar cubes and Asbach brandy, topped with whipped cream and chocolate shavings. A drink was provided for everyone present.

"I am going to find that brandy and make this for my friends when I get home," Sophie announced. "I bet Dad will like this, too," she said to her sister, drawing her into the conversation.

"He probably will," Sierra said.

Her enthusiasm and her smile had slipped to the bottom edge of lukewarm. It looked like this cruise was losing its shine for Sierra Johnson. Catherine wished there was something she could say or do to help.

If anyone else was noticing how subdued she was no one was saying. Which was what you did in situations like this with people who were acquaintances. Sierra was doing her best to hide her feelings and when someone did that you had to pretend they were well hidden.

"If I buy you some of that brandy will you make me Rüdesheim coffee when we get back to Seattle?" Charlie asked Denise.

"I might," she said coyly, and Arnold, who was with them, frowned and took another drink of his.

Sierra finished hers, then excused herself. Her sister bit her lip as she watched her go.

"Are you and your sister going to join us on the monastery tour?" Catherine asked Sophie.

She pulled her gaze back from the sliding glass door. "No, I think we'll walk around the town." She downed the last of her coffee and excused herself, as well.

"We'll see you later tonight, then," Catherine said as she left.

"I hope so," she murmured.

"Whatever is going on with the girl, you're not her mother

and you can't fix it," Denise said to her that evening as they got ready to leave for their tour of the Erbach Monastery and the wine tasting and dinner to follow.

"I know," Catherine said.

"She's young. The young are resilient."

"Resilient or not, I hate to see anybody sad on a trip like this."

"Right now, making sure you don't get sad is all I care about," Denise said. "Come on, let's go."

Catherine felt far from sad as she walked in the monastery's cloister. She could almost feel the presence of the monks who had once lived there. She thought of the old saying God is in His heaven and all is well with the world. Taking in the simple beauty of the place reminded her that her life was in hands bigger than hers. Whatever lay ahead, surely she could face it with if not a smile at least courage.

After the wine tasting, their group, along with several other cruisers, was taken to the restaurant on the monastery grounds and served a meal with traditional German bread and salad and steak in a sherry-mushroom sauce.

"I'm going to explode," Catherine said to Denise as they followed the others back onto the ship later.

"Don't do that. Think of the mess for the maid. Come on, let's ditch our coats and get a seat for the glassblowing demonstration. It will take your mind off your overstuffed stomach."

In addition to shedding their coats, the two women also brushed their teeth and freshened their makeup.

By the time they entered the lounge the glassblower already had samples of his work on display—everything from jewelry to ornaments. Catherine was glad to see Sierra there. She and Sophie were perusing the ornaments. So was Athena, her father by her side.

"Let's go look at the pretties," Denise said.

Catherine half feared that if she went over to look Rudy would feel the need to buy her something, and she didn't want him to think she was the kind of woman who came on a trip like this looking for a wallet.

"You go ahead. I'll help Trevor hold seats for everyone," Catherine told her.

Trevor had thrown a coat over a couple of seats and was sprawled across the love seat. He looked relieved to see Catherine.

"I'm glad you're here," he greeted her. "People were starting to give me dirty looks."

"We can't have that," Catherine said, and settled into another chair. She'd brought her purse along just in case she felt tempted by something she saw, and she put that on the chair next to her.

"That was some meal, wasn't it?" he said.

"Amazing." Like the rest of the trip so far.

She wondered what the kids were doing. Did they miss her? She hadn't had an email or text from either of them. Not that she expected one from William. Once he'd married he'd delegated the family chats to his wife. Although he'd been quick enough to ask for money when he needed it, Catherine thought with a frown. And Lila. It would have been nice to at least get a text asking if she'd arrived in Amsterdam in one piece.

But really, if the plane had crashed it would have been in the news, so texting to ask, "Are you all right?" would have been a little silly. Still...

Denise was right. Catherine's kids were twits.

"You okay, Catherine?"

She recalled her wandering thoughts. "Hmm?"

"You okay?" Trevor repeated, looking at her in concern.

"Yes, I'm fine," she said. "But I think I need a repeat of that fancy drink I had the night before."

"You got it," he said, and called over a waiter.

Five minutes later Catherine had her drink and was thanking Trevor for picking up the tab.

He waved away her thanks. "Gotta keep the ladies happy."

"I think you're doing a good job of that," she said.

"I could do better," he said, his easy smile looking a little less easy.

She followed his gaze to where the glass ornaments were laid out. Sophie had joined Rudy and Athena and was chatting happily.

"Don't give up," Catherine advised. "Sometimes it takes a while for things to sort themselves out."

"You're a wise woman, Catherine."

"Not really," she demurred.

"Yeah, you are. By the way, feel free to run interference for me," he cracked.

"I'll try my best." Distracting Rudy from Sophie—tough job, but someone had to do it. Ha ha.

The others drifted over and found seats, Rudy taking one next to Catherine and Athena flanking his other side. Sierra and Denise both sat down, leaving the chair next to Trevor free.

"I have chocolate," Trevor said to Sophie, patting the seat, and she dropped onto it.

"I couldn't eat another thing," she said. Then, as he pulled the bar from his shirt pocket, she added, "Maybe just one bite."

"Anyone want to try the Catherine special, ladies?" he offered. "I'm buying."

Sierra shook her head and murmured a "No, thanks." She

was such a subdued version of the woman who had joined them the first day of the cruise. Did it have something to do with the husband who hadn't been able to join her?

Her sister seemed to be trying to balance the social scales with smiles and enthusiasm. "It looks fabulous. What was it called?" she asked Catherine.

"A Winter Wonderland," Catherine said.

Trevor summoned the waiter back. "One of these for the rest of the ladies."

"You don't have to," Athena protested.

"I know. I want to."

"That's really nice of you," Catherine said to him.

"Nah. It's really selfish. I like feeling like a big man."

Generous, humble, fun-loving—Trevor was a gift from Santa, for sure. Catherine hoped Sophie woke up to that before the cruise ended and it was too late.

The demonstration began, the glassblower talking about glassblowing in general and his region of Germany specifically. He inspired many oohs and aahs as he blew an elegant, long-stemmed candleholder.

Catherine had been one of those doing the oohing and aahing, and when he was done, he asked her name.

"Catherine," she said.

"The Great," Trevor added, lifting his glass to her.

"Would you like this, Catherine the Great?" asked the glassblower.

"Oh, yes," she said.

"Well, then, you may have it," he said. "My assistant will box it up for you."

"Lucky you," Sophie said to her.

"I've never won anything," she confessed. Here was another lovely memory to add to the ones she was collecting.

"Don't let Lila see it," Denise cautioned. "She'll expect to get it for Christmas."

The mention of Lila and Christmas in the same sentence dulled the shine of the moment. Catherine wouldn't be with her daughter at Christmas. She wouldn't be with either of her children.

If only this cruise went through December 25. She could stay busy seeing sights and drinking fancy cocktails. But it didn't. In fact, the cruises stopped by then so crew members could be with their families.

Who needed family togetherness, anyway? Not her. She had…a glass candlestick.

Face facts, Sophie told herself. Rudy was not interested in being with a younger woman and he was smitten with Catherine. There would be no un-smittening him. Really, who could blame him? She was a nice lady.

Studying her, Sophie detected sadness in her eyes. With the demonstration over, people moved to the display tables to get serious about purchasing the various goodies. Catherine stayed seated and Sophie remained with her.

"Catherine, are you okay?"

"Me? I'm fine."

"Are you sure? You don't look fine."

"You're sweet to ask. I just get a little blue sometimes."

"You miss your husband?"

"I do. Not that our marriage was perfect—no marriage is—but I miss the companionship."

"You have kids, though, right?"

"Oh, yes, but they have lives of their own."

Sophie thought of how close she was with her parents. She and her brother and sister had lives of their own, of course, but their mom and dad were still an integral part of those lives. Why weren't Catherine's kids on this cruise with her?

Any number of reasons. Maybe they couldn't afford it. Maybe Catherine couldn't afford to take them.

"I bet they think you're fabulous," Sophie said, determined to cheer her up. She sure wanted to cheer up someone.

"Oh, I don't know about that."

"Well, I think you're fabulous. Hey, want to adopt me?"

That did bring a smile. "I doubt your mother would want to share."

"Sure she would. Anyway, you can't have too many moms, right?"

"Oh, yes, you can," said Athena, who had returned in time to eavesdrop.

Catherine's smile vanished. "I'm feeling a little tired. I think I'll say good-night," she said.

"Don't go, Catherine," Sophie urged.

"No, really. It's been a long day. I'll see you in the morning," Catherine said, then got up and threaded her way through the throng of shoppers.

"That was classy," Sophie said.

Athena pretended not to hear. *Bitch.*

Sophie left her to sit by her bitchy self and went to join her sister at the display table.

Trevor slipped in next to her. "Find anything you like?"

"Found something I didn't like," she said, glaring across the room at Athena. "That woman leaves a bad taste in my mouth."

"We'd better put something good in it, then. Fancy another drink?"

"May as well," she said.

There was sure no point trying to talk to Rudy. He was

all about Catherine. And anyway, look what came with him. Would she want to be related to Athena?

"Want to join us?" Trevor asked Sierra, who was half-heartedly fingering a paperweight.

"Nah. You two go ahead and enjoy yourselves. I'm going to head back to the room."

To mope. "Already? Why don't you hang out with us for a while," Sophie urged.

"I want to be rested up for Heidelberg. I'll see you later."

"I hope she doesn't just go to the room and text Mark," Sophie said, watching her go.

"Mark?"

Sophie bit her lip. She shouldn't have been voicing her thoughts out loud.

"Hey, none of my business," Trevor said easily. He pointed to the glass art in front of them. "Anything catch your eye?"

"Nope," Sophie said, and picked up the paperweight.

"Uh-huh."

"It's for my sister." As if a paperweight could counter the heavy weight on Sierra's heart. Sophie bought it, anyway.

"Trevor," someone called, and she turned to see his number one fan moving in their direction.

Trevor was suddenly deaf. "Come on," he said to Sophie, "I see a seat in the corner." He put a hand to the small of her back and steered her away.

"You can run but you can't hide," she joked.

"I can try," he said.

As they settled in Sophie did a quick scan of the room, looking for the girl. She'd been waylaid by a husky guy in jeans and a T-shirt. It looked like Trevor was safe for a while.

"I think you dodged the bullet," she said.

"I hope so."

"It's got to be tough to have women throwing themselves at you all the time," she teased.

"Funny." He shook his head. "What is it with people always going after someone who's not right for them?"

"Maybe you're right for her and you don't know it."

"I'm way too old for her," he said in disgust.

"Not necessarily. After a certain point, age doesn't really matter," Sophie argued.

"And after a certain point it does again. Age gaps don't matter so much in the middle of life, but they do in the early part and they do again at the end. You kinda want to reach the finish line together."

There was that. But still. "Lots of people manage quite well in spite of their age difference."

"You think so, huh?"

"I do," she insisted.

A waiter arrived and Trevor ordered drinks for them—beer for him and a Winter Wonderland for Sophie.

"There's something to be said for being with someone who grew up listening to the same music, watching the same TV shows, experiencing the same events in history. It's a bonding thing."

"There are all kinds of ways to bond," she argued. "Shared hobbies, similar values."

"So, what do you value, Sophie Miles?" he asked.

"Family, friends. I think it's important to be loyal," she added, thinking of her sister and her husband. "If you're in a relationship you owe it to the other person to really be there for that person."

"Absolutely," he agreed. "Once you make that commitment you stick to it. Which is more than I can say for my dad," he added. "Are your parents still together?"

"Oh, yes. Happily."

"Lucky you. Are they the same age?"

"Daddy's two years older."

"Same generation, though."

"Yes," she admitted.

"There you have it," he said. The server arrived with their drinks and Trevor took a slug of his.

"What about you?" she asked. "What do you value?"

"I'd say pretty much the same thing as you. Family first, loyalty."

"Must be willing to watch romantic comedies," she challenged.

"Must like going to car shows."

"Must be willing to play games with the family."

"Must like chocolate."

"That's easy," she scoffed.

"How about the car shows?"

"Oh, yes." She'd gone to a few of those with her dad and brother and had enjoyed seeing all the restored cars.

"Hiking?"

"You could get stung and have an allergic reaction." She'd gotten stung once when her parents rented a cabin on Lake Crescent. Granted, she hadn't gone into anaphylactic shock. But she could have!

"That's what antihistamines are for."

"You have an answer for everything, don't you," she said, frowning at him.

"Not really. Just some things. How about this for a requirement? Want to be with someone who makes you laugh?"

"For sure," she said.

"Okay, let me see if I can think of a joke." He paused a

minute, as if thinking. "Never mind. I'll just give you another drink and then everything I say will be funny."

"I'll just get myself another drink and then you won't have to try so hard."

And she did get another drink, and insisted on paying for one for him, too.

"I hate when women buy me drinks," he said after the server left. "It makes me feel so cheap. Are you trying to get me drunk and take advantage of me?"

She snickered. "You are good at making people laugh."

"After you've finished that you'll think I'm hilarious," he predicted.

She was getting a buzz. It was a pleasant buzz, though, so she kept right on enjoying herself.

He finally said, "We'd better get you back to your room while you can still walk there on your feet instead of your face."

"I'm fine," she said, waving away his concern. Then she stood and, whoa, was the ship spinning in circles?

"Here, let me help you," he said, slipping an arm around her.

"I am not drunk," she informed him.

"No, but you're definitely buzzed."

"Buzz, buzz," she said happily. "I hope you have some antihistamine with you for in case I sting you." Ha ha, wasn't that funny?

"There is no cure for what I'm coming down with," he said. "You'd better down a big glass of water before you conk out for the night or you're going to have a monster headache in the morning."

"Yes, doctor," she said. Doctor. "I need a doctor."

"You feel sick already?"

"No, I mean I need to be with a doctor."

"Do you have some disease?"

"Well, no. But I tend to get sick."

"Ah. Well, that doesn't mean you need to be with a doctor. It just means you need to be with someone who will take you to the doctor."

Good point. "That's what my sister says." Her poor sister.

"Your sister's a very smart woman," he said.

"Not that smart." She'd picked Mark.

They reached the room and Sophie leaned her dizzy self against the door and studied him. Those eyes. They were almost too pretty for a man. Big and brown with lots of lashes. She knew women who paid a lot for lashes like those. And that jaw, it was so…manly. So was his chest.

She tapped it with her finger. "Do you work out?"

"Gotta work off the chocolate."

He leaned an arm against the wall and smiled down at her. Trevor March had a beautiful smile. Trevor March had a beautiful everything.

"Has anyone ever told you that you are very, very gorgeous?"

She was cute, but gorgeous was stretching it. "Think so?"

"Yes, I do." He was looking at her lips.

"Do you want to kiss me?" she asked.

"Yes, I do," he said.

"I'd like that, but after all those drinks…"

"Worried you won't be able to feel your lips? Let's see." He moved in closer, threaded a hand through her hair and kissed her. Beautifully. But…

"How was that?" he whispered.

"I feel…" She'd had way too much to eat. And drink. "I think I'm going to… Oh, no! My room key." She fished the card out of her bra where she'd stuck it and quickly turned to the door.

"You okay?" he asked.

She barely got out the word "Norovirus!" before dashing into the room and to the bathroom.

11

SOPHIE WASN'T AT BREAKFAST THE NEXT MORNING but her sister was. "Where's the sis?" Trevor asked.

"Hungover," Sierra said. "How much did she drink last night after I left?"

"Only two, I swear," he said.

"That on top of the wine she had at dinner, plus the drink before the glassblower started talking." Sierra shook her head. "She's not a big drinker."

"I'll remember that in the future and just buy her pop," Trevor promised.

Sierra cocked her head and studied him. "Thinking of a future with my sister?" she asked with a smile.

"Maybe," he said, smiling back. "She's pretty amazing."

"Yes, she is."

"Think she's going to be up to seeing Heidelberg?"

"I don't know. Right now she's in bed and sure she's dying."

"Asking for a doctor?"

"How'd you guess?"

Trevor grinned. "Did I mention I took a first aid course in college? I know a couple of cures for a hangover."

"I bet you do." Sierra reached around and pulled a key card out of the back pocket of her jeggings. "She's going to be pissed if she misses seeing Heidelberg. See what you can do, doc."

"I'm on it," he said, taking the card.

He went to the pastry table and collected a croissant, then he got some coffee and made his way to the girls' room. Juggling the food, he managed to knock on the door, then unlocked it and pushed it open. Eased in cautiously to make sure she was presentable.

Sophie was under the down comforter, on her back with an arm over her head. "Are you back already?"

"Yes," Trevor said in a falsetto.

The arm came down and Sophie opened one eye to see him approaching the bed. "Trevor! What are you doing here?"

"I've come to cure your hangover."

"I'm dying," she groaned. "And I look terrible. But then people do look terrible when they're dying, don't they?"

"Come on," he urged, "try and sit up."

"I can't. The bed's spinning."

"I brought you some coffee. It will help with the spinning. And some carbs."

"Carbs. I ate way too many carbs yesterday."

"This will help your brain. Come on."

She sat up, the covers falling away. She was wearing some

kind of sleep shirt, red with little Santa faces all over it. No bra. *Don't look.*

"I can't eat," she groaned.

"Then start by drinking." He held out the coffee, making a valiant effort to keep his eyes on her face. A very cute face, with hair falling over it.

"Drinking—don't say that word," she protested, and pushed her hair away.

Don't look below her chin. He looked. Okay, so he was human.

"I'll, uh, get you some water," he said, setting down the croissant and moving away from the bed. "Keep drinking that coffee." He fetched water, then returned and set it on the nightstand along with the croissant. "Got any aspirin? That's best for hangovers."

"In my purse. I like to be prepared for anything," she added.

"Where is your purse?"

"On the counter," she said, and groaned.

The one she'd had the other day, a red fake leather number was, indeed, sitting on the counter. He picked it up. Good Lord, what did she have in the thing, weights?

"How do you carry this around without your arm going numb?" he muttered.

"It's not that heavy." She took another sip of coffee.

He tried looking for the aspirin. It had to be in there somewhere but where? He saw a pink wallet, a couple of travel-size bottles of hand sanitizer, hand lotion, tissues, a small brush, her cell phone, mints, antacid, a little emergency sewing kit—all that was missing was the partridge in the pear tree. She was definitely prepared for anything.

He gave up and set the purse next to her. "You'd better look. It's a jungle in there." She handed over her half-finished coffee and opened the purse, rooted around and came out with a small bottle of aspirin, then groaned and fell back against the headboard.

He took the bottle, opened it and shook out two pills. "Here you go. Breakfast of champions." She downed the aspirin and water and he made another try with the croissant. "Okay, carb time."

"Ugh. I can't think of food," she said, rubbing her forehead. She handed back the empty coffee cup and started to slip back down under the comforter.

"No, no," he said, grabbing her arm. "Carbs first. It'll help. Trust me."

"I did that last night and look where it got me." Her cheeks turned pink. "I'm sorry I ran off so quickly."

"Understandable under the circumstances," he said.

Her cheeks got pinker. "It was a lovely kiss. I wish I'd been in more of a position to appreciate it."

"We'll have to try again, when you feel better," he said, and smiled at her. "Now, how about another bite of that croissant? You don't want to miss Heidelberg."

"I don't," she admitted, and took the croissant and bit off a piece.

"My brother's doing the castle tour with his students, then he's turning them loose and he and I are going to do our own thing. You and your sister can join us if you want."

"Brother time? We don't want to interrupt that," she protested.

"You won't be interrupting. You'll be the frosting on the cake."

"Chocolate?"

Dang but she was adorable. "Of course," he said. "Drink some more water, take a shower. You'll feel better soon."

"Yes, doctor," she joked. Then she took another bite of

croissant and slid back down the bed. He took that as his cue to leave and slipped quietly out the door.

He hoped she'd feel good enough to leave the ship. He was up for seeing the city with his brother, but he really wanted Sophie to join them. The woman was more addictive than chocolate. And for a chocolatier, that was saying something.

Denise and her fan club finished breakfast and went to their respective rooms to primp, leaving Catherine and Sierra alone at the table to finish their coffee and pastries.

"I'm surprised we haven't seen Rudy and Athena yet," Sierra said.

After the previous night Catherine really had no desire to see Athena. "Maybe they already ate," she said, then quickly changed the subject. "I hope your sister's going to feel well enough to tour Heidelberg."

"If Trevor has anything to say about it, she will. He seems like a great guy. I hope Sophie doesn't blow it."

A text came in on her phone and Catherine watched Sierra's face turn pale as she read it. "Bad news?"

Sierra looked on the verge of tears. "It's nothing."

"Of course it's none of my business," Catherine hurried to say.

"My husband says we need to talk when I get back." Sierra's voice was barely above a whisper. A tear slithered down her cheek.

A text saying they needed to talk. Catherine understood the significance of that. "So it wasn't just work keeping your husband from taking this cruise with you?"

"I thought it was. I guess I thought wrong," she added bitterly.

"Maybe it's not what you think," Catherine said. Rather a stupid thing to say. It probably was exactly what she thought.

Sierra shook her head. "We don't have the same goals anymore. I don't even know how that happened."

"I'm so sorry," Catherine said. "We like to think we'll stay the same as we were when we were first young, but people do change."

Bill had. Somewhere along the way the responsibilities of a family had whittled off much of the carefree attitude he'd had when they were first dating, exposing some sharp edges. But she'd learned to balance them, and in the end they'd rubbed along fine, especially after becoming empty nesters. She'd so been looking forward to starting a whole new life once he retired. If she'd known she was going to lose him she'd have lobbied for not waiting for retirement to start checking off the items on the bucket list. He would have enjoyed this cruise.

"I still love him," Sierra said, wiping away another tear.

Catherine found a tissue in her purse and handed it over. "Sometimes you can reassess and renegotiate. I'm sure you already know that marriage is all about give-and-take."

"What if it's too late for that?"

"Then you'll reassess yet again. Don't give up yet, though," Catherine urged her. "Every marriage goes through rough patches but you can get through a lot if you're determined to stay together and remember what brought you together in the first place."

Sierra heaved a sigh and wiped away another tear. "I think he's forgotten."

"Then maybe you can remind him. Love can work miracles."

"You are a wise woman, Catherine," Sierra said.

Sierra was the second person who'd said that to her. Catherine wasn't about to tout herself as wise, but it made her feel good to know someone appreciated her advice. Someone actually wanted to hear what she had to say.

"I don't know about that," she said. "I'm sorry you're going through this."

"I shouldn't have dumped it on you," Sierra said with a sniff. "Good grief, you hardly know me."

"I don't mind."

"I don't usually barf my troubles all over people I've just met," Sierra said, embarrassed. "It's just that…I feel like I've been punched." She dabbed at another tear and blew her nose.

Catherine handed over another tissue. "It's okay."

Sierra caught back a sob. "He's breaking my heart."

Catherine laid a hand over hers. "I know how it feels to be heartbroken. I felt that way when my husband died."

"Sounds like you had a great marriage."

"We had a good marriage. We always managed to work out our differences." Not that they had that many left after almost forty years together. They'd grown accustomed to each other's flaws and idiosyncrasies and settled into a comfortable cohabitation. Bill had always been there for her. Always there, period. "It's so much easier to go through hard times when you have someone by your side," she said sadly. "I wish I had him now."

Sierra turned her back on her own unhappiness and looked at Catherine with concern. "Are you going through something hard right now?"

Catherine wished she'd kept her big mouth shut. "Just a little health challenge."

"Why am I thinking it's not little?"

"I'll get through it."

"I hope you do."

"And you'll get through what you're dealing with, too, I'm sure of it."

"I hope so. Thanks for listening. Again, I'm really sorry about boring you with my problems."

"I didn't mind," Catherine assured her.

Sierra nodded, blew her nose one last time, then said, "I guess I'll get back to the room and see if my sister's feeling better."

"I hope she'll feel well enough to go on the castle tour. And you, too."

Sierra shook her head. "Not sure I'm in the mood anymore."

"It's a shame to let tomorrow rob you of today's joys," Catherine said. Now there was a pearl of wisdom she needed to hang on to.

Sierra sighed. "I think it already has. Thanks again. For being there."

"Anytime you want to talk," Catherine said.

Sierra left just as Rudy approached the table, his daughter following behind like a sheep dog. Or rather, a rottweiler.

"May we join you?" he asked Catherine.

"Of course," she said. It was difficult to include Athena in her smile, but she managed.

Athena gave her a small one in return.

"Great," he said. "I think I need an omelet," he added, and went off to stand in line at the omelet station.

Athena chose yogurt and some fruit and was back at the table while her father was still waiting in line to put in his order. "I imagine you'll be spending the morning in Heidelberg with your friend," she said casually. "She must be feeling neglected."

Yes, with her two admirers, Denise was feeling terribly neglected. Arnold had bought her an ornament the night before and both men had plied her with drinks. Both had made sure she was going on the castle tour.

"I suspect Charlie and Arnold are going to demand a lot of her attention," Catherine said.

Athena looked far from happy with that answer.

Now was the perfect time for a talk. "Athena, I suspect you're worried that I might have designs on your father."

Athena didn't bother to deny it. "Don't you?" she challenged.

"I have to admit, I've been lonely since my husband died, and I'm very much enjoying your father's company. I'd like to be able to call him a friend, but I have no plans for getting involved romantically. I have some health issues I'm dealing with."

Athena almost looked contrite. "Nothing serious, I hope."

"I had uterine cancer. It was pretty advanced. After Christmas I'll be starting chemo."

For the second time that morning Catherine saw a woman's face go pale. "Oh, my God. I'm so sorry."

"Don't be. I'm coping with it."

"I..." Athena stared down at her yogurt.

"I understand you not wanting to share your father with another woman. Your mother sounds like she was someone very special."

"It's not just that. Daddy is..." Athena hesitated, and Catherine could tell she was searching for the right words. "Vulnerable. Watching my mother die, not being able to save her and him a doctor—it about killed him."

"It had to be hard for you, too," Catherine ventured.

Athena bit her lip, nodded. Both women sat in silence a moment, then Athena continued, "He was lost after Mom died. It made him easy prey."

Was that how Athena thought Catherine saw her father?

"His second wife only married him for his money," Athena said with a scowl. "She was young enough to be his daughter and beautiful, and she knew how to turn on the charm. He'd thought she loved him but she didn't. She was shallow and selfish and in the end she left him for somebody with more money. It about broke his heart."

This explained so much. "And you don't want to see that happen again."

"People can be deceptive and my father is so trusting. I..." She sighed. "I've probably come across as a real bitch."

Yes, she had.

"But I don't care. I'll do anything to keep Daddy from being hurt again."

"Your father's lucky to have such a loyal daughter. And you don't need to worry about me making a grab for him," Catherine promised even though a part of her would have liked nothing better than to get grabby. "I'm sure I'll come through all of this just fine." Surely with all the extra measures the doctors were taking she would. "But I don't want to drag someone else through what lies ahead of me."

"Do you have kids nearby who can help?"

"If I need help, I'm sure they'll find a way. They're very busy."

Athena's brows rose. The girl had one of those expressive faces and the message it was telegraphing at the moment was a shocked *Too busy for you?*

And what was Catherine's expression saying? *I'm afraid so.* But it was wrong to think that of her children. Yes, they could be self-centered, but they weren't heartless. Surely, if she really needed them to they'd come through.

"It is a busy time of year," Athena said, taking the polite

route and helping Catherine set up excuses for her children in advance. "At least you'll all be able to enjoy Christmas before the chemo starts."

Catherine could feel her face heating up. The fact that her children wouldn't be with her at Christmas was embarrassing. If only she hadn't been such a drama queen the year before.

"It will be a quiet Christmas," she said, and left it at that.

"I hope everything works out for you," Athena said.

Now that she didn't have to worry about protecting Rudy, the dragon lady was gone and Catherine could glimpse a young woman who had some manners, after all. And a heart, dedicated to keeping her father's heart safe. Athena wasn't jealous or possessive, she was concerned. How different her behavior looked when seen in that light.

"Thank you," said Catherine. "And you're right about today. I should spend more time with Denise." She stood. "Please give my excuses to your father."

She left the dining room before he could join them at the table. There would be more than one bus leaving the dock for Heidelberg. She'd make sure she was on a different one than Rudy and his daughter.

Another sick woman. After what her father went through he wouldn't want anything to do with Catherine, Athena knew that. She should tell him.

Somehow, though, when he arrived at the table asking what happened to Catherine, she couldn't bring herself to tell him about Catherine's situation. "She left. She's going to spend the day with her friend."

Daddy looked disappointed and Athena felt responsible for that disappointment.

Although, really, she shouldn't have. There would have

come a point when Catherine would politely push Daddy away. Better the pushing happened sooner than later. Still, Athena felt badly over how unfriendly she'd been to the woman. She had so misjudged Catherine.

Funny how different someone's behavior looked when you had all the facts. Catherine had been enjoying being with Daddy, but she hadn't been angling for his attention or strategizing some subtle method to get her hooks into him. She simply was what she was—a nice widow who was trying to enjoy a getaway before facing something horrible.

And what was the deal with her kids? A quiet Christmas? *If I need help, I'm sure they'll find a way.* What did that mean? The kids weren't already planning on helping her? Athena had been to every one of her mother's treatments. What kind of offspring did Catherine Pine have, anyway?

Shits, that was what kind.

Like what Athena had been to her. Maybe it was time she stopped jumping to conclusions and judging people.

If only Catherine wasn't going through what she was going through. If only she had...anything but cancer.

"I'm going to stay on the boat and bag seeing Heidelberg," Sierra told Sophie.

Sophie was feeling almost human now that she'd eaten, dressed and showered. But seeing her sister upset, that hurting head was nothing compared to the ache in her heart.

She sat down on the bed next to Sierra and put an arm around her. "You can't just stay here and mope. Come on, come with me."

Sierra shook her head. "I need time to process what Mark said."

Outside was a view of snug German houses with tiled roofs,

flower boxes and shutters at the windows, and lawns with manicured hedges. An old castle ruin and a beautiful city awaited them. Her sister should have been having a wonderful time.

With Mark. "Maybe he wants to work things out. Maybe that's what he meant by that text."

Sierra shook her head. "Then he would have said that."

"You don't know that for sure." Although she was probably right. Was it better to encourage her sister to delude herself or have her face the ugly probability right then? It was the emotional equivalent of slowly pulling off a bandage or yanking it off fast and being done with it.

"It's over. I think I've known it for months. I just didn't want to admit it." Sierra wiped at a tear sneaking out the corner of her eye. "You know what really hurts is him waiting until I'm over here and supposed to be having fun to say this. No, I take it back. What hurts even more is how he pretended everything was okay before I left, like he felt so bad he couldn't take time off. 'Go, have fun with your sister,' he said, making it sound like he was being such a good sport. I guess what he really meant was go."

If Mark had been on the ship with them Sophie would have pushed him overboard. Of course, if he'd been on the boat it would have meant there was no problem. Her sister would have been happy.

"If it is over, then it's all his fault and he's a fool," Sophie said vehemently.

Sierra gave her a watery-eyed smile. "You're the best sister in the world."

"No, that award would have to go to you. I wish I could make it all better."

"I wish *I* could make it all better." Sierra heaved a sigh. "I'll get through this."

"Yes, you will. Start by coming with me and seeing the castle."

Sierra shook her head. "I'm just going to hang out on the ship. And eat. Maybe Trevor will leave me a supply of chocolate. Speaking of, he's waiting."

Sophie couldn't go skipping off to have fun when her sister was so miserable. "I don't want to go. I'll stay with you."

"You will not," Sierra insisted. "I don't want you underfoot being all irritating and chipper."

"You shouldn't be alone."

"I want to be. Seriously. So pleeease, go away. Spend some time with a great guy with my blessing."

"It feels all wrong to abandon you." Even if Sierra did want to be alone, Sophie felt like a traitor. She was going to go have fun while her sister stayed behind with a broken heart.

"I need some time alone. Really. Get my money's worth and go have fun."

"Like I can do that when your life is falling apart."

"There's no point in both of us being miserable. And I'm serious. I've already embarrassed myself dumping on Catherine. And now you. I need some time alone to think and pull myself together. So go. I want you to."

"Okay, I will, but only if you promise to go out with me on our next port of call."

"I'll think about it," Sierra said, making no promises.

Think, shmink. Sophie was going to make sure her sister got out and forgot her troubles. Or at least shoved them to the back corner of her mind.

She finally gave up the battle when Sierra threatened to

smack her if she didn't get out of the room, but she wasn't exactly skipping when she went down the hallway.

"Where's your sister?" Trevor asked when she met him in the lobby.

"She's not feeling good."

"She's sick?"

Only at heart. "She'll feel better later," Sophie said.

What a bunch of baloney. If that text from Mark meant what Sierra thought it meant, it was going to be a very long time before she felt better.

12

ATHENA CONTINUED TO WRESTLE WITH THE dilemma of whether or not to tell her father about Catherine. The longer Catherine delayed and the closer they became, the harder her news was going to be on Daddy.

But telling him wouldn't be right. She needed to let Catherine share her situation in her own good time. Meanwhile, maybe a little distance between them wouldn't hurt.

Her father had no intention of keeping his distance, however. He found Catherine when everyone was loading onto the buses and made sure they were on the same one as her.

Athena reminded herself that the situation was out of her hands as they settled into their seats behind Catherine and Denise. At least Catherine wasn't a fortune hunter. Somehow, she didn't find that consoling.

She did find it mildly consoling that Catherine was trying to stick close to her friend and not encourage Daddy. Of course it didn't work. Denise got distracted with her men friends and Daddy and Catherine were soon walking side by side again as they all got off the bus and started for the castle.

Wars dating as far back as the 1600s along with two lightning strikes had taken their toll on Heidelberg Castle, but even though it was mostly a red stone ruin, it was worth touring. It offered an incredible view of the city below with the Neckar River ribboning its way through the city. Caught up in the beauty of it all, Athena set aside her concerns for her father and allowed herself a moment to take pictures.

"Take one of all of the old people, will you?" Denise asked her, handing over her phone.

"Sure," Athena said.

They all posed, Denise and Catherine front and center, surrounded by the three men. Athena noticed Daddy had a hand on Catherine's shoulder. Both of them were smiling. They could have been an old married couple celebrating an anniversary.

Athena's heart cracked. There was no future for her father and Catherine. Catherine didn't want one.

The crack widened as Athena thought about how much she missed her mother, how happy Mom and Daddy had been and how wrong it was that he was alone now. Life was about both loss and gain, but Athena was convinced that losing a mother was one of the largest losses of all. It filled you with pain and then, once the pain dulled, it filled you again, with loneliness.

It wasn't hard to understand why her father so desperately wanted to find someone. Daughters could only staunch so much unhappiness. He'd come on this cruise on a quest, hoping to somehow heal a wounded heart, still trying to recover, and he had. But the woman he'd met would leave him even more miserable than he'd been before.

Athena handed back the phone to Denise, who looked at the picture and pronounced it good. "We don't look too bad," she told the others, and turned the phone so they could see.

"No, we don't," said Daddy. "Will you send that to me?" he asked Denise.

"Sure. What's your email?"

Daddy passed it on. Then, as Denise was getting the other two men's emails, he handed his phone to Athena. "One more, honey. Take one of Catherine and me."

"Oh, no," Catherine said, pulling away. "Let me take one of you and your daughter."

Catherine really was a class act.

Athena tried for her happiest smile as they posed, but she knew it had never reached her eyes. A blizzard of emotions swirled inside her—unhappiness over the loss of her mother, guilt over her earlier attitude toward Catherine, worry about her father—and she half wished she'd never invited herself along on this trip.

Catherine handed Daddy's phone back to him and was about to hurry off to start walking down the hill with Denise and Arnold and Charlie, but Daddy stopped her. "One more picture. Something to remember our time here."

Catherine looked to Athena as if asking permission.

"A good idea," Athena said. Let them have their moment. It would end soon enough.

She told herself the same thing when, once they were in town, they stopped in a little jewelry shop and Daddy bought both her and Catherine another charm, this one of the castle.

"Another memento," he said, beaming at them.

"It's very kind of you," Catherine murmured. "It will be a lovely reminder of both of you."

Yes, a class act.

Trevor's brother planned to join up with him and Sophie after the castle tour, once the bus had unloaded them all in the city. Meanwhile, Trevor and Sophie trailed behind the kids during the tour, stopping like everyone else to take pictures in front of the fortress's huge wine barrel, the largest in the world.

"This will be a fun post for Instagram," she said as they walked away.

"So you're on Instagram? Me, too."

"Do you post lots of pictures of chocolate?" she asked.

"Of course."

She did a search on her phone. Yep, there was Cupid's Chocolates. "Oh, wow," she said, checking it out. "You sure know how to pack temptation in a picture."

"Good temptation, though," he said. He, too, was searching his phone. "And there you are. I see you've already put up some pictures."

"Of course."

"So, what else are you on?" he asked.

"Everything. Twitter, Facebook, Pinterest. That's my favorite. I love those foodie pins, especially the ones featuring baked goodies."

"Oh, yeah. I seem to remember you mentioning something about French silk pie," Trevor said. "Is that your specialty?"

"No. Cupcakes are my specialty. I make a fabulous chocolate one with white chocolate frosting flavored with rose water."

"White chocolate and rose water?"

"It's a fabulous combination. Maybe you should think about it for one of your chocolate bars," she said.

He nodded thoughtfully. "Intriguing. I'll have to look into that."

Okay, giving a chocolatier advice on chocolate treats. How was that for tacky?

"Look at me, giving advice to the expert," she said, her face heating up.

"Hey, I'm always open to new ideas," he said.

Silly how pleased she felt by his reaction to her suggestion. Growing up as the baby of the family, she hadn't always been taken seriously. Maybe she wasn't now, either, but if Trevor was faking his reaction to her suggestion, he was doing a great job of it.

They moved on to the thick wooden door leading to the residential courtyard. "Here's an interesting legend," Sophie read from the guidebook she'd purchased. "It's said that the castle will be handed to anyone who can bite through the door knocker."

"Yeah? Let's try it," Trevor suggested.

"Eeew," she said in disgust. "I don't even want to think about how many germy mouths might have touched that."

"Hey, you have to be brave to win a castle," he said, and sunk his teeth into the door knocker.

It was so thick even a horse couldn't bite through it, and she found herself giggling.

"I guess nobody will be giving me the keys to the castle," he said as he stepped away and wiped his mouth.

"If it's any consolation, it says here that even a witch tried to bite through it and she failed."

"Oh, well," he said. "This place would take a lot of work to fix up and I have a business to run."

"A very important business," she reminded him, making him smile. It didn't take much to make Trevor March smile. She liked that about him. She liked a lot about him.

Once they got outside the castle, Harriet the pest attached herself to them, spouting much of the same information from the same guidebook Sophie had been reading, all the while casting hungry looks at Trevor.

She was an irritant, but who was Sophie to judge after the way she'd stalked Rudy? She got that whole determination thing, the hope that someone who seemed so right would turn out to be your soul mate. But Rudy's soul had leaned in a different direction.

And here was easygoing, easy-to-talk-to Trevor the chocolate king, making Sophie's soul do some leaning of its own. And he'd made it pretty clear how he felt. Poor Harriet was out of luck. Still, Sophie could be magnanimous.

"Looks like great minds think alike," she said to Harriet, holding up her guidebook. "I like learning about new places, don't you?"

"I like learning, period," Harriet said, and Sophie wondered if that comment was supposed to make her look superior.

They started to stroll across the flagstone courtyard to take in the view, and Harriet strolled right along with them. Next thing Sophie knew Harriet was pumping her for more information about her life, wanting to know where she lived and worked. She finally got down to the main question: Did Sophie have a boyfriend?

"She's working on it," Trevor answered for her, and caught Sophie's gloved hand in his. The contact, along with his grin, made her heart start skipping.

No heart skipping for Harriet. Instead, she scowled. "How old are you, anyway?" she demanded when Trevor left to talk to his brother and it was only the two of them standing together, looking at the view below.

Maybe instead of German Harriet should have been taking a course in manners. "How old are you?" Sophie countered.

"I'm nineteen." She may as well have added, *Compete with that, old broad.*

"Cheer up," Sophie quipped. "You won't be nineteen forever."

"Yeah, and you won't be…whatever you are, either," Harriet retorted. "It sucks to get old."

Okay, Sophie was beginning to dislike this kid.

Trevor was back. "Harriet, Herr Professor wants a word with all of you. Thank God," he murmured as Harriet reluctantly left them to join the rest of the class.

"I think she feels you'd be better off with a younger woman," Sophie said.

"I'll bet. I should never have given her chocolate."

"Give a woman chocolate and she'll follow you anywhere. You're like the Pied Piper," Sophie teased. "Except she's not really a rat." Just a bit of a brat.

"She's something," Trevor said, shaking his head.

The class made their way to the bus and Kurt began walking toward Trevor and Sophie. Harriet fell in with him.

Sophie heard him say, "Harriet, you don't want to fall behind the others."

"I thought I'd come with you," she said. The girl was bold, Sophie would give her that.

"Actually, I'm going to be spending some time with my brother. You know. Family time."

Harriet pointed to Sophie. "She's not family."

Kurt stopped just short of where Sophie and Trevor stood.

"Not yet. Oh, and I'm hoping you won't mind doing me a favor."

Harriet looked eager at that. "Sure. What do you need, Herr Professor?"

"Make sure Hugh and Bristol and Megan all get back to the boat on time."

Harriet rolled her eyes. "I can't believe I paid all this money to babysit." But she marched off, in search of the other students.

"I was thinking the same thing," Kurt said, turning to Trevor and Sophie. "Bringing along my German class seemed like a good idea at the time."

"I could have told you how that would turn out," Trevor said.

"Yeah, you tell me a lot of stuff, most of it useless," Kurt shot back with a teasing grin.

"Oh, well, you're saved now," Sophie said, then decided to give the two brothers some quality time. She'd find Denise and company and hang out with them. "You two enjoy yourselves."

"Wait a minute. Where do you think you're going?" Trevor demanded.

"I'm going to let you enjoy your family time," Sophie said.

Kurt put an arm around her. "We share," he said, and winked at his brother.

Trevor pulled her away. "We don't share that much," he said, making her giggle.

"Come on, let's all go check out the city," Kurt said.

Sophie was entranced with the stately brick homes with their gables and shuttered windows, many of them looking like miniature castles, as they made their way down the cobblestone street from the castle ruins to the town. She was delighted with the Christmas market, especially the giant pyramid that towered above all the booths. Sierra would have loved this, she thought wistfully.

Shopping for a treat for her sister was her first order of business, and she found an elegant silver tree ornament shaped like a pine cone that she was sure Sierra would like. As if an ornament was any kind of consolation for what Sierra was going through. Still, it was all Sophie could think to do.

She bought both brothers Glühwein. They, in turn, insisted on buying her lunch, taking her into a restaurant with enough inviting aromas to keep her mouth watering for months.

"Would you like a beer?" Kurt asked her as their dirndl-clad waitress approached.

"No," said both Sophie and Trevor in unison.

"After the hangover I had this morning I don't think I'm ever going to drink again," Sophie said. "At least not today. Thank God Trevor knew what to do for a hangover."

"He knows something, huh?" Kurt grinned across the table at his brother.

"Jealous, always has been," Trevor said to Sophie. "It's because he's adopted. Bank robbers left him on our doorstep." He smacked his forehead. "Damn! Mom told me not to tell."

Sophie snickered and Kurt said, "Pay no attention to him. He's delusional."

The waitress had arrived. *"Zwei Bier, bitte, für ihn und für mich,"* he said to her. Then, to Sophie, "I have the perfect drink for you. *Und eine Spezi*," he told the waitress.

"What's that?" Sophie asked.

"It's a combination of cola and orange drink. You'll like it."

"Und dreimal Schnitzel, bitte," Trevor added, then held up three fingers. *"Und Pommes frites auch."*

"You speak German, too?" Sophie asked him, impressed.

"Not as well as the old guy here," Trevor said, "but some. One of our grandmas was an import. She had us speaking it when we were two."

"So what did you just ask for?" Sophie wanted to know.

"Good stuff," Trevor assured her. "The *Pommes frites* are French fries and the schnitzel is pork, pounded thin, breaded and fried. Our grandma used to make it."

"Pork?" she said weakly. "Trichinosis."

"Don't worry, they cook it well," Trevor assured her. "Germans eat this stuff every day."

"And how many of them have little worms in their stomachs?" she retorted. She was not a big fan of pork.

But she became a big fan of schnitzel, salty and crispy on the outside and tender and moist on the inside. "I could eat this every day," she declared after her first few bites. "Thank you for introducing me to schnitzel," she said to Trevor.

"I have all kinds of things I can introduce you to," he informed her, his voice smooth as milk chocolate.

She could already imagine. Was it suddenly hot in here? She needed another Spezi.

The more time Trevor spent with Sophie Miles, the more he liked her, he thought as they strolled the Christmas market after lunch. She looked so cute in her red knitted cap. Her parka covered her butt but not her legs. They were hugged by skintight leggings and they were a work of art. So was her smile.

Yeah, she was a little obsessed with germs and getting sick, but everybody had their flaws and he'd sure dated women with worse: everything from drama queens so insecure they drove him nuts constantly checking up on him, to self-centered divas who excelled at manipulation. Someone who was health obsessed beat those kinds of women any day.

Trevor also appreciated Sophie's willingness to stop at whatever booths he and Kurt wanted to, offering to take pictures of them and buying them treats. That, in addition to seeing how she treated her sister, were all good indicators that she wasn't selfish. And he got a kick out of her eagerness to learn the German language as they visited the different market booths.

"Just be sure you ask everyone, *'Ist das in Deutschland gemacht?'*" Kurt advised her.

"What does that mean? Something about Germany, right?" she asked.

"It means, 'Was this made in Germany?' Not everything you see was handcrafted, so if you want authentic German items it's good to ask."

"I definitely want the real thing," she said, and was happy to try out her new sentence when they stopped at a booth selling candles.

She had a flair for language. Her pronunciation was flawless when she repeated the words to the woman selling the candles.

So flawless that the woman replied in German with far more than a simple, *"Ja."*

"Um." Sophie turned to Trevor. "What did she just say?"

"That she and her husband make these candles themselves."

"Oh. What can I say back? Something easy."

"Sehr gut."

"Sehr gut," Sophie said to the woman with an enthusiastic nod.

"How many do you want?" Kurt asked.

"One for my mother, my grandmother and my sister."

"Okay, tell her, *'Ich möchte drei, bitte.'*"

Sophie parroted what he'd told her and the woman got busy wrapping them for her.

"That was fun," she said when she'd finished conducting her business. "I may have to take your German class."

"You don't need to bother with him," Trevor said. "I can teach you all the German you want to know."

"If you don't want to know much," Kurt teased.

"Funny," Trevor said back. "Who invited you along, anyway?"

"He's very insecure," Kurt said to Sophie.

Oh, yeah, big brother was in rare form.

Trevor didn't mind, though. His brother was his best friend and he was pleased that Kurt and Sophie were hitting it off.

"I like her," Kurt approved later, once they were all back on board the ship and the brothers were in their room, unloading the presents they'd bought. "She's nice."

"She is," Trevor said. "Total hypochondriac, though. She's convinced she needs to be with a doctor."

"Doesn't a first aid course count?" Kurt asked, shrugging out of his jacket.

Trevor tossed his coat on his bed. "It should."

"It better. You don't have time to go to med school." He kicked off his boots and slipped into loafers. "You can thank me anytime for making you come on this cruise."

"And you can thank God I didn't kill you for sticking me with Harriet."

"I didn't do that. She stuck herself. Anyway, you're free of her now."

"For the moment."

Kurt shrugged and started for the bathroom. "She'll get tired of chasing an old man. Just don't feed her any more chocolate. You should have known better than that. It only takes one to get hooked."

"That's for sure," Trevor said. But he wasn't thinking about candy bars. He was thinking about kisses, and that one he'd enjoyed with Sophie the night before sure had him hooked, possibly for life. Sadly, the moment had been cut short, but he intended to make up for it in the very near future.

13

THE NEXT DAY'S STOP WAS THE CITY OF FREIBURG, which Catherine quickly decided was her favorite so far. Although much of the city had been bombed during World War II, the people had taken great care to restore the buildings and it had a medieval feel to it. She was delighted by the Christmas decorations, lights and giant fir boughs strung between buildings on each side of its cobblestone streets making a canopy of green, and by the network of tiny streams that ran through the center of town. According to the guide on their walking tour, they had been originally created in the Middle Ages as a source of water for livestock.

But the cathedral, built in the sixteenth century and said to have the most beautiful spire in the world, was her favorite stop. She stood in awe, taking in the stained glass windows, the panels, sculptures and art treasures.

"It's beautiful, isn't it?" she said to Sierra, who had tagged along with her, Rudy and Athena, as well as Denise and her men, leaving Sophie free to hang out with Trevor.

"It is," Sierra agreed, although she didn't sound as impressed as Catherine. Or even as interested.

Catherine understood. It was hard to muster up an interest in the world around you when your own world was teetering on its axis.

"Standing in a beautiful, old cathedral like this reminds me that there's something, someone, bigger than me out there, and it gives me comfort," Catherine said.

Sierra nodded. "Right now I'll take all the comfort I can get."

"I understand," Catherine said. "I had a terrible time after losing my husband. I still miss him, but the pain has lessened. One thing I'm finding is that God has a way of bringing along just what we need to start healing and moving forward."

"I don't want to move forward," Sierra said miserably. "Not without Mark."

Catherine put an arm around her. "I know you don't, but no matter what, forward is always the only way we can go."

Sierra bit her lip and nodded. "I'm sorry I keep dumping on you."

"I don't mind."

"I guess it's because you're so easy to talk to. It's a little like having my mom along."

"That's one of the nicest compliments I ever had," Catherine said.

"I'm glad we met."

"Me, too."

"I hope we can stay in touch after the cruise."

"I'd like that," Catherine said.

She'd come on this cruise thinking it would be something to fill her empty days, a nice getaway. It was filling that emptiness, certainly, but it was becoming so much more. The people she'd met had unwittingly pulled something dark and heavy off her soul. Christmas this year would come wrapped in wonderful memories, and it looked like she'd be taking home some new friends.

Even Athena seemed open to friendship now that she'd been assured Catherine wasn't out to make a grab for her father's money or break his heart. Later, she appeared at Catherine's other side in the Christmas market as she and Sierra looked at cottage-shaped incense burners while Rudy stood in line for Glühwein.

"Are you buying one?" Athena asked.

"I'm considering it," Catherine replied.

"They're really unique," Sierra said. "You should definitely get one."

"You won't find these in the States," put in Athena.

Catherine nodded. "I think I will. And one for my daughter, too." She smiled and pointed to the ones she wanted and the woman behind the counter nodded, wrapped them in paper and slipped them into a bag.

"Your kids didn't want to come on this cruise with you?" Athena asked as Catherine handed over her money.

"It was a spur-of-the-moment decision," Catherine said. "Denise had booked the room for two with another of our friends, and that friend dropped out so she invited me to join her. Anyway, the kids already had plans." She wondered if Lila ever found a babysitter so she could go to that Christmas party.

Athena's brows pulled together. "I'm surprised they let you

go off all alone like this when you've been…" Aware of Sierra on Catherine's other side, she shut up. But once Sierra got busy purchasing an incense burner for her mom she asked, "Didn't they want to spend time with you after everything you've gone through?" She bit her lip, then said, "It's just that I'd sure want to be with my mother under the circumstances."

"We can't always make things work out the way we want," Catherine said. "Anyway, I'm not alone. I'm here with my best friend and I'm making some very nice new ones."

"I haven't exactly been one of them, I know." Athena's cheeks got a little rosier as she picked up an incense burner and examined it.

"You're just watching out for your father," Catherine said.

"Someone needs to. He's so…trusting."

"That's not a character flaw," Catherine said gently.

"Only when it comes to picking the right woman." Athena shook her head and set the incense burner back down. "I guess it's understandable. If you could have seen how miserable he was after Mom died."

"I can imagine," Catherine said. "I've been there."

Athena's cheeks turned rosier still. "Of course. I'm sorry."

"Don't be."

"I think he still misses her. I know I do." She pulled a tissue from her coat pocket and dabbed at her eyes.

"It's only natural that you would," Catherine said. "I remember when I lost my mother. It was a year before I could think about her without crying. I miss her to this day."

"He's all I have left." Athena frowned. "All right, that's not true. I have a son, and he's the best. But he's busy with school."

Yes, busy, thought Catherine. It was what happened when children grew up. They found lives of their own.

"And parents are different," Athena continued. She chewed

on her lip a moment. "I worry about him. I really don't want to see him hurt."

"I'm not going to do that," Catherine assured her.

"You wouldn't intentionally."

Catherine knew exactly where she was going. Rudy had already buried one wife. He wouldn't want to bury another. *Cancer* was still one of the scariest words in the English language.

"Your father will find someone perfect for both of you eventually, I'm sure," she said.

Under different circumstances she'd liked to have been that someone. But there was no sense going there. Much better to keep living in the moment.

Sierra was done with her purchase and Catherine picked up another little cottage. "I'd better get one of these for my daughter-in-law, too. I wouldn't want her to feel left out."

"You're a kind woman, Catherine," Athena said. "My mother would have liked you."

Surely the highest praise one woman could give another. Catherine decided she liked living in the moment because this was certainly a good one.

It was even better when Rudy gifted her with a charm for her bracelet shaped like a beer stein. "You really shouldn't," she scolded, but it was half-hearted.

"If you're going to have a charm bracelet you have to have charms to go on it," he said.

Sound reasoning. She looked to where Athena stood with Sierra, checking out a booth displaying all manner of honey and beeswax products. Hopefully, Athena would approve of her father buying Catherine yet another gift now that she knew Catherine wasn't a threat.

Rudy followed her gaze. "Don't worry. I got my daughter one also. I would never want her to feel left out."

"Were you concerned about that?" Catherine asked.

"I guess maybe I have been. She'd been acting a little, well..." He stopped, obviously not wanting to say anything bad about his daughter.

"Not jealous, I assure you," Catherine said in case he'd been thinking that was the case. "I think she just wants to look out for her daddy."

He smiled ruefully. "I know she does. She's a good daughter. And I have to admit, I've given her cause for worry in the past. My second wife was...a mistake."

"We all make mistakes," Catherine said.

"Some of us make dumber ones than others." He shrugged. "But water under the bridge, as they say."

Athena and Sierra returned to them, both bearing little gift bags. "We each got beeswax lotion bars," Athena said. "They're supposed to be great for dry skin. I think Aunt Millie will really like this," she said to her father. "She's always having trouble with cracked heels."

"So's my mom," Sierra said. "This will make a nice Christmas present for her."

"Did you girls get anything for yourselves?" Rudy asked.

"This is all about Christmas shopping," Sierra said, then added, "Now," and her smile lost its shine.

"Hey, we're going to make the most of it," Athena said to her, and Catherine wondered if Sierra had confided some of her troubles to the other woman. They'd been spending a lot of time together that day.

Maybe the two of them would become friends. California wasn't that far from Washington, and these days it was a small world thanks to social media. She quickly veered away from applying that to her and Rudy. *In the moment, in the moment.*

How she wished the moment could last forever.

Denise, Charlie and Arnold came into sight as Catherine was finishing up buying some spiced almonds for her son at another booth. Denise was looking elegant in her formfitting black parka, leggings and boots, the red scarf Charlie had bought her around her neck. She was carrying a little bag.

"What's in there?" Catherine asked her as they all gathered in front of the booth.

"A little gift from Arnold," she said, smiling at him, and making Charlie frown. Then she transferred her smile to Charlie. "And Charlie bought me the most beautiful earrings, which I intend to wear tonight."

Oh, yes, Denise certainly was enjoying herself.

"You really are a stinker, leading both those men on," Catherine told her once they were in their room, showing each other their new acquisitions.

"I'm not leading them on. I like them both. We're pals."

"They're probably both hoping you want to be more."

"You know, maybe I do. I'm getting pretty darned fond of Charlie. But never mind me. What about you and Rudy? That's the third charm he's bought you."

"I know," Catherine said, and suddenly felt sad.

"Hey, why the long face? You've got a treasure of a man interested in you, and even his daughter seems to be coming around."

"Only because she knows this isn't going anywhere."

"Why not? He's single. You're single." Denise narrowed her eyes. "I hope this isn't about Bill. He'd want you to be happy."

"I can't commit to anyone when I have no idea what the future holds."

"Who does?" Denise argued. "You'd let a little thing like that stop you from enjoying a relationship with someone? Forget the oncologist. You need a shrink."

"It wouldn't be fair to Rudy," Catherine said.

"Maybe you should let him make that decision. Have you told him?"

"No." She needed to. She would. Soon. But not yet.

First she intended to enjoy the taste-of-Germany dinner buffet in the dining room. After a quick nap.

The quick nap stretched into two hours and Catherine barely got freshened up and to the lounge in time to hear their cruise director, Elsa, talk about the next day's activities. Her group had claimed their usual spot and she saw that Rudy had saved her a place. She tried not to feel conspicuous as she threaded her way through the various groups of people already settled and listening to Elsa, who had been telling them about the next day's off-ship adventure option.

"So I hope you will all enjoy your excursion to beautiful Baden-Baden. I'm sure you will want to do the walking tour so you can burn off enough calories to enjoy our final port of call the following day where we will take you into the Black Forest with its beautiful mountain landscape and rolling meadows. There you will see a cuckoo clock–making demonstration and learn how to make the popular Black Forest cherry cake. Once you try the cake you will understand why I encourage you all to take tomorrow's walking tour," Elsa concluded.

"Black Forest cherry cake. Be still my taste buds," cracked Charlie.

"My mouth is already watering," Denise said. "At the rate I'm going none of my clothes are going to fit by the time we get off this ship. I'll have to walk down the gangplank in a beer barrel."

"I'd like to see that," Charlie said, waggling his eyebrows.

"Don't let me have dessert tonight," she told him.

"It's all traditional German food. You don't want to start dieting now," he told her.

Once they got to the dining room Catherine couldn't help but agree. The aromas that greeted her as she walked in were a gourmand's delight. The tables gleamed with the usual glassware and silver, but had been laid with festive blue-checked tablecloths, baskets of giant pretzels on each one. Their servers were all dressed in traditional German dirndls and lederhosen, and a couple with an accordion and violin, also dressed in traditional Bavarian garb, were already strolling among the tables, serenading diners.

"This is a feast," Catherine said to Rudy as they filed past the main-course station, which offered them everything from schnitzel to bratwurst and German potato salad, warm and spicy with vinegar, onions and bacon.

"The perfect ending to a perfect day," he said.

"The whole cruise has been perfect. I'm so glad Denise talked me into coming."

"I am, too."

Her heart turned over at the way he looked at her. She had to tell him what lay ahead for her.

Tomorrow. She didn't want to think about it tonight.

At her sister's urging, Sophie had left to sit with Trevor at another table, which left room for Charlie to squeeze in at theirs. Arnold had to settle for sitting at the next one over. As it was a group of women traveling together, he didn't seem to be suffering too much, obviously enjoying talking with a busty middle-aged blonde in a sequined red top. Meanwhile, Charlie was in an especially chipper mood, cracking jokes and slipping a possessive arm over the back of Denise's chair.

Denise certainly didn't seem to mind, not the way she was smiling at him. Sierra was actually managing to smile a little, too, which Catherine hoped meant she had set aside her worries for the moment.

Even Athena looked happy. She had a lovely smile. In fact, she was a nice-looking woman. It was too bad she hadn't met someone on the cruise.

Catherine said as much to Denise when they went to the dessert table, to choose from the various cakes on display.

"Maybe she would have if she hadn't been so busy guarding her father," Denise said. "For a while there I was wondering if the poor guy was even going to be able to go to the men's room by himself."

"I can understand her wanting to protect him."

Denise shook her head. "Kids should keep their noses out of their parents' love lives."

"I think it's kind of sweet that she cares enough to watch out for him."

"There's caring and then there's smothering," Denise said.

Catherine thought of her own children. No one would accuse either of them of smothering, that was for sure. She hadn't expected to hear from her son but she had thought maybe she'd at least get a text from Lila. Out of sight, out of mind. She almost felt jealous of Rudy with his overprotective daughter.

After dinner everyone made their way to the lounge for the evening's festivities. Kurt managed to escape his students and joined Catherine's group, a glass of beer in hand. Charlie ordered champagne for everyone, but Catherine was too stuffed from dinner, and opted for nursing a club soda. Sierra, she noticed, had gone through several desserts at dinner and quite a bit of wine, and was now digging into the bag of chocolate truffles Trevor had brought to share.

Her good spirits seemed forced, and she was inhaling chocolate like it was a drug. Catherine wondered if she'd gotten another text from her husband.

When Elsa arrived, took the mike and bubbled, "Who is ready for a game?" Sierra excused herself.

"Where are you going?" Sophie asked, her voice threaded with concern.

"To the room. I'm pooped. And I think I shouldn't have had so much of that chocolate. I need an antacid."

"I'll go with you," Sophie said, and started to get up.

Her sister gave her a gentle shove back into her seat. "I think I can manage to take an antacid by myself."

"Are you sure?" Sophie asked.

"Yes, I'm sure, you goof. Have fun."

Sophie watched her go and bit her lip.

"Maybe she needs a little time to herself," Catherine said gently.

"I don't know if it's a good idea for her to be alone," Sophie fretted.

"Sometimes you can feel more alone in a crowd of people than by yourself," Catherine said. She'd heard that before, but never realized how true it was until she became a widow.

Sophie frowned. "Her husband is such a jerk."

"But she's got a good sister. Whatever lies ahead, she'll have you to help her through it," Catherine said.

"I hope I can. It doesn't seem right that we're all having fun and she's so miserable."

"It never does."

Catherine remembered the first time she ventured out of the house after Bill's memorial service. It hadn't been much of an outing, just a trip to the supermarket for coffee and yogurt. Inside the store people were pushing carts up and down the aisle, chatting with each other and the clerks at the checkout stands. It had all felt so wrong. Someone had laughed and she'd wanted to shout, "Stop it, all of you!" For her it was the end of the world. For everyone else, business as usual.

Still, she'd survived somehow. She knew Sierra would, too.

"Your sister's very lucky to have you," she told Sophie.

"I'm not helping her very much."

"I bet you're helping her more than you realize. She knows you're there for her and that you care. That's huge. And I'm sure whenever she wants to talk you're there to listen."

"Sometimes listening doesn't seem like much."

Catherine remembered the times she wanted to reminisce about Bill and got only voice mail when she called her daughter. "It's more than you realize."

"Now," Elsa was saying, "I have papers here with a list of popular songs. All my teams, send someone up to me to get one. Then I want you all to list in order what songs the most people will get up and dance to. I will be counting the dancers at each song, and the team who predicts correctly who will dance to what songs will win a prize from the bar."

"Piece of cake," Charlie assured them all.

The list of dances included many that Catherine was sure their younger group members had never heard of.

"'Shout'?" asked Sophie, raising both eyebrows.

"That's a great one," said Charlie. "Otis Day and the Knights." He began to sing, doing a rather impressive shimmy and stamping his feet, and Denise joined him.

Denise sure knew how to work a shimmy. It helped that she still had such a great figure, Catherine thought, just the teensiest bit jealous. Until she reminded herself that Denise worked hard to keep that figure. Catherine had once had a pretty nice figure herself, and she could again if she'd lay off the carbs.

"Sounds like a top dance number," Trevor said.

"But so is this," said Denise, pointing to "Stand by Me." "One of the best slow dance songs ever written."

One of the best songs ever written, period, if you asked Catherine. She loved the message of the lyrics. No need to be afraid during the dark times when someone was with you. She couldn't help looking in Rudy's direction. He was looking at her, as well, and the expression on his face made it clear that he liked what he saw. Oh, my. It was suddenly feeling warm here in the lounge.

"Every couple in the room will get on the dance floor for that," Charlie was saying.

"'Country Girl (Shake It for Me),' I know that one," Trevor said. He smiled at Sophie. "Will you get up and shake it to that?"

"Maybe," she said, her cheeks turning pink.

"'Thriller,' that should go somewhere near the top," said Denise.

"I know what the number one song will be," Catherine said.

"What?" asked Kurt.

"'YMCA.'"

"Even I know that one," Kurt said.

"The song that won't die," said Denise. "You're right, Catherine, everybody will get up for it. Put it down as number one," she said to Arnold, who had rejoined them and was acting as team secretary.

"How about the 'Electric Boogie' as number three?" Charlie suggested. "Everyone knows that."

"I don't," Sophie said.

"You'll pick it up," Denise assured her. "It's easy."

"I think 'Thriller' will top it," Kurt said. "That's still a monster flash mob favorite at Halloween."

"No pun intended?" Charlie said to him, and Kurt shook his head and groaned.

"Okay, 'Thriller' before the 'Electric Boogie,'" Arnold said.

"And, guys," Denise said to everyone, "we have to get up and dance on the dances we picked if we want to win."

"I'm up for the slow dances," Trevor said, and winked at Sophie.

"Me, too," said Rudy, smiling at Catherine.

"We have to dance to *all* of them," Denise said sternly.

"I don't know about the fast ones," Sophie fretted. "My ankle."

"I think you'll be fine. The swelling's gone and you're still wrapping it," Trevor said easily.

Sophie turned to Rudy. "What do you think, Rudy?"

"I think you'll be fine as long as you don't get too carried away," Rudy said.

"You just get up there and the rest of us will do the getting carried away," Denise said to her. "Oh, put the 'Chicken Dance' as number two. Everyone will get up for that."

"Denise's theme song should go near the top," said Charlie.

"What's that?" she asked.

"'Pretty Woman,'" he replied, and Denise actually blushed. "Everybody loves a pretty woman," he added.

"They sure do," said Arnold, not to be outdone in the flattery department. Although, after watching his behavior at dinner, Catherine suspected that Arnold had no problem liking more than one pretty woman at a time.

They finally had their list compiled and Charlie ordered more champagne for everyone to enjoy while they waited for the other teams to finish their lists.

"I'll take another 7UP," Sophie said to the server.

"On the wagon, huh?" Charlie cracked.

"Forever," she said fervently.

Elsa announced it was time to begin and Jacques played a fast rock song that brought several people to the dance floor. Sophie started up but Denise reached over and pulled her back down. "That's not on our list. We don't want to swell the numbers."

But they did all get up to swell the numbers when it came time for the "Electric Boogie," Denise leading them all, teaching them the steps as they went. Plenty of other people joined them, as well, which had her chortling and claiming success as they returned to their seats.

Kurt was right about "Thriller," which packed the dance floor pretty well, but nothing like the "Chicken Dance." Catherine felt both silly and lighthearted as she bounced around the dance floor, hands tucked into her armpits, flapping her crooked arms like wings.

She felt sixteen, singing "YMCA" with everyone. So many people swarmed the dance floor for that song there was barely room to move, and being part of a crowd of happy people enjoying life was a tonic. She found herself in between Athena and Sophie, grinning and going through the motions for all she was worth. Then Jacques slowed down the music and began to play "Stand By Me" on the piano, and the next thing she knew she was in Rudy's arms, smiling up at him.

"I could dance like this all night," she said.

"Could you?"

"Oh, yes."

"And how about tomorrow night?"

He drew her a little closer. He was comfortingly warm and solid. Funny how a woman could feel young again, dancing with a handsome man.

"I think so," she said.

"And after that?"

"We'll be getting off the ship."

"Doesn't mean we can't go out dancing."

"Didn't you say you lived in California? Washington is a ways to go to find a dance floor."

"Not so far to come to find a sweet woman."

They were wandering into territory they shouldn't. She needed to keep things light in fairness to him. Shipboard romances never went anywhere, anyway. Once they were back in their respective homes the enthusiasm would burn down into nothing but a warm memory. And that was how it had to be.

She merely smiled.

She kept smiling when, later, her team won the game and was awarded a bottle of champagne to share. More champagne? Why not? She sipped hers and let the bubbles dance on her tongue.

People stayed on after the game was over and the enthusiastic Elsa had departed. Jacques continued to play at the piano.

Sophie was one of the ones who stayed but she felt guilty over it. What a subpar sister she was, enjoying herself when Sierra was now so miserable.

Sierra had enjoyed the cruise in fits and starts. Mostly, though, it was a bust. It was so unfair. This should have been a dream trip for her.

Maybe she and Mark could work out their differences. Maybe he'd find a way to make up for the hurt he was causing her.

Or maybe not, because, really, it was always all about Mark.

Always had been, probably. It was just that nobody had noticed it at first. Sierra had been besotted and Sophie had been happy for her. He'd seemed like such a nice guy—polite to the parents, friendly with the sis, said all the right things. He'd been the image of near perfection. Until the selfishness began to float to the surface.

Images. You couldn't trust them.

Which just went to show you that you had to be careful when picking someone to spend your life with. That seemingly perfect someone could turn out to be a waste of good love.

What about Trevor? Would he be a good investment or a waste? So far he sure looked like a good investment.

He pointed to Sophie's red top when Jacques started playing "Lady in Red" and said, "They're playing your song. How's your ankle holding up? Want to dance?"

Guilt or no guilt she had to say yes. Happily, her ankle was in total agreement.

"This is a great nightclub two-step," he said. "Know how to do it?"

"You can nightclub?" she asked eagerly. A past boyfriend had taught her how and she'd loved the dance. She'd thought she loved him, too, until he dumped her.

Trevor grinned and took her hand. "Come on."

He was smooth on the dance floor and, dancing with him, Sophie felt like a star. Good dancer, good kisser, good-looking, good-natured—he sure seemed to be the whole package.

"Ooh, that was fabulous," she said when the dance ended.

"I'd say we make a pretty good dance team. Wouldn't you?"

Yes, they did. She soon discovered he not only knew how to nightclub two-step, he was also a rock star swing dancer and a good teacher, showing her steps and then helping her through moves and making her look pretty darned good herself.

"Where'd you learn to dance like that?" she asked as they paused for a drink. (Beer for him but cola for her.)

"Took a class in college. My stepdad used to say the guy who can dance goes home with the girl."

"You'd have been able to get girls if you had two left feet," she said.

"Maybe, but dancing is a guaranteed girl magnet. Kind of like having a dog."

Crudballs. "Do you have a dog?"

"No, but I've thought about getting one at some point." His smile fell away. "Please don't tell me you hate dogs."

How much did she want to tell him? "I was allergic as a kid."

"That had to suck."

Not as much as not being able to breathe.

"Did you have any pets growing up?" he asked.

"We had a cat for a while."

She'd loved Matilda the cat, but Matilda's cat dander hadn't loved her. A cat and childhood asthma hadn't been a good combination. Matilda had been sent to live with the cousins in Puyallup.

"I like cats," he said. Before she could say anything more Jacques started another slow song and Trevor caught her hand. "Come on, let's dance."

Dancing was more fun than talking about her health issues, anyway.

She caught sight of Harriet dragging a husky guy wearing a long shirt over bagging jeans onto the floor. "It looks like you've been dumped for a younger man," she said to Trevor.

"Thank God. Propinquity finally saved me," he said, drawing her to him.

"Pro…what? It sounds like a disease."

He chuckled. "It has to do with being close to someone. You can't help but fall in love eventually. Or maybe even sooner."

As his lips moved close to that sensitive spot behind her ear she decided there was a lot to be said for propinquity. "I wish you were a doctor." She sighed.

"You know, I do see that you have a certain condition, but I'm not sure you need a doctor to treat it."

"What condition? What do you mean?" she asked suspiciously.

He tightened his hold on her. "Okay, now don't take this as an insult, but I think you might be a hypochondriac."

She scowled at him. "That's what my sister says."

"I concur with her diagnosis," he said.

Well, who asked him, anyway?

"Hey, lots of people are. By the way, did I mention that I majored in psychology in college? I'm practically a shrink. I can help when you have a bout of hypochondria."

"I am not a hypochondriac," she insisted, frowning at him. "I just happen to be in tune with my body."

He considered that. "Okay, and what do you do when you get sick?"

"I go to urgent care. Or the emergency room." She'd been there more times than she cared to remember.

"I have a car and I can drive fast. I can have you at the emergency room in no time."

"How about if I couldn't breathe? What would you do then?"

His brows drew together. "Are you planning on not being able to breathe anytime soon?"

"You never know. It's happened." Okay, time to tell him. Let him know up front what he might be getting into. "I had asthma bad when I was a kid. I can remember some really scary trips to the emergency room."

"Do you still have it?"

"My doctor said I'm one of the lucky ones and I outgrew it. But I read online that only a third of the people who have it as children do outgrow it. The symptoms can return in adulthood."

"But you're symptom free."

She nodded. "So far."

"Maybe for the rest of your life."

"Maybe," she conceded.

"Still, health is a big concern for you."

He said it so kindly, was being so understanding, unlike her last boyfriend, who'd told her to get over it and quit being so paranoid. Unlike her family, who all loved her but, when it came right down to it, didn't take her concerns seriously. Even Sierra, close as they were, didn't understand about that shadow of fear that lurked at the edge of her life. Not being able to breathe was a terrifying experience, one that was hard to forget.

"It is," she said.

"Understandable. You went through some scary stuff as a kid. But maybe, instead of a doc who has his nurse take your body temperature, what you really need is someone who can keep tabs on your emotional temperature."

Now, there was an interesting thought.

He smiled down at her. "Doctors are arrogant asses. You don't really want to be with one."

"I don't, huh?" she said. Maybe she didn't.

"Anyway, I've got something a doctor doesn't have," he continued.

"What?"

"My own chocolate company. And you know, chocolate makes everything better."

He had a point there. Maybe what she really needed was an almost psychologist who owned a chocolate company.

That *maybe* leaned closer to *for sure* when he strolled back to her room with her and kissed her. He had a magic mouth, and his fingers slipping through her hair lit up her nerve endings like holiday lights.

"You are a good kisser," she murmured when they finally came up for air.

"I'm a good everything," he replied with a grin. Then he gave her nose a playful tap. "Try and dream of me, okay?"

"I'll give it my best shot," she said.

It wouldn't be hard. She was warm all over, and boneless. Human syrup, that was what he'd turned her into, she thought as she let herself into the room.

But the euphoria faded at the sight of her sister. Sierra had left a bedside light on, but she was laid out under the covers, facing away from Sierra. Asleep?

"Si?" Sophie whispered.

No answer.

She crept to the bed and leaned her sister's direction. "Sierra? Are you okay?"

Again, no answer. It was a stupid question, anyway. Sophie already knew the answer. Her poor sister.

Maybe she was wrong about Mark. Maybe things were fine between them and he really had to work. And needing to talk didn't necessarily mean needing to split up.

And maybe Santa didn't wear red.

Sophie dreamed that night, but not about Trevor. She dreamed Mark was on the ship with them, wearing red underwear and a Santa hat and chasing all the college girls around the ship. Sophie found him at the stern of the boat with an older woman, who was dripping with diamonds, telling her how beautiful she was.

"I love older women," he said. "I love all women. Except my wife."

"You rat!" she'd said, and pushed him overboard. Ha ha. Drowned rat.

14

THE SHIP'S NEXT PORT OF CALL WAS BADEN-Baden, a spa town in Baden-Württemberg, southwestern Germany, near the border with France. Catherine fell in love with the park-lined Lichentaler Allee, the town's central promenade, and the Trinkhalle with its loggia decorated with frescoes.

"You have to taste the water," Denise said to her when they all stopped at the mineral water fountain. "It's supposed to have curative powers."

If only Catherine could substitute those waters for chemo. She gave it a try. And shuddered.

"What does it taste like?" Sophie asked her.

"Dirty socks and salt water."

Sophie wrinkled her nose. "Eew. Just. Eew."

"Think of all the curative powers," Denise said to her.

"Eat chocolate instead," Trevor joked. "Antioxidants."

"You've kept us well supplied in those," Denise told him. "You marvelous man, you."

"Uh-oh, I've got competition," Charlie joked.

But it looked like some of the competition was dropping out. Arnold had fallen away from Denise's side and was strolling with the group of women he'd sat with at dinner the night before. Denise didn't appear to be missing him.

The Christmas market wasn't huge like the ones in Cologne and Heidelberg, but it was Catherine's favorite. The wooden booths were all trimmed with greenery and festive lights, and good smells danced on the air along with conversation and laughter of the many shoppers. Tiny snowflakes began to float down like little fairies, adding to the magical atmosphere.

She treated everyone to Lebkuchen hearts and she and Denise took a selfie next to a life-size wooden nutcracker soldier in his guard booth. She managed to take the walking tour of the city also, and then was pooped.

But after a nap when they got back on board the ship, she was ready for another gourmet meal in the dining room and some more dancing in the lounge. One more day, she thought as she and Rudy swayed on the dance floor. Why did such wonderful times have to fly by so quickly?

"I can't believe it's already almost at an end," she said to Denise the next morning as they dressed for their tour of the Black Forest.

"I don't think everything's at an end," Denise said. "I guarantee you'll be seeing more of Rudy."

Not once she told him what her new year held. She was going to have to tell him. Tonight, she thought miserably.

Tonight was still a long way off. She'd focus on enjoying today.

Everyone who had signed up for a bus ride into the Black Forest disembarked the ship to find buses waiting for them. Catherine, Denise and their new friends boarded a bus and clumped together, occupying seats toward the front, Catherine and Denise seated by each other and Rudy and Athena behind them, the rest of the gang in seats on the other side of the aisle.

It was fun to watch romance blooming between Sophie and Trevor, who were laughing about something as they got on the bus, and Catherine was also happy to see Harriet slide into a seat next to the young man named Hugh. He slung an arm around her as soon as she settled in and she seemed pretty happy about it. Catherine couldn't help remembering an old rock and roll song that advised if you couldn't be with the one you loved to love the one you were with. Maybe not such bad advice for Harriet.

Love was a bit like those old choose-your-own-adventure books Catherine's kids had enjoyed growing up. One choice took you down one road, another choice took you in a different direction. Remember that, she advised herself. Rudy was a lovely adventure for the moment. She didn't have to feel badly that this adventure was bound to end. She'd get through chemo and radiation and then she'd choose another adventure, take an enrichment class at her local community college, learn to line dance. Surely her story wasn't over yet.

"It's so green," Athena said to her father as the bus wended its way up a mountain road past pines, beech and elm.

"It makes me think of the Cascades," Denise said to her. "Let me tell you, there's no place like Washington."

"Never seen much of it," said Rudy.

"You'll have to come visit," Denise said. "We could show

you around," she added, and Catherine wanted to kick her. She was only making things harder.

"I'd like that," he said.

"Me, too," said Athena, and Denise rolled her eyes.

Yes, the guard dog. But after talking to her, Catherine understood. Athena was dedicated and loyal, and hopefully, whatever lucky woman her father wound up with would appreciate that and understand that father and daughter came as a set.

They finally reached their destination, which was nothing more than a few houses in the middle of nowhere camped around a huge tourist trap. But it was a pretty tourist trap, a large Alpine lodge that, on one level, offered an entire floor of cuckoo clocks and other souvenirs for purchase. The lower level held restrooms and a sort of cafeteria, which was where the visitors would see a Black Forest cherry cake being assembled and then have an opportunity to enjoy a slice.

First it was time to watch a demonstration on how cuckoo clocks were put together. Catherine wasn't as interested in that as she was checking out the clocks for sale, and she eventually wandered off, leaving Athena and Rudy to listen.

The shopping area offered clocks of every imaginable size and price range. Catherine was almost overwhelmed by the selection. Many were styled to look like chalets, with figurines in traditional German garb coming out from inside the clock and circling the miniature balcony to go back in again. Some clocks were carved to represent sawmills, some to look like barns. But the one Catherine fell in love with was a simple, dark wood clock, embellished with carved leaves and birds, with heavy pine cone pendulums, a simple little cuckoo coming out of a tiny door to count the hours.

"I love this one," she said to Denise, who had joined her.

"Sweet and simple." Denise checked the price tag. "Not a bad price, either."

"Do you ship to America?" Catherine asked the salesman.

"Oh, yes," he assured her.

"Then I'll take it," she decided. Every time that little cuckoo popped out she'd remember this trip.

Rudy and Athena joined them. "Did you find something you like?" he asked Catherine.

"I did," she replied.

"I wonder if you'll like it as well as the clock I bought for you," Rudy said.

"Oh, no," Catherine began, horrified at the thought of him making such a large purchase.

"You'll want this one," Athena said. "He bought me one, too."

The minute Rudy produced the little gift bag, Catherine knew what would be in it. Sure enough, it was another charm—a sterling-silver cuckoo clock with tiny, swinging pendulums. How could she refuse, especially when Athena herself was on board with her father's gesture?

"Thank you," she said. "It's very kind of you." Even though his daughter had warmed to her, Catherine still felt like a bit of a gold digger and decided she needed to curb the man's generosity. "But you really don't need to," she added.

"I know. I want to."

"Let's make this the last one, then," she said.

Silly thing to say. This was their last stop. The next day they would be disembarking and the magical adventure would be over. Catherine's smile suddenly tasted bitter. *Tonight he'll talk about seeing you in the future. Tonight you have to tell him what your future holds.*

* * *

After seeing the clocks, it was on to the cafeteria where the cake demonstration would be held. Sophie's mouth was already watering as the group of friends settled at a long table near the stage up front where a thin, swarthy man wearing an apron and chef's toque was setting up his supplies.

"Is that whipped cream?" she wondered, taking in the giant bowl of white fluff. "Cardiac arrest in a bowl."

"But you'd die with a smile on your face," Sierra said.

At the rate she was going Sierra was going to eat herself to death. She'd insisted she didn't want to talk about Mark anymore when Sophie tried to see how she was doing that morning, so Sophie hadn't pushed. But she was worried all the same.

The cafeteria filled quickly, with not only people from their bus but from buses sent from other river cruise lines, and soon the room was almost roaring with conversation. Until the chef began his demonstration. Then an awed hush fell over the room.

Layers of chocolate cake, sprinkled with Kirshwasser, a cherry liqueur, and spread with cherry jam and cherries—the cake was a work of art. And, oh, the whipped cream. The entire huge bowl of it got used.

As the baker created a chocolate snowstorm, grating chocolate on the top of the cake, Trevor leaned close to Sophie and whispered in her ear, "See? Everything's better with chocolate."

And with Trevor, she thought. She only wished her sister was enjoying the day more. Sierra had been a sport, coming along on this final outing, even managing a smile when one was called for, but Sophie knew her heart wasn't in it.

"We have slices for sale for any of you who would like to

enjoy one," the chef finished, causing a stampede for the serving area.

"You don't have to call this pig to the trough twice," Charlie said, getting up. "Let's go check it out."

"You two stay put. This one's on me," Trevor said to Sophie and Sierra, and joined the others in the race for cake.

"Think we should make that for Christmas this year?" Sophie asked Sierra, trying to keep her sister focused on happy thoughts.

"Do you see our brother being happy if we don't have red velvet cake?" Sierra replied. "Some traditions you can't break."

Mark liked red velvet cake, too. Was her sister thinking that? Sophie hoped not.

Trevor returned with their cake, three plates on a plastic serving tray. "Those pieces are ginormous," Sophie said, looking at them. "I'll never be able to finish mine."

"I will," said her sister, taking one. "And I'll eat what you don't want of yours. Thanks, Trevor."

"You girls probably need something to drink, too," he said. "Coffee or hot chocolate?"

"Chocolate," Sierra said for both of them.

"Good choice," he approved, and went off again.

Sophie couldn't keep quiet any longer. "Are you sure you're okay?"

She hated seeing her sister bottling up all her misery. It was always so much better when you could talk about your troubles, feel like someone was sharing the load. When it came to problems, big sister Sierra had always only shared so much. Then she went all stoic...and ate everything in sight.

"What makes you think I'm not?" Sierra demanded, and stuffed a monster-size piece of cake in her mouth. She chewed and groaned in ecstasy.

Sophie wasn't impressed. Every woman knew how to fake it.

"The way you've been eating. You've practically single-handedly emptied the cookie bin. Last night you inhaled more at the buffet than Charlie. You took a chocolate overdose in the lounge, and now you're going to eat a slice of cake the size of the Texas panhandle with enough whipped cream to frost Mount Rainier."

"So what? Eating makes me happy. I deserve to be happy."

Yes, she did. No sense arguing that point. "I know you only eat like this when you're upset. You don't know that you and Mark are through," Sophie said gently.

"You're right, I don't know. But I *know*." Sierra shook her head. "I've been in denial, probably for the last year, and I wish I'd never bought this stupid cruise." She made a face. "That didn't come out right. I'm glad you're with me and I'm glad you're having a good time."

Sophie was having a great time. When she wasn't feeling guilty about it or feeling badly for her sister.

"I'm sorry I haven't been more supportive."

"You have been. You've been trying to cheer me up, and you've been buying me presents at every port of call like you're a trust fund baby."

"But here I am, partying away when your heart is breaking. You have a really selfish sister."

"No, I have a really good sister," Sierra said, nudging her shoulder. "I'm glad you're with me."

"Me, too. And I'll always be with you."

"Which is probably more than I can say for my husband." Sierra stuffed another giant piece of cake in her mouth.

"If he doesn't want to stay, then he's a fool," Sophie said

vehemently. "Just remember that. And he doesn't deserve you and you're better off without him."

Sierra stared at her plate. "I wish I could feel that way."

If only Sierra was jumping to conclusions. But that last text from Mark sure hadn't looked encouraging. And no "I love you's," no "I miss you's."

Trevor was coming their way, bearing three mugs of hot chocolate, grinning like he thought he was Santa Claus. She tried to imagine him ever pulling the stunt Mark had pulled, leaving his wife to take a dream trip without him, and couldn't. He was simply too good-hearted.

"Here you go, ladies," he said, setting the mugs down in front of them. "Drink up."

Sierra took a sip of hers. "It's delicious."

"How's the cake?" he asked, pointing to her half-consumed piece.

"Amazing," she said.

"We are going to completely clog our arteries," Sophie predicted. But sweets were her Achilles' heel and she couldn't resist taking a bite of hers.

"Oh, who cares?" said her sister. She stuffed more cake in her mouth, closed her eyes and chewed. Then groaned again. "Chocolate orgasm. Better than sex."

Trevor looked shocked. "I don't know if I'd go that far."

"Don't mind her," Sophie said. "She's..." She stopped herself. The last thing her sister needed was an open discussion of her love life. She forked off another bite of her slice. "It is good, though."

"It is, but sex is better," Trevor said.

Sex with Trevor March, that sure sounded like a treat. Any man who made the kind of chocolate goodies he did had to know a lot about the other one of life's greatest pleasures. And he'd already given a pretty good indication that he did, indeed, know plenty when he'd kissed her.

Sierra finished her cake, then eyed Sophie's. "Are you going to finish that?"

"No, I'm done," Sophie said, and pushed it her way, then watched in amazement as her sister shoveled the remains down like a starving woman.

In a way she was. Starving for affection.

"That was fabulous," she said when she'd finished. "Thanks, Trevor."

"You're welcome," he said, looking a little dazed at how quickly a piece and a half of cake had disappeared.

"You know what? I think I'm going to go buy me a cuckoo clock," Sierra announced. "I'm worth it."

"You are," Sophie agreed. "Want me to come with you?"

"No. I want you to get me another piece of cake."

"I guess she liked it," Trevor said as Sierra marched away.

"She's been a little stressed," Sophie said.

He nodded. "Stuff happens."

Yes, it did. Sophie chewed her lip and watched her sister go. Had Sierra heard from Mark again and not wanted to tell her? If he was leaving her what kind of Christmas would Sierra have?

A darned good one, Sophie decided. She'd take her sister to see the gingerbread house display at the downtown Sheraton, drag her to lunch at the Pink Door in the Pike Place Market, organize a chick flick night with her friends. Talk about all the bad things they'd like to have happen to her rotten husband. Yes, she'd find a way to make sure Sierra got through the holidays.

Trevor's hand over hers brought her back into the moment. "Your sister will be okay," he said. The man was psychic.

"She's…wait. How do you know?"

"That something's not right? Not too hard to figure out. She's married, got the ring on, but she's doing this cruise with her sister instead of her husband, and for these last few days she's looked like she's having trouble smiling. It doesn't take a Sherlock Holmes to figure out she's not exactly in a happy place right now."

"She's not," Sophie admitted.

"And you're wishing you could rush in and make everything better."

"I wish I could do…something." Find a magic wand and wave it over her sister, beat up Mark.

"Sometimes people have to figure out their problems on their own," Trevor said.

She supposed he was right. There were some things you went through hand in hand with people. Others you went through alone, even when other people were present. No one traveled down the birth canal with you and no one escorted you into the next life except God Himself. She supposed it was the same with the death of a relationship. In the end you had to wrestle with the pain yourself.

"It just stinks that he didn't come on this cruise with her. It was supposed to be his Christmas present but he said he couldn't get time off."

Trevor didn't say anything, just nodded to show he was listening.

"Do you think that's the case?" Sophie asked hopefully.

"I dunno."

"She's worried he's going to leave."

He frowned. "It sucks when people split up. We were kids when my dad left. It felt like a bomb had been dropped right in the middle of our lives. Blew everything to hell."

"I can't even begin to imagine how hard that must have been."

"Let's just say it didn't put him on the top of our Christmas list. I don't want to ever do that to my kids. Or to the woman I promise to love. When I get married it'll be for keeps and I sure want to find someone who feels the same way and is willing to work through our problems."

"I think that's admirable," she said.

"It's just the way it has to be, so I won't rush into anything because I do want it to be for keeps. Good relationships are like making good chocolate. You gotta work at them."

"I like that analogy."

"And I like you. What do you say to working at a relationship after the cruise?"

"I say I think that's a good idea."

Did she really need to be practical and marry a doctor? Doctors worked long hours. She could wind up marrying one, then go into cardiac arrest when he was in the middle of surgery or with a patient and she'd have no one to drive her to the hospital. So what good would that do? And marrying a man who knew all about the body didn't guarantee he'd know all about the soul. Trevor March, with his insights and kindness, was a man who knew about the soul. She owed it to her soul to really give him a chance.

"Come on," he said. "Let's help your sis pick out a clock."

Yep. Trevor March was no doctor, but he was an expert in a lot of the things that mattered.

15

BACK ON THE SHIP, TREVOR LOOKED IN VAIN FOR Sophie in the lounge. He concluded she was having a sister shrink session. He didn't see them in the dining room, either, when he joined his brother at the students' table. Thank God propinquity had worked. Harriet had glommed on to the kid named Hugh and was happily giving him a pop quiz, making him name various items at the table. The giggler was still giggling, and correcting Hugh's grammar every once in a while, and two other guys at the table were getting loud and Kurt had to settle them down.

"I think I'm ready to go home," he said under his breath to Trevor.

"It hasn't been that bad," Trevor said.

"For you. You got to escape." He saw the sisters come in

the same time as Trevor and said, "By the way, you gonna keep seeing Sophie when we get back?"

"I am."

"Good decision."

"Our mama didn't raise no fool."

"I guess not, but I was beginning to wonder," Kurt teased.

Trevor kept an eye on Sophie's table, and once it looked like she and Sierra were ready to leave, he said *Auf Wiedersehen* to the students and went to join them.

"Are you ladies ready to stake our claim on our seats in the lounge?" he asked.

"I think I'll go back to the room and pack," Sierra said.

"Oh, come on, join us for a little while," Sophie urged. "It's our last night and they're decorating the tree in the lounge."

Sierra didn't look all that enthused about tree decorating, but she nodded and went with them.

Poor kid, Trevor thought. A pretty shitty vacation for her. Seeing Germany while your husband was back in the States.

He was sure glad she hadn't canceled, though. Otherwise, he'd have never met Sophie.

"It's hard to believe it's our last night," she said as they settled in.

"It may be the last night of the cruise," Trevor told her, "but it's not our last night."

"Portland's not that far," Sierra said, and smiled at her sister, then at him. Nice woman. Even though she was worried about her own love life she had enough class to be happy for her sister.

"I know you two are going to want to come down and take a tour of the Cupid's Chocolates factory."

"Oh, yes," Sophie said enthusiastically.

"Sounds fun," Sierra said. Not enough emotional energy for enthusiasm but she was, at least, smiling.

The others joined them and got busy ordering drinks. Even though they'd just eaten, Charlie dug into the little bowl of cocktail munchies on their table. "We're going to have to all stay in touch," he said before popping a handful in his mouth.

"For sure," said Denise. "I don't have any contact information for you girls," she said to Sierra and Sophie. "Do you mind sharing?"

"Not at all," Sierra said.

Sophie had her phone in hand. "Denise, are you on Facebook?"

The next few moments were taken up with friending and sharing other contact information. "Isn't it funny?" Sophie said when they were done. "You go on one of these things expecting to have a good time, but you don't necessarily plan to come away with so many good friends."

"No, you don't," agreed Rudy. "I'm sure glad we came," he added, smiling at Catherine. Oh, yeah, those two would keep what they'd started going.

And so would Trevor and Sophie. He was going to make sure of it. Like Sierra had said, Seattle and Portland weren't that far from each other, only a little over a three-hour drive apart.

Everyone chatted for a while, and then Elsa made her appearance, ready to oversee the last bit of fun and games. "As you can see," she said, "our poor tree needs decorating. We have ornaments and we would love each of you to sign your names on them and then hang them on the tree. So please, help yourselves to an ornament and a marker and help us remember this lovely cruise we have all enjoyed together."

"Fun idea!" enthused Denise, and hopped up.

Charlie was quick to follow her, and they drifted over to

the tree. Arnold, who had joined them, stayed behind, visiting with Athena.

Good God, don't go for him, Trevor thought. What was it with old men and young women, anyway?

"Let's go sign our ornaments," Sophie said to her sister. "And take a selfie to remember our time together."

Sierra agreed, and the two sisters went to the tree and dug out ornaments. Catherine and Rudy followed, and Athena broke away from old Arnold and went after them.

Trevor remained where he was and watched as everyone in the group selected markers, wrote their names and hung their ornaments. He watched as Rudy and Catherine and Athena all passed an ornament back and forth between them, each one signing it. He smiled as he watched Sophie take a selfie of her and her sister in front of the tree. The two sisters were close, obviously good pals, just like his brother and him. What were their parents like? They had to be pretty cool to have raised such nice women.

Sophie hung the ornament, then Sierra said something. A discussion of some sort ensued. Finally, Sophie hugged her sister and Sierra headed for the sliding glass door. Sophie returned to Trevor alone.

"Had all the fun she could stand, huh?" he asked.

"She says she wants to pack. She doesn't have that much to pack." Sophie frowned. "I'm sure she's going to text Mark again." The frown turned into a sigh. "He's breaking her heart. It's so not right."

"It never is."

"She'll get through this," Sophie said with determination.

"With a little help from her sister?"

"With a lot of help from her sister. And her brother."

"Whoa, you didn't tell me you had a brother."

"I do. He's great. And really buff. He was a wrestler in college. Scared?" she teased.

"Wrestlers don't scare me."

"He's a cop now. How about cops?"

"No problem. Cops don't scare me, either. Bring on the whole force. And bring on a fire-breathing dragon, too." It would take more than that to keep Trevor away.

"And an evil king?"

"The eviler, the better," he said. "I'll bribe him with chocolate."

"Chocolate, huh?"

"Chocolate fixes everything," he said with a grin.

"Maybe not everything," she said, then looked wistfully in the direction her sister had gone.

Jacques had settled in at the piano and was playing Savage Garden's "Truly Madly Deeply." "Come on," Trevor said. "Let's dance."

He held out his hand and she took it and let him lead her onto the dance floor, and into a nightclub two-step.

But partway through the dance he stopped with the fancy steps, snugged her up against him and whispered in her ear, "Would you like to stand with me on a mountaintop, Sophie? Bathe in the sea?" Her hair was soft against his mouth and her perfume was getting him high. Not to mention the closeness of her body. This woman had to be God's best creation.

She turned her head and smiled at him. "I think that sounds pretty awesome."

Her lips were practically touching his. It would have been a waste not to take advantage of that.

So he did.

Catherine definitely wanted to stay in touch with her new friends. She'd enjoyed getting to know everyone, and the idea that the fun was coming to an end made her more than a little sad.

People didn't linger in the lounge as long as they had other nights. There was packing to be done, purchases to stow away. Catherine had packing to do also, but this was her last night with Rudy, so she lingered. Eventually, it was just the two of them, sitting side by side on a love seat.

"Do you have plans for New Year's?" he asked.

You have to tell him. Tell him now. "I do." He looked disappointed. "Not the kind you think," she said.

Oh, dear. He looked both relieved and eager. He'd be neither once she explained.

"I'm afraid I can't get involved with anyone right now." This was so hard. She bit her lip. What to say next? "I should have told you sooner."

His smile fell away. "So there is someone."

She shook her head. "No."

"What, then?" he asked. "Is it still too soon after losing your husband?"

She shook her head again. Tears burned her eyes. "I had cancer. I'm scheduled for chemo and radiation in the new year."

The color bled out of his face. "My wife had cancer."

"I know," she said.

"I..." He shook his head. "I don't know what to say."

Say that it doesn't matter.

He didn't.

"I'm afraid you've had some hard bumps when it's come to women," she managed. There was an understatement. The poor man had buried one and been left by another. "I don't want to add to that. I would wish you a smooth road."

He gave a snort. "There's no such thing."

"Some roads are smoother than others." She could feel a tear leaking out of one eye.

He reached up and wiped it away. "I'm sorry you've had to go through this," he said. "What kind of cancer?"

"Uterine."

"The best kind to get if you have to have it," he said, and wiped away another tear. He frowned. "Usually a hysterectomy does it."

"Not this time. This had chewed halfway through the uterine wall and my doctor wasn't comfortable leaving it at that."

He nodded, took her hand and looked at it. What was he thinking? She was afraid to ask. Almost afraid to speak. Fresh tears were welling up. She wasn't sure how much longer she could keep them dammed up inside her.

They couldn't sit here forever in silence. They couldn't sit here forever, period. How she wished they could!

She cleared her throat. "I've had a lovely cruise, and a lovely time with you and your daughter."

His jaw was clenched. He nodded.

"I want to thank you," she added, "for all your kindnesses, for making this such a special time for me. It's been...magical."

"I feel the same," he said.

"Then we'll both have some beautiful memories to take away with us."

"Just memories." It was a statement, not a question. He was still holding her hand, staring at it.

She gently pulled it free. "I should go."

"I wish you didn't have to," he said. "Stay a little longer?"

She couldn't. This was like pulling off a bandage painfully, slowly.

"I think it's best I leave," she said.

Now he did look up, and his expression brimmed over with misery.

Before she could say anything more, he took her face in his hands and kissed her. It made her foolish heart flutter with hope.

"Let's stay in touch," he said, but the words sounded hollow.

She nodded, but she knew they wouldn't. That kiss hadn't said *au revoir.* It had said goodbye.

She pulled away, and now it was her not looking at him. She could barely see for the tears in her eyes. She murmured a shaky, "Goodbye," then fled the lounge. It was nearly deserted, a room filled with the lingering scent of women's perfume, a giant treasure chest, closed on the collective experiences of a group of travelers gathered together for a short time. She started past the tree. Many people had taken their ornaments when they left. The next day she and everyone else would disembark and whatever was left would be taken down and thrown away and it would be as if this night had never happened.

She didn't want anyone throwing away the ornament she and Rudy and Athena had signed. She stopped long enough to remove it. It wouldn't be as if this night had never happened for her. She would remember it for the rest of her life.

The rest of her life. The tears broke loose and she hurried away.

She was too embarrassed to go to the room in tears, so she went above deck, to the top of the ship, and leaned on the railing, crying as she watched the homes on the bank slip by. Most of them were dark. People were in their beds, sleeping, resting for whatever the next day held. Below her, the ship cut through the water, a dark wake rushing past its side.

It made her think of her own life, rushing by so fast, feeling suddenly dark and hopeless. It wasn't all darkness, she reminded herself. This cruise had been a bright spot. She'd go home, wear her charm bracelet and hang this ornament on her tree and be thankful for the time she'd been given. The tears were gone and night air was not welcoming. It was time to go back inside.

She got to the room to find Denise finished with her packing, in her pajamas and lying in bed with a book, a romance by Melinda Curtis, one of her favorite authors.

"You sure closed down the lounge," she greeted Catherine with a grin. Then she squinted at Catherine and frowned. "You look like you've been crying."

Catherine shrugged and turned to pull her suitcase from the closet.

"Okay, what happened?" Denise demanded, her voice filled with concern.

"I told him."

She didn't have to explain what she told Rudy. Denise sat up and frowned. "And?"

"And we said goodbye."

"Goodbye?" Denise echoed in disgust. "What does that mean?"

Catherine fell onto her bed. "It means this was a wonderful cruise and I'll never forget it."

"Or him?"

"Or him."

"Catherine," Denise said sternly, "did you sabotage this relationship?"

"No, of course not. I just was truthful. Rudy's had enough heartbreak."

"Oh, honestly," Denise said in disgust. "You have got a martyr complex."

"I do not," Catherine insisted. "Anyway, he didn't exactly push to see me when we get back."

"And here I thought he was such a noble specimen of manhood," Denise said in disgust.

"I don't blame him. Why would he risk more unhappiness? My future is too uncertain."

"Everyone's future is uncertain," Denise snapped. "Nobody has any guarantees."

"You're right. All we have is right now. Thank you for making mine so good."

"You're going to have a lot more good right-nows," Denise insisted.

"I hope so." Catherine looked at the cheap little ornament in her hand. She would wrap it with extra care. It was priceless.

16

ATHENA HAD ENJOYED HANGING OUT WITH HER new friends in the lounge. Well, all except Arnold, who she decided didn't qualify for friendship. The old coot had actually hit on her when Denise wasn't looking and she'd opted out of exchanging contact information with him. If there was a slightly older version of Trevor walking around she'd sure happily latch onto him. Trevor gave men a good name.

So did her dad. He deserved to be happy. He was probably not going to be very happy by the time this night was over. When Athena had left the lounge, he and Catherine had been on the dance floor, totally wrapped up in each other. Seeing them, she'd felt like she was watching some tragic movie and waiting for the awful final scene.

Athena was finished with her packing and she was done

reading the mystery on her e-reader, but not finished wondering what was going on with those two. Had Catherine told him what was waiting for her in the new year? Were they still in the lounge?

They could be. It was open for another hour.

If they were still talking she didn't want to interrupt, but if they were done, if all was not well… She decided to go poke her head in and see.

No one was left in there but her dad, who was sitting at the bar, hunched over a drink. Athena felt her heart turning in her chest, heavy like the wheel she'd seen in that windmill. Catherine had told him.

Ironic how she hadn't wanted Catherine and her dad to get together, and now here she was, wishing they could. If only things had been different.

She slipped into the chair next to her father.

"What can I get you?" the bartender asked her.

A double order of happiness for my father. "Nothing," she said.

"I thought you'd be in bed," Daddy said.

"I thought you would be, too. Are you all right?" Of course he wasn't, but she could hardly start their conversation off saying, "I knew Catherine was going to dump you." Not *dump*, that wasn't the right word. Catherine was simply trying to spare them both from heartache.

"I'm half wishing I hadn't taken this cruise," he said. He swirled the whiskey around in his glass, then took a drink.

"What about the other half?" she asked.

He made a face. "The other thinks it's the best thing I've done since losing your mother."

Catherine was responsible for that. Sweet, unassuming Catherine. She'd won both their hearts, and now look at them. Athena wanted to slap her.

"Did Catherine tell you she's going to be doing chemotherapy in the new year?" Daddy asked.

Athena wished she was a better liar. She should have ordered a drink. She could have stalled by taking a sip. Her silence said it all.

"I guess she did." He took another swig. "She's a lovely woman—humble and unassuming. She seemed a little lost when we first met her, didn't she?"

"Yes, she did," Athena agreed. Unsure of her future, in need of someone who really cared. Maybe her kids did, but if you asked Athena they had a funny way of showing it.

"I wanted nothing more than to help her find herself. Now... God, what kind of man does it make me that I'm put off by the fact that she's had cancer?"

"The human kind? You went through so much with Mom, and then you lost her."

"I never thought I'd find anyone who could hold a candle to your mother. Nicole was sure a mistake. But Catherine." He rubbed his forehead. "I could have told her I wouldn't let what she was dealing with scare me away, but I didn't. I think your old man has become a coward," he said.

"No, you're not. You're the bravest man I know." *So be brave. Take a chance.*

She couldn't say that, of course. What if she did urge him to pursue what he'd started with Catherine and things went all wrong?

But things had already gone wrong. Her father had come on this cruise, met someone wonderful and built up his hopes only to have them crushed. So much for her resolve to protect him. How could you protect someone from falling in love?

He grunted, shook his head, finished his drink. Then he looked at his watch. "I guess we should turn in."

She stood up with him. "I guess so."

They left the lounge and walked down the hallway to their rooms in silence, her arm linked through his. "Try not to feel bad, Daddy," she said when they reached his door.

He smiled a sad smile for her. "You're a good daughter, Athena. I don't know what I'd do without you."

"Me, either," she said, hoping to inspire a smile.

She didn't. He kissed the top of her head, wished her pleasant dreams and went into his room.

You got what you wished, she thought as she went into her own room. She hadn't wanted her father to get entangled with anyone. He was definitely unentangled now. And miserable. So was she. What a mess.

Catherine slept fitfully. Her dreams were a mishmash of horrible tableaux. In one she was back at Heidelberg Castle, standing on the stone wall and looking down at the city below. Rudy was with her, begging her to come down from where she stood.

"I'm scared," she said. Then she lost her balance and fell. She could hear him calling her name. "Help me!" she cried. But she was out of reach.

She awoke before she hit, but her soul felt broken. She finally fell back asleep again, only to find herself in a hospital, wandering up and down the halls in her hospital gown, looking for her doctor.

"You won't find him," said the nurse who suddenly appeared at her side. "It's too late."

Too late. Catherine awoke a second time, with the words ringing in her ears. It was seven o'clock in the morning, time to get up.

Denise was already up and dressed, wearing a black sweater

and winter-white slacks, a gold chain around her neck and matching hoop earrings. "You look like you hardly slept," she said to Catherine.

"I feel like I hardly slept," Catherine admitted.

"Hurry up and get dressed. We'll get some breakfast and maybe that will help you feel better." She frowned. "Oh, what am I saying? As if an omelet can cure a broken heart. I'm sorry, Cath. I wish things had worked out for you and Rudy."

"It's all for the best. I need to focus on getting well."

"You will," Denise assured her. "You're going to come out of this just fine."

Maybe she would. Maybe she shouldn't have burned her bridges, telling Rudy about the cancer and what lay ahead. But there would have been no hiding it. He'd want to come visit. When he did, he'd see her bald, with a scarf around her head, or wearing a wig, and would know instantly. Then he'd resent the fact that she hadn't been up front with him.

She'd been right to warn him off. She was a bad risk. Even after all the treatments the cancer could still come back. The doctor would be monitoring her every three months, then every six and after that every year until she reached the five-year mark safely. That wasn't exactly finishing treatment with a clean bill of health. Five years of anxiety, it was too much to put a man through. She didn't even want to go through it.

"I'm not going to think about the future," she vowed. "I'm going to focus on being grateful for the present."

"An excellent idea," Denise approved.

Catherine only hoped the present wouldn't include seeing Rudy one last time.

Liar. Of course you want to see him.

It would be best for both of them if they didn't meet, though. Would he be at breakfast?

Denise was still talking. What had she said?

"I'm sorry. What did you say?" Catherine asked.

"I said maybe don't think about the near future, but think about what you're going to do to reward yourself once you're through all of this. Like maybe another cruise. Have I got you hooked now? It's nice to have someone to split the bill with."

"I think you do."

"Then my work here is done. Let's do one to celebrate once you're done."

"The way Charlie was talking last night I suspect you'll have someone new to cruise with," Catherine said.

"I think we're going to be buddies."

"What about Arnold? Did you give him the heave-ho?"

Denise shrugged. "He dropped out of the competition. Just as well. I think he's a belt notch cruiser, out to see how many women he can collect. The male equivalent of me," she added with a wink. "But I don't think I could collect anything better than Charlie. He's a sweetheart."

"Yes, he is," Catherine agreed. So was Rudy.

They'd had such a short time together. Catherine thought of her friend Lisa, who she'd worked with in the school office. Lisa always signed her emails, *Don't cry because it's over, smile because it happened.* Good advice. She showered, dressed, then put on her makeup. And a smile.

But the smile faltered when she and Denise arrived in the dining room and saw only Athena and Sierra taking seats at their usual table. She scanned the dining room, looking to see if Rudy was anywhere there. Perhaps standing at another table, visiting with someone? Or in line for an omelet. She didn't see him anywhere.

It was all for the best. He probably knew that. He'd been smart to stay away. Catherine wished she had.

Athena greeted her with the same kind of wan smile she was wearing. "Daddy isn't feeling too well," she said, "but I wanted to see you all one more time."

"It's gone by too fast," Catherine said politely.

"But we'll all stay in touch," Sierra insisted, and Athena looked at Catherine almost hopefully.

Did she want to stay in touch? "Of course we will," Catherine said. Then, "I think I'll enjoy one last omelet. Anyone want to join me?"

"Sure," said Denise.

"Come on, Sierra," said Athena, "we may as well live it up while we can."

"I guess," Sierra said.

She hardly looked like a woman wanting to live it up. Catherine suspected all she wanted to do was get home and begin sorting out her life. Even if that sorting turned out to be painful it would probably be better to know where she stood.

Charlie came up to the table just as the women were about to go in search of eggs. "Here we are," he said, "the beginning of a new day and new adventures when we all get home."

Sierra and Athena didn't appear to be cheered by his words. Catherine wasn't, either. The last thing she wanted was to think about the new adventures waiting for her.

She left Charlie and Denise at the pastry table and followed the other two women to the omelet stand.

"I hope things work out for you when you get home," Catherine said to Sierra, who wound up standing in front of her.

"Me, too," she said.

"Even if they don't, I know you'll be all right."

The expression on Sierra's face showed what she thought of Catherine's prediction.

"Life does go on after the bad parts."

"You're right. Yours has."

Catherine was hardly the poster child for happy endings. "Look at Denise," she said, nodding to where she stood with Charlie, hovering over a basket of crusty rolls.

That did bring a slight smile. "She seems to be enjoying herself."

"She is. Now. She was crazy about her husband and was beside herself when he died. She swore she'd never meet anyone like him. And then she met a dance host on a transatlantic crossing and fell madly in love."

"What happened to him?"

"He died, too. But they had ten wonderful years together before she lost him," Catherine added. "Now it looks like she's found another soul mate. There are plenty of wonderful people in this world to love, Sierra. I hope, if things don't work out with your husband, that you'll remember that."

"I'll try. And thanks again for being a listening ear."

"Anytime," Catherine said. "Stay in touch."

"I will."

People always promised to stay in touch in situations like these but then got drawn back into their lives. Sierra and her sister had their own parents, their own family. They didn't need any more family members. Catherine wished they did, because she sure wouldn't mind adopting those two.

Sophie and Trevor joined them, chatting and grinning like a couple of lottery winners. When it came right down to it they were. They'd won the love lottery, which was the best one of all.

Once Catherine was back at the table she found she didn't have much appetite. Seeing the empty chair where Rudy had sat stole it from her. Athena didn't look all that joyful herself, and left her omelet uneaten, settling instead for yogurt.

"I guess I'd better go find Daddy," she finally said, and stood. She looked at everyone. "It's been great."

Sierra stood, too. "Don't forget to text me," she said as the two women hugged.

"I won't," Athena assured her. Then she surprised Catherine by coming around to her side of the table, bending over and hugging her. "I hope everything goes well," she whispered. "You deserve to be happy."

Her words brought tears to Catherine's eyes and she could barely murmur her thanks.

Later, as people were disembarking, she saw Athena and her father, already off the boat and walking toward one of the buses waiting to drive people to the airport.

"You haven't seen the last of them," Denise predicted.

Catherine just shook her head. *Don't cry because it's over, smile because it happened.*

Trevor was on the same flight back to SeaTac airport as Sophie and Sierra, which meant they were all at the same gate in the Basel airport. They'd been bused straight there, so all they'd seen of Switzerland had been from the bus windows. And much of what they'd seen had looked a lot like Germany.

He decided he'd have to come back, check out Zurich, Geneva and Lake Lucerne. Maybe Sophie would like to join him.

"You owe me big-time for making you come," Kurt teased as they went in search of coffee.

"Yeah, I do," Trevor said, opting out of a smart-ass answer. He was going home with presents for his mom and aunts and a cool stein for Kurt's collection. Best of all, he was going home with a very special woman.

They returned to where the sisters were sitting and he handed over the eggnog lattes he'd bought them.

"One of the good things in life," Sierra said after thanking him. "Right up there with sisters and men who make chocolate."

He couldn't help admiring how she was trying not to look like she wanted to jump from the plane once they were airborne. A strong woman. She'd be fine.

Speaking of fine, he thought, looking at Sophie. She was the whole package—cute, enthusiastic, kindhearted. She was happy to be with Trevor, but she wasn't letting that happiness blind her to her sister's misery, and she kept trying her best to distract Sierra with talk of the presents they'd bought.

"Drew's going to love that beer stein, and I think Dad will love those smoked nuts," she said, and Sierra nodded.

Sophie searched her phone, then turned it so her sister could see. "Look, here's a recipe for Lebkuchen. We should try to make it. Dad would like that, too."

"It's a lot like gingerbread cookies," Sierra said. "Those were Mark's favorites. Are," she corrected herself. Her lower lip began to wobble and she took a quick sip of her drink.

Sophie turned to Trevor, probably hoping to rope another person into the conversation and distract her sister. "What's your favorite cookie?"

"Those frosted sugar cookies, hands down," he said. "And mint chocolate chip."

"Chocolate, of course," she said, and smiled at him. Then she turned back to her sister. "Let's have a baking day tomorrow."

"We'll be jet-lagged," Sierra protested.

"We won't be jet-lagged all day."

"Maybe later in the week. I need to spend some time with Mark."

Sophie pressed her lips into a tight line.

Sierra turned her head, pretending to look around at their fellow travelers, and took a surreptitious swipe at the corners of her eyes. Poor kid. Trevor hoped she'd be able to work out her problems with her husband.

"Gosh, I hate waiting for planes," she said after a moment, turning back to him. "I imagine you two will have to take a Horizon Air to Portland after we land," she said. "That'll make a long day for you, won't it?" So, chin up and subject rerouted from the husband to air travel.

"It will for Kurt and his class," Trevor said. "I've got my car waiting."

"That sounds more exhausting than being on a plane."

"But that's the price you pay for being a jet-setter, right?"

"Yeah, that's you, Mr. Workaholic," teased his brother.

"You're looking at a new me," Trevor told him. He could easily picture himself seeing more of the world with Sophie.

"I wouldn't mind being a jet-setter," Sierra said. "Maybe I'll see Paris next year if..." She cut herself off.

"If you can get the time off," her sister supplied. "I'll go with you."

"You so will not," Sierra said firmly. "You should wait and go with someone special," she said, and managed a smile for Trevor.

Yep, a class act. Trevor liked Sierra.

But he was crazy about Sophie. Looked like he'd be making a lot of weekend trips to Seattle in the new year.

Kurt had just left for the bathroom when Harriet plopped onto his vacated seat next to Trevor. Déjà vu all over again.

"Have you got any chocolate left?" she asked.

"Afraid not. It's all gone."

"That sucks," she said. "Your chocolate's better than anything we had on the cruise." She looked to his other side where Sophie sat talking with her sister. "But your taste in women is so trite."

Yep, that was him, trite. "What can I say, Harriet? I'm under the influence of propinquity." And he intended to be under the influence a whole lot more in the new year.

17

EMPTINESS GREETED CATHERINE WHEN SHE walked back into her house, dragging her suitcase and carry-on. She felt as if she'd stepped into a museum as a dispassionate observer of someone else's life.

The living room was filled with artifacts from Christmases past. The tree was decked out with ornaments she had collected over the years. Some the kids had made, either with her supervision or in school.

Framed holiday photos sat on top of the entertainment cabinet. One was of her with Santa when she was pregnant with William and beaming like a woman waiting to receive a special award. Another was of both the kids with Santa when they were small. And there was her favorite family portrait, one Bill had taken of all of them in front of the tree when the kids were in grade school. It had been a lighthearted moment. He'd barely made it back into the picture before the timer on the camera went off, tripping over a present on his way. The camera had caught all of them in midlaugh.

She'd arranged some flicker candles and fake greens along the fireplace mantel but the only stockings hanging there were hers and Bill's, the ones she'd made from red felt the first year they were married. The kids had taken their stockings when they moved out and seeing those two stockings was depressing. Bill was gone and she was the lone survivor here in the Pine residence.

She sighed and towed her suitcases into the bedroom. Then she pulled back the bedspread, flopped on the bed and fell asleep. Jet lag had its benefits. It saved a woman from thinking of all the good times that had ended.

She woke up at eleven to a very silent night. These were the times when being alone always hit her hardest, late at night, when she had no daytime activities to distract her.

She knew she wouldn't get back to sleep so she got up, showered and put on the flannel pajamas her daughter had given her for Christmas the year before. Then she went to the kitchen and made herself some hot chocolate. It made her think of the little beverage bar on the ship.

She pulled the carry-on where she'd stored all the presents she'd purchased in Germany back into the living room and opened it. It was a holiday treasure trove and she began sorting out her various purchases, spending some time reminiscing over each one. She already had some presents under the tree for the kids and grandchildren. What she'd gotten at the various Christmas markets would be bonuses.

The last thing she found was the ornament from the ship's tree, bundled up in a scarf. Signed and dated. If only she and

Rudy had met at a different time, under different circumstances.

She padded out to the living room and hung the little blue globe on the tree, another artifact to add to the others.

Don't cry because it's over, smile because it happened.

Such wise advice. Smiles were so much more satisfying than tears.

She dug out wrapping paper and ribbons and got busy wrapping presents. By the time she was finished she had the gifts all neatly stacked under the tree, ready for her children to come pick up. She wished she could see everyone's faces as they opened their gifts.

Knowing that she wouldn't be with any of her family made her want to throw a nice, big pity party for herself. She could invite the Grinch.

Actually, no. Even he'd reformed. He wouldn't want any part of her misery.

She didn't, either. She was going to have a fine Christmas with Denise and her daughter and children. They were like second family, and second family was better than no family, right?

She finally went back to bed around three in the morning and managed to crawl into a fitful sleep. She was actually dreaming herself back on the cruise ship when her ringing phone awakened her at nine. Seeing the name on the caller ID cheered her up. It was Lila.

"How was the cruise?" her daughter wanted to know.

"It was lovely."

"Good. I want to hear all about it. I thought I'd come by this morning and pick up presents. I assume you'll be around."

"I will. I was thinking about making some frosted sugar cookies." Lila loved those cookies and they'd often baked them together when she was still living at home. Not so much once she moved out, but maybe she'd like to revive the tradition. "Want to help?"

"I can't. I've got so much to do before the kids are out of school and we leave."

She probably did, but Catherine still felt a little hurt. "Oh, well. It was just a thought."

"It was a great thought. Sorry I can't do it."

"That's okay," Catherine said. "When were you planning on stopping by?"

"In about an hour or so."

"All right. I'll have the espresso machine ready."

"Great," Lila said, and ended the call. She didn't have time to bake cookies, but enjoying one of her mother's homemade lattes was another thing altogether.

Oh, well. When you had grown children you took what you could get. Catherine hurried out of bed and into the shower. Then she threw together a coffee cake because you couldn't have lattes with nothing to go with them.

An hour later she had just taken the coffee cake out of the oven when Lila's voice came to her from the front hall. "I'm here. Where are you?"

"In the kitchen," Catherine called.

In breezed her daughter, looking Christmassy in red plaid leggings under a black top and a red coat, the cap Catherine had knitted for her two Christmases ago perched over her carefully straightened hair. Lila had been slender as a teenager and as a bride, but she'd inherited her mother's sweet tooth, and her addiction to cake, cookies and doughnuts had plumped her up. She still thought a little extra weight looked good on Lila. She was a pretty woman, much prettier than her mom, with an easy smile. Always fun to be around. And yes, maybe a little self-centered, but when it came down to it wasn't everyone?

"Something smells good," Lila said, pulling off her hat. "Is that your streusel coffee cake?"

"It is. I just took it out of the oven. Do you have time for a piece?"

"I can stay long enough for that." Lila shed her coat and dropped her purse next to a chair. "Eggnog lattes?"

"I haven't had time to get to the store and pick up any eggnog," Catherine said.

"Darn."

"How about your usual caramel?"

"Sure. Why not?" She got plates out of the cupboard while Catherine made her latte. "So, tell me about the cruise. I can't believe you went on one without me."

"You were too busy." Did that sound a little accusative? Was it meant to? Maybe. "Anyway, there was only room for one more in Denise's room," Catherine hurried to add.

"I suppose she picked up a man," Lila sneered.

"She had fun."

"You had to feel like a third wheel. What a drag."

Lila cut herself a hefty piece of coffee cake and one for Catherine, as well, and set them on the table. Fork in hand, she sat down and dug in, not bothering to wait for Catherine.

"I met some nice people." Catherine decided not to go into details, especially about Rudy. What was the point?

She set a mug in front of Lila and she picked it up and sampled the latte, nodded approvingly. "I'm glad you had fun. What all did you get?"

"Oh, all kinds of things," Catherine said, sitting down opposite her.

Lila grinned. "Are some of the all kinds of things in those boxes under the tree?"

"As a matter of fact, yes."

"Sweet," Lila said, and took another sip of her latte.

"And I bought a cuckoo clock."

"Who'd you buy that for?"

"Myself."

Lila nodded. "I guess you can't go on a trip like that and not come back with something for yourself. Speaking of something for yourself." She bent over and pulled a large envelope out of her purse. "Open it now."

"If I do I won't have anything under the tree."

"Yes, you will," Lila assured her. "I stuck something under there. Come on. Open it."

Catherine opened the envelope and found a gift card for the Fifth Avenue Theater, a beautiful, old downtown theater loved by Seattle residents for their musicals. "Oh, how sweet!" Bill would have been proud of her daughter's unselfishness.

"I thought we could go together," Lila said around a mouthful of coffee cake.

That was her girl. Always thinking of others…and herself.

"I'd like that," said Catherine.

"Great." Lila took another bite of coffee cake and downed a healthy slug of her latte, then said, "I've got to get going. I still have to buy ski pants for Carissa and I'm supposed to be helping in Joey's classroom today. Then tomorrow I have to deliver cupcakes for Carissa's class party. Like I have time for that. I don't know what I was thinking when I let myself get suckered into all this stuff."

She'd barely been there and now she was leaving. Catherine sighed inwardly. "We'd better get your presents gathered up, then," she said.

She grabbed a couple of paper shopping bags from under the sink and followed her daughter out to the living room.

"This is going to be a lot to pack," Lila said. "Maybe we'll open some before we leave."

For a moment Catherine entertained the hope that her daughter would suggest she come over and watch them, but she didn't. They'd probably open the gifts on the fly and then move on to the next adventure. She'd thought her life had been busy when the kids were growing up but it couldn't compare to Lila's frenetic pace.

Someday the top will stop spinning so fast, she thought, *and you'll find yourself wondering when it began to slow and how you missed that. And you'll wish someone would sit with you and watch it do its final dance.*

"Thanks, Mom," Lila said, leaning over and giving Catherine a quick kiss on the cheek. Then she started for the door.

"Have fun," Catherine said, trailing her.

"We will. The kids are really excited." She opened the door and breezed out, calling over her shoulder, "See you in the new year."

And that was that. Catherine went back into the living room, feeling let down. She'd hoped her daughter would have a little more time for her. The tree, with all the ornaments dangling from its branches, seemed to mock her. *Memories, that's all you're going to have to keep you company this Christmas.*

Well, there was a cheery thought. She frowned, disgusted with herself. Life was what you made it. So was Christmas, darn it all. She'd take her holiday cake to Denise's, drink eggnog and listen to Denise's granddaughters sing "Santa Baby." There would be games and probably a holiday movie to watch. She could have fun without her children. She was a big girl.

To distract herself, she picked up her iPad and checked her email. She found a short one from Sophie.

I already miss everybody! Sophie enthused. *I hope we can get together in the new year. Meanwhile, have a great Christmas. By the way, I'm going to Portland to tour the Cupid's Chocolates factory. Bet you can't guess who will be my guide.* ☺

Sierra had also written. Her email started out happy enough—so glad they'd met, was Catherine busy getting ready for Christmas? etc., etc. Then she came to the real meat of the message.

Mark and I are splitting. Now I know why he couldn't take off work to go on the cruise with me. He's been having an affair with his boss. Is that even allowed in the workplace? Stupid question. Affairs shouldn't be allowed anywhere.

I should have seen this coming. I knew we were growing apart. We both want more out of life. Our definitions of more just happen to have stopped matching up. I should be glad I found out now that this marriage isn't going to work, but all I want to do is cry. How do you go into the holidays feeling like this?

Good question.

It's not easy, Catherine responded. *We always think that because this is such a happy holiday what's happening in our lives should match up. But it doesn't always, does it?*

There was an understatement. Nothing had matched up for her the year before. She'd gone into the holidays miserable and had left them behind feeling the same way.

This year she was not going to do that. Was not. She refused.

She turned her attention back to Sierra's email. What to tell her?

This won't be the happiest holiday ever for you and I'm sorry about that. I'm sorry you and your husband aren't able to reconcile. Who would want to under those circumstances? But I know you have people in your life who love you and they'll be there for you. Trust me, you will get through this.

Catherine read what she'd written, deleted her last sentence and retyped the words in upper case, bold letters. Then she added, Anytime you need to talk, I'm here.

She was smiling when she shut down the iPad. Even if her own children couldn't make time for her there were still people who wanted to share their lives with her and who appreciated her input. She may have been sitting in her living room by herself but she wasn't alone.

She decided to bake those sugar cookies. Her Christmas may not have been what she'd have liked the year before and it wasn't going to be what she wished for this year, either, but it didn't have to be miserable. She'd bake brownies and snowball cookies and maybe even some gumdrop cookies. So what if her children and grandchildren weren't going to be around to eat Christmas cookies? The neighbors would appreciate some.

Two hours later her kitchen table was covered with baked treats and she was exhausted. She went into the living room, turned on the TV and flopped on the couch. Found a holiday movie on Hallmark and promptly fell asleep.

She didn't wake up until her doorbell rang at seven. Who on earth?

She made her groggy way to the front door and opened it to find her son standing on the doorstep. He was holding a little white dog with button brown eyes and floppy ears.

"Hi, Mom," he said. "Sorry I didn't call first but Lila said you were home so I figured it was okay to come over."

"Of course," Catherine said, stepping aside to let him in. "What have you got here? Is this a new member of your family?" And did he want her to watch it while he was gone?

"No, actually, it's a new member of yours." He set the dog down and it gave a little bark and tried to climb his leg. "No, not me," he said to it. "You want her."

No, not her, either. "William..." she began.

The little dog barked at her and wagged its tail.

"She likes you," he said.

"What is this about?" she demanded.

"Uh, it's your Christmas present?"

"A dog? What makes you think I need a dog?" *Or want one.*

"Let's go in the living room," he suggested. "Come on, Cookie." He started for the living room and the dog fell in line, prancing along behind him.

"Gabby and I thought you might like the company," he said.

As if an animal could substitute for a person? Not in her book. *Thank you, Gabrielle.*

"I'm not looking for a dog," she said, her irritation bleeding into her voice. There were some presents people shouldn't buy for you and pets fell in that category.

"She's already housebroken," he said. "She's a mix, part Maltese and something else. The woman at PAWS thought maybe a spaniel because of the ears. She said both breeds are really good with seniors."

"William, I don't want a dog." Catherine didn't care how sweet the dog was. He could just take her back to PAWS. "And I'm not *that* old," she added, and plopped on the couch.

"She's pretty sweet, Mom. The kids fell in love with her."

"Good, then they can have her."

Now he looked hurt. "I thought you'd like her."

Catherine looked down at the little dog sitting on her

haunches, looking up at her, stubby tail wagging tentatively. "What am I supposed to do with her if I want to take a trip?" Who knew? Maybe she'd want to take another cruise with Denise.

"Lila or I can watch her."

"And when I'm doing chemo?"

"Chemo?" he said sharply.

Oh, dear. Now look what she'd done.

"Wait a minute. I thought you only had to have surgery."

"Well, I don't," she said crossly. Which of them she was most cross with she wasn't sure. "I have chemo starting in January and radiation after that. I don't have time for a dog."

Her son's smile vanished. "Shit, Mom. You might have told us."

"I didn't want to bother you. You're all so...busy." Yes, there was the accusation again.

He looked at her, horrified. "You need to tell us this stuff. We're your kids."

She shrugged. "I don't see that much of you." The little root of bitterness that had been lurking in her ever since her children each told her of their plans for the holidays sprouted up into a full-grown plant, refusing to be ignored any longer.

He sat next to her and put an arm around her. "I'm sorry, Mom. Why are they doing this? I don't understand."

He looked so worried. *Shame on you*, she scolded herself, *dumping all this on him right before Christmas.*

"The doctor was worried they might not have gotten everything with the surgery."

He pulled away, leaned forward, elbows on his knees, shut his eyes tightly and swore. Rubbed a hand over his forehead. A grown man determined not to cry in front of his mother.

"Mom, you should have told us."

"I didn't want to worry you." And now here she was worrying him. She was pathetic.

"It will be all right," she assured him.

He scowled at her. "Yeah, right. That's why you didn't tell us, 'cause it will be all right?" He swore again.

She thought she'd been unhappy that her children were taking off for the holidays. That was nothing compared to how unhappy she felt now. She was a two-legged Christmas wet blanket.

"We shouldn't be leaving you," he said, shaking his head.

'Tis the season for a guilt trip. Fa-la-la-la-la la-la-la-la. She should never have let it slip about the chemo. She hadn't planned to tell her children about it until the new year if at all, and now here she was, spilling toxic news all over her son.

Cookie put a paw on Catherine's leg and looked up at her with a whimper. She picked up the little dog and settled her in her lap.

"I'm sorry," she said. "I shouldn't have said anything."

"Yeah, you should have. You need to tell us this stuff. How can we help you if we don't know?"

He did have a valid point. Maybe her children didn't give enough because she didn't ask enough. Maybe she needed to stop being a martyr and act a little more like a queen.

"Does Lila know?"

Catherine shook her head.

"When were you going to tell us about this?"

"Eventually."

"I'm canceling our trip." He pulled out his phone.

And then she'd have one of her children with her for Christmas. Wouldn't that be a triumph, binding her son and his family to her with guilt, ruining a getaway they'd been looking forward to?

She put a hand over his to stop the frantic texting. "No, don't do that. You go and have fun."

"How the hell am I supposed to do that when I know you've got this coming up?"

"The same as you would have if you hadn't known. I shouldn't have told you."

"Yes, you should have. And you should have told Lila, too. She's gonna shit a brick when she hears."

"I'll tell her after the holidays." She'd work on getting in touch with her inner queen come the new year.

"You can't be by yourself."

"Darling, I was going to be by myself before you heard about this," she said, and his cheeks turned russet. Oh, dear. That was thoughtless.

"It was Gabby's idea. I shouldn't have gone along with it."

"Yes, you should have, especially in light of our miserable time last Christmas. Happy wife, happy life. Remember?"

"Like I can be happy now? I'm sorry, Mom. It was wrong to go off and leave you. I thought Lila was going to be here. By the time I found out she wasn't we'd already made the arrangements and..." He stopped talking, frowned, shook his head. "I can't believe this."

"It's all right, really. I'm going to Denise's Christmas Day, and it looks like I'll have company on Christmas Eve," Catherine said, looking down at the little dog curled up in her lap.

"You want to keep her?" he asked eagerly.

"I'll keep her through Christmas. Then your family can have her."

"I bet by the time we get back you won't want to give her up," Will said.

"A dog is a lot of work and I'm going to be...busy."

"Like I said, we'll help you take care of her. At least see if you like her."

She hadn't had a dog since their old basset hound, Sherlock, died. The kids had been in high school then and she and Bill had opted out of getting another pet.

Catherine sighed. "Animals are a lot of work. I'm going to have to go out and buy dog food."

"No, you won't. I've got it in the car. And a dog bed, travel crate, leash, chew toy. You name it. Gabby went crazy. Oh, one more thing." He reached inside his jacket pocket and pulled out a check. "Sorry it took me so long to pay you back."

The money she'd lent him. "You didn't have to," she said. But it made her happy that he did.

"Yeah, I did. I know I don't tell you often enough, Mom, but I really do appreciate all you've done for us. All you do. Anything you need once you start chemo, you just say the word."

She nodded, her throat too clogged with emotion to speak.

"Hey, I'll go get Cookie's stuff. Okay?"

"Okay." Not that Catherine was going to keep the dog but the poor thing had to stay someplace until Will returned. "And I'll fill a plate with some cookies for all of you," she said. "I just baked this afternoon."

"The boys will love that," he said.

Her son went to fetch Cookie's things and Catherine went out to the kitchen to load treats into a cookie tin. The dog trotted after her and sat observing while she worked.

"I bet you think you're going to get some of this," Catherine said.

Cookie's tail thumped.

"Well, you're not. These wouldn't be good for you. They

won't be good for me, either, but I'm a human and I get to make bad choices."

Listen to her. She was already talking to the dog like they were boon companions. Good grief.

She gathered the presents for Will's family into another couple of shopping bags while he brought in all of Cookie's things, set the dog bed on the floor in Catherine's bedroom and stowed the dog food in the pantry after pouring some into a double-dish dog bowl, along with water.

"I took her for a walk before we came so she should be good to go for tonight. But if you're worried, you can let her out in the backyard."

Where she would make a mess. Just what Catherine wanted to be doing, shoveling doggy-do. Or worse, walking the dog, plastic bag in hand, ready to do poop patrol. She was not—was not!—keeping this dog.

She handed over the treats for the family, as well as their presents, and walked her son to the door.

"You need to tell Lila," he said.

"I will."

"If you don't, I will," he threatened. Then he bent over, gave her a hug. "We'll FaceTime you Christmas morning. Okay?"

"Okay," she said. FaceTime was better than no time.

She thought for sure the little dog would want to trot out the door after him, but Cookie stayed by her side, then followed her back into the living room, settling at her feet once Catherine was back on the couch.

"You're awfully well behaved. You know that?" Catherine said to the dog, and Cookie barked and wagged her tail. "I suppose you'd like to sit up here with me."

Another woof and tail wag.

"All right. But we're not going to make a habit of this," Catherine said, and picked up the dog. She set Cookie next to her and scratched behind her ears. Cookie promptly fell onto her back, eager for a belly rub. "What's your story, anyway?" Catherine asked as she obliged. "Somebody must have loved you. Did your owner die? I guess we'll never know. You'll make a nice houseguest." And that was all Cookie was going to be because her son was getting this dog back as soon as he got home.

Meanwhile, though…the house suddenly didn't seem so empty.

"Let's watch a movie, shall we?" Catherine asked. She picked up the TV remote and Cookie snuggled up against her and laid her head in Catherine's lap. "Something with a dog in it, I'm thinking. What do you think?"

Cookie's ears went up.

"Yes, definitely something with a dog in it."

It took a while to find a movie where the dog didn't die. "The kids liked this one," she said to Cookie, and began to stream *Beethoven*. "Now, there's a dog I'd never have," Catherine said. "Saint Bernards are terrible slobberers."

The movie was cute and Catherine enjoyed it. She also enjoyed having the little dog with her on the couch. But what a nuisance it was having to let her out to go potty later. And what a nuisance to have to feed her the next day and take her out for a walk.

"Dr. Dimatrova did say I needed to walk a mile every day once I start chemo, whether I feel like it or not," she informed Cookie as they started down the sidewalk in the morning fog. "If I have you with me I'll have to do that, won't I?"

Oh, no. Was she really thinking about keeping this dog?

After their morning walk she had another email from Si-

erra. Let me know when you start chemo. I'll bring you chicken noodle soup.

And that afternoon a text from Sophie. *I just toured Cupid's Chocolates. Yum!*

"It's good to hear that things are progressing nicely between Sophie and Trevor," she said to Cookie. Cookie barked her agreement and wagged her tail.

Actually, it was good to hear from both the sisters. Two days before Christmas she heard from them again, this time via the mail. Sierra sent a box of lavender-scented soap and Sophie sent a box of chocolates from Cupid's Chocolates.

To be remembered by such new friends warmed her heart. "You have a lot to be thankful for," she told herself.

And what a difference in attitude that was from the Christmas before. Not that she didn't have her moments when she wished Bill was still with her, when she didn't look at the mantelpiece with the two empty stockings hanging from it and tear up, but she was starting to use the good moments to counterbalance the bad ones.

She wrote thank-you notes to both sisters, stuck them in her mailbox for pickup and then did a little shopping of her own. Online. She found a book for Sophie on herbal medicines and an inspirational book for Sierra on how to get past a breakup, then had them shipped. Then she took a bath and enjoyed using the lavender soap.

And tried not to think about the fact that she hadn't heard from either Rudy or Athena. She had, on impulse, sent Athena a Christmas card. Probably a silly idea. Those two would go on the list of people who merely passed through your life, the human equivalent of a cruise ship, headed for a new destination.

Then, Christmas Eve, the postman delivered a package. From California.

18

THE RETURN ADDRESS ON THE BOX SAID SANTA Monica. Rudy and Athena both lived in Santa Monica but she didn't remember the rest of either of their addresses. She carried it out to the kitchen, Cookie trotting along behind.

She got scissors and opened the box, her heart thumping in rhythm with Cookie's tail. Something from Rudy? Was it possible?

Inside it was another box, wrapped in shiny red paper and tied with raffia ribbon. On top of the box sat a red envelope. She opened it and pulled out a Christmas card. Inside it was signed, *Merry Christmas from Athena.*

No *Rudy* added to the signature and that was disappointing. Although it shouldn't have been. She'd known what they'd started was done and would fall into the category of Christmas past.

Still, it warmed Catherine's heart that his daughter had thought of her. "Isn't that sweet?" she said to Cookie. "I'll put it under the tree to open Christmas morning."

Except Cookie was liable to eat the ribbon. She'd just have to open the present right then and there. She worked the ribbon off the box, pulled away the wrapping paper and lifted the lid.

There sat a large version of the hand-painted glass globe candleholders she'd bought for her daughter and daughter-in-law. This one was blue, featuring a night sky over a small-town snow-covered street. The houses made her think of Germany. She'd admired a globe just like this one but refrained from spending the money on herself. Now here she had one, and from such an unexpected source.

She gave it a place of honor on her dining room table, then sat down at her little kitchen desk and wrote a thank-you note to Athena.

> Dear Athena,
>
> I just received the most lovely surprise in the mail today. How kind of you to think of me! Needless to say, I'm thrilled, and your thoughtfulness has helped to make this Christmas very special. I do hope you'll have a wonderful one. Give my best to your father.

Oh, no. That was not a good idea. She tossed the note in the wastebasket and wrote a new one, leaving out any mention of Rudy. If he'd wanted to continue things he'd have signed his name to the card, as well. Unlike the relationship that was slowly growing with the sisters, Catherine doubted this one with Athena would last. Still, she would treasure the present, almost as much as the bracelet and charms Rudy had bought her. More artifacts.

So what? she decided. Artifacts were valuable things.

Christmas Eve at the Miles residence was always a night for laughter and good-natured teasing. Someone always threatened to report Sophie, Sierra or Drew's naughty behavior to Santa. When the Miles siblings were little, it had been Dad, telling them he was going to call Santa's hotline and instruct him to pass by their house if they didn't settle down and go to sleep. As the years went by the methods of communication changed to email. Now that they were grown the warnings turned to teasing and threats of texts, and with naughty behavior a thing of the past, both Dad and kids settled for promising to report suspicious behavior. Dad loved playing the suspicious behavior card, partly because Drew was a cop, but also because he could stay vague. Suspicious behavior ranged from snagging the last piece of pumpkin pie at Thanksgiving to doing too much gloating when winning at cards.

This Christmas Eve, the teasing felt a little forced and it was limited to Sophie and Drew.

Sierra was trying to be a good sport, but Sophie found her sister's attempted smiles and laughter harder to bear than if she'd cried.

Family tradition allowed opening one present on Christmas Eve, and the three siblings knew what that would be—the same as it had been since they'd been small—Christmas pj's. This year's version were holiday elf pajamas, featuring green tops over green striped bottoms. Elf ears completed the ensemble.

"Got to add this to the picture collection," Dad said. "Next year, maybe we'll have another elf in the family, eh?" he added, winking at Drew. They all knew of Drew's plans to spring an engagement ring on his girlfriend New Year's Eve. "Okay, kids. Everyone on the couch."

The sisters sat on either side of Drew, his arms draped over them. "Say Christmas pickle," Dad coached, aiming his phone at them.

"Christmas pickle," belted Drew and Sophie.

"Christmas pickle," said Sierra, a faint echo.

"Take one for me, too," Sophie said to her father, handing over her phone.

"Okay, Christmas pickle one more time," he said.

Once more Sophie and Drew tried to inject extra enthusiasm into the moment to make up for their sister's lack of it. They didn't quite succeed.

No one should be unhappy at Christmas, Sophie thought, especially her sister. It was so wrong. Thank you, Mark. She hoped, wherever he was, someone fed him peppermint bark laced with reindeer poop.

"Clam chowder is ready," their mother called from the kitchen.

"All right," Drew said, rubbing his hands together. "Let's eat." He pulled Sierra off the couch. "Come on, sis, let's drown your troubles in chowder."

Sierra rallied enough to eat chowder and garlic bread and sample several of the Spritz cookies Sophie had brought. Maybe she'd be able to enjoy the rest of the evening.

After dinner was finished and the siblings had done kitchen cleanup, their dad put in the DVD that Drew had made for the parents, a compilation of pictures from Christmases past. For background music, he'd inserted snippets from favorite holiday songs. "Grandma Got Run Over by a Reindeer" accompanied shots of the two grandmas enjoying Christmas cookies. Bittersweet. One grandma they'd see the following day. The other was no longer with them. "White Christmas" played as several pictures faded in and out of the siblings playing in the snow, and "We Wish You a Merry Christmas" accompanied several shots everyone had taken from different angles the year Dad dropped the turkey on his way to the dining room table.

They were laughing uproariously as "Do You Hear What I Hear" played over shots of various people being subjected to torture with the whoopee cushion Drew had given their dad two years earlier.

Until one shot showed Mark sitting on it, looking disgusted. Sierra instantly teared up and Drew's face turned Christmas-stocking red. "Shit," he muttered.

"Never mind that loser," Dad said gruffly, then decided maybe they should watch the rest of the DVD another time.

"I'm sorry, sis," Drew said as their mom hurried to fetch more cookies. "I thought I got all of his out of there."

"It's okay," Sierra said bravely.

"If I wasn't a cop I'd beat the shit out of him. I wish I could arrest him for being a jerk."

"How about at least staking out his house, then following him and giving him a speeding ticket?" Sophie suggested.

"I'd rather see him in jail," said Sierra. "Handcuff him and make him eat Grandma Sanders's fruitcake till he barfs."

"Just looking at Grandma Sanders's fruitcake is enough to make me barf," said Drew.

"Tie him up with strings of Christmas lights," put in Sophie. "Make Santa shove him down a chimney."

"Yeah, one where they've built a fire in the fireplace," Sierra said, beginning to smile.

"Best revenge, take a picture of yourself in these hot pj's so he can see what he's missing," Drew teased.

Sophie gave a snort, but her sister's smile went away.

Drew sobered. "He is missing a lot. He's a fool, sis."

Sierra bit her lip and nodded.

Their mother came into the room with a plate of cookies in time to hear. "Living well is the best revenge," she reminded Sierra. "You work on making your life great in this new year and everything will work out."

Sierra sighed and nodded.

Later, when the two sisters were back in the room they'd shared growing up, snuggled under the covers in their twin beds, Sierra said, "I am thinking of doing something to make my life great once I get through all this."

"Another cruise?" Sophie guessed.

"No. Adopting a child."

"Really?" It was the last thing Sophie had expected her sister to say, although why she wasn't sure.

"Do you think it's a bad idea?"

"No, of course not. You'll be a great mother. And Mom's ready for grandkids. I'm ready to be an aunt, too."

"I'm not going to rush into it instantly, but I do want to check out options. At the rate I'll be going you'll probably be married and pregnant before I ever have a child."

"*Moi?* Married. I can't imagine who you might be talking about," Sophie joked.

"Oh, no, hardly at all. Marrying into your own lifetime supply of chocolate. Lucky you. That's better than marrying a doctor. Although what you really need is a shrink."

Sophie decided not to tell her sister what Trevor's college major had been. She'd sure never hear the end of that.

Catherine's Christmas Eve had been a quiet one. She spent the morning shopping for ingredients for a Black Forest cherry cake, then managed to use up a chunk of the afternoon baking it. That night it was just her and Cookie and a frozen turkey dinner, watching old Christmas movies on TV.

By the time she let Cookie outside for her bedtime bathroom break she discovered that the snow the weatherman predicted had arrived. Not so much that she'd be afraid to drive the next day, but it was enough to qualify for a white Christmas. The pretty sight made Catherine smile.

Cookie wasn't into white Christmases. She did her duty and then was back immediately, ready to be inside and warm.

"I guess this means you don't want to go out and play in the snow with me," Catherine said, and Cookie wagged her tail and barked.

"No more treats," Catherine said sternly. "You already had your dog biscuit and half my turkey. That's enough. For you, anyway," she added, then helped herself to a brownie before going upstairs to bed. Calories didn't count at Christmas.

William and his family checked in on Christmas Day. They all looked tan and happy and relaxed. Gabrielle was delighted with Catherine's gift and quick to invite her out to lunch after they returned home. The boys were buzzing on sugar highs and bouncing around the hotel room like little gremlins. Will asked how Catherine and Cookie were doing.

"We're great."

"Still want to give her back?" he teased.

"Maybe not, but you're going to have to promise to dog-sit next Christmas when I go away for the holidays."

His wife suddenly had to go calm the boys down and Will looked embarrassed. "Let's not make a habit of that, okay?"

That was fine with her.

Lila didn't FaceTime but she did text. We're off to the slopes. Kids loved their prezzies. Me, too. Love U.

Short, sweet and not all that satisfying. But at least she'd checked in.

"Okay, Cookie, we've heard from everyone," Catherine said to the dog.

That was it for family time, and a meager helping of time it had been. But no pity parties. Catherine had someplace to go. She wouldn't be alone.

She dressed in slacks and a red sweater, then went bold and settled a Santa hat on her head. She loaded up her presents for Denise and her daughter and the granddaughters, along with the Black Forest cherry cake, left Cookie to enjoy the chew toy Santa had brought her and drove the few blocks to her best friend's house.

The mixed sounds of squeals and Christmas songs playing on the TV were almost loud enough to drown out the doorbell, but not quite. A moment later the door flew open and there stood Denise's granddaughters, wearing matching red velveteen dresses, ruffled socks on their feet, their shoes already off. Ten and eight, they were bouncing up and down with excitement. Eleanor, the oldest, held a new iPad and Pearl Ann clutched an American Girl doll.

"Merry Christmas, Aunt Catherine!" they chorused.

"Look what I got," Eleanor said, holding out the iPad for Catherine to see.

"I got this," said her sister, determined not to be left out of show-and-tell.

Denise rounded the corner into the front hall. "Good grief, you little heathens. Somebody offer to help her with her things."

"Sorry," Eleanor said. "Can I help you?"

"You can take this bag of presents," Catherine said to her.

"Ooh, presents," Pearl Ann squealed, and reached for the bag.

"I'm helping her," Eleanor said, and grabbed it.

"I want to help," protested Pearl Ann.

"Would you like to take the cake out to the kitchen?" Catherine asked.

Pearl Ann nodded soberly and held out her hands, and Catherine gave her the cake carrier.

"Don't drop it," Denise cautioned.

Pearl Ann nodded, and started walking slowly toward the kitchen, her sister shadowing her, the guardian angel of cakes.

Denise smiled fondly, watching them. "Those girls," she said, shaking her head.

"Are adorable, of course," Catherine finished.

"Yes, they are. Here, give me your coat. Did you hear from your kids?"

"Oh, yes, everyone checked in."

"They'd better do more than check in next year or they're going to hear from me," Denise said. "Go on in. Carrie brought her fabulous Christmas tree appetizer and there's actually a few bites left. If you hurry you might get one."

In addition to the appetizer, Denise's daughter, who had been a single mom for the last two years, had brought along a new boyfriend. He seemed like a nice man and Carrie's smile was lit up like, well, Christmas. Catherine thought of Sierra, whose marriage was ending. That was life for you. Somewhere a relationship ended while somewhere else a new one began. Maybe, down the road, Sierra, too, would find someone who would make her smile look like Christmas.

The day included a huge meal with a standing rib roast taking center stage, a hunt for miniature candy canes and other tiny Christmas treasures Denise had hidden around the house, as well as a game of Trivial Pursuit and some singing of carols.

They were about to cut the cake when Charlie dropped by

with a gift for her. Her daughter looked at him suspiciously and then at her mother when Charlie informed Denise he had reservations at the Space Needle for New Year's Eve.

"How about joining us, Catherine?" he suggested.

"I'm sure you'd like that," she scoffed.

"Of course I would," he said. "Two beautiful women, one for each arm."

"I'm afraid you'll have to settle for one empty arm," Catherine told him. Something was definitely blooming between those two and she had no intention of stunting the growth of what could turn out to be a very special relationship.

Thoughts of Rudy tried to intrude, but she pushed them firmly away. She had plenty of good people in her life. She was fine just as she was.

Altogether not a bad day, she thought later as she drove home. Not the Christmas she'd have planned but a nice one, anyway. It was also nice not to come home to an empty house. Cookie was there to greet her. And she'd only chewed up one sofa pillow. Yes, not a bad day at all.

Catherine spent the rest of the night on her couch, reading, Cookie snuggled by her side. A quiet finish to the day, much as it would have been if Bill was still alive. She could live with that.

She could live with a quiet New Year's Eve, too. She and Bill hadn't done much when he was alive, anyway. They'd usually watch a couple of movies—*Die Hard* and *Groundhog Day*, their respective favorites. Then it would be a glass of champagne, a kiss good-night and off to bed. Knowing there would be no kiss good-night made her sad, but at least she had company now. And she could still watch movies and drink champagne.

"I think you should go out with Charlie and me," Denise

said as they sat in the Westlake Mall Starbucks the next day. "You don't want to be alone on New Year's Eve."

"I won't be alone. I'll have Cookie."

"Dogs don't count," Denise said.

"Sure they do," Catherine said, then changed the subject quickly.

Denise hadn't been impressed with William's present, labeling it a sop to his conscience. Maybe it had been or maybe it had been a thoughtful present. Either way, Catherine didn't want to discuss it.

They shopped a few after-Christmas sales, then went back home, Denise to get ready to entertain Charlie for dinner and Catherine to…entertain Cookie.

William called the next day on his lunch break to see how Cookie was settling in. "You ready to give her back?" he asked.

"Not quite."

"I knew you'd like her."

"Just remember, you're still going to have to dog-sit once in a while," Catherine warned.

"We can handle that. The boys'll love it," he said. Then he whiplashed them into new conversational territory. "Have you told Lila about the chemo?"

She didn't even want to think about the chemo, let alone talk about it. "No, but I will."

"Sometime before it starts would be good," he said irritably. "I don't want to be the only one dealing with this."

Funny, she'd thought she was the one dealing with it. "I'll be fine," she said as much to herself as him.

"I know you will," he said. "But don't shut us out. We want to help."

"I know." It was good to hear him say it.

"Tell her today, Mom," he commanded.

"Don't worry. I'll talk to you later," she said. Then she hung up before her son could find anything more to lecture her on.

"You know, Cookie," she told the dog, "this is a fine example of how you should be careful what you wish for. Here I was feeling neglected and now all of a sudden my son is turning into a helicopter child." Although, really, it was rather nice to have William hovering. Once in a while, a woman needed her children in her airspace, needed to know they really did care.

Lila called that evening. "Why didn't you tell me the doctor didn't get everything when they did the hysterectomy?" she demanded. "What were you thinking?" Catherine tried to speak but her daughter didn't give her the chance. "I had to find out from William. William! I'm your daughter. You're supposed to tell me these things. I mean, when were you going to tell me? Ever?"

"Of course I was going to tell you at some point. You've been a little preoccupied."

"It has been the holidays, you know," Lila said defensively.

"Yes, I do," Catherine said. *And you've been way too busy with your own life to care about what was happening in mine.* Oh, how those words wanted to come out, but Catherine resisted the temptation to send another child on a guilt trip. "So there was no sense bothering you with this."

"Bothering? Mom, are you kidding? When does it start? I've got to get the dates on my calendar."

"Why on earth do you need to put them on your calendar?"

"I'm taking you, of course. How else are you going to get there? Where are you having it done?"

"Virginia Mason, downtown. But you don't have to take me."

"I want to take you. Anyway, don't you have to stay hooked

up to that… IV drip or whatever? You don't want to sit there all by yourself, do you?"

Catherine had been spending a lot of time by herself in the last year. What were a couple more hours, give or take?

"They do let people come in the room with you, right?"

"They do."

"Okay, then. We can play cards or something. Mother-daughter time."

Mother-daughter time. Catherine smiled. "I'd like that." *See, Bill, our children aren't so very selfish, after all.*

"Good. That's settled, then. Text me the dates. By the way, I hear William gave you a dog. What was he thinking?"

"That I'd enjoy the company."

"I guess," Lila said dubiously. Then, to her daughter, who Catherine could hear in the background. "I know. I'm coming! Okay, Mom, I've got to run. I promised Carissa we'd go shopping for jammies. She's got a slumber party on New Year's Eve. I'll talk to you later."

New Year's Eve. Catherine hadn't had the opportunity to ask what her daughter was doing, but she was sure Lila would have something planned with her husband. William and Gabrielle would be doing something, too.

Which was as it should be. Everyone should celebrate the beginning of a new year with someone they loved.

The thought of spending the night alone wrapped her in melancholy. "But I'm not going to say anything to Lila or William," she said to Cookie. "I already said enough to upset them."

She could handle seeing in the new year alone. She could handle a lot of things alone.

The melancholy began to slide off. "We don't mind being on our own, do we, Cookie?"

Cookie thumped her stumpy tail and lifted a front paw, giving Catherine a little doggy wave.

"I knew you'd agree. You know, I'd never really been alone before Bill died. I lived at home when I was going to college and then I got married. Sometimes I feel a little like a sheep, looking for the rest of the flock. I don't know if alone suits me."

Still, one had to make the best of things. She'd find something to do New Year's Eve.

Take down the tree, read a book. Maybe start a new knitting project. And...what else? She'd think of something.

19

IT WAS EARLY AFTERNOON ON NEW YEAR'S EVE when Catherine got a text. She had to read it twice to make sure she wasn't hallucinating.

This is Rudy in case you don't recognize the number. I'm in town and wondering if you have plans for New Year's Eve.

Rudy? Plans? She blinked. She had to be hallucinating. She read the text again. *Oh, my.*

She texted back…several times, thumbing in a reply and then deleting it, her heart thumping all the while. She finally settled for something innocuous. It would be lovely to see you.

What a bland response in light of the crazy excitement she was feeling. It was as if she'd been thrown back in time, and was once more on the dance floor of that cruise ship, in his arms, falling in love for the second time in her life.

The first had been Bill, and she remembered those butterflies she'd felt when they'd stood on her front porch after their second date and she'd known he was going to kiss her. Time changed a woman on the outside, but never on the inside. The butterflies always returned. And now, here they were.

What did that text mean? Surely it could only mean one thing, that he wanted to keep what they started going. But she was afraid to hope. How, she was dying to know.

Okay. I'll make reservations.

They set a time, she gave him her address. It was a done deal.

New Year's Eve with Rudy. What was she going to wear? She hurried to her bedroom closet and stood a long time looking at the clothes hanging there. She didn't have anything fancy, at least nothing that fit anymore. She hadn't needed anything fancy for the quiet New Year's Eves she'd spent with her husband. You hardly had to get dressed up to watch TV.

"I need to go shopping," she told Cookie.

An hour later she was at Ross Dress for Less, sifting through the dresses on the rack. She finally found a simple black dress with long, lacy sleeves that didn't make her look too much like the proverbial sack of potatoes. She still had some black heels that would do and a rhinestone necklace and matching earrings. All she needed was pantyhose.

Ugh. Pantyhose were one of fashion's instruments of torture. She read the measurements on the back of the packages with knit brows. How much did she weigh now? She hadn't gotten on her scale since the cruise. Actually, she hadn't gotten on her scale in the last year, and she'd been afraid to look every time she went to the oncologist and the nurse weighed her. She finally bought two different packages, deciding it would be best to have options.

Then she drove home, set her bedside alarm clock for two hours, fell back on her bed and…lay there, staring at the ceiling, her mind whirling. She should rest. She'd be exhausted.

She was too excited to sleep.

She finally gave up. She called her son and asked him to come pick up Cookie for an overnight.

"You going out?" William asked.

"Yes, I am."

"With Denise?"

"No, someone else."

"Who?" he asked suspiciously.

"Just a friend."

"What does that mean? What friend?"

"Someone I met on the cruise."

"On the cruise! You never told me you met someone on the cruise."

"I met a lot of nice people."

"Is this a man?" Will demanded.

"Well, yes."

"Mom, you've got to be careful. What do you know about this guy, anyway? For all you know he could be a fortune hunter."

Catherine thought of Athena and smiled. She and William had a lot in common.

"Don't worry. He's fine. Now, are you going to come pick up Cookie?"

"Yeah," he said, not sounding happy. "We're going out but

the babysitter and the kids can watch her. Jeez, Mom. You don't tell us anything."

"I didn't think you'd be interested."

"I want to know if some fortune hunter's after you."

She chuckled. "If that's why he's after me he'll be sorely disappointed since I don't have a fortune. Maybe he wants me for my body."

"Mom, stop it," William said, shocked.

"I've got to get ready. Thanks for watching Cookie."

"Yeah, yeah," he said irritably. "I don't like this."

"I know," Catherine said, and smiled.

She took a bath, fixed herself a little snack, then got busy doing her hair and makeup. Struggled into the pantyhose. By the time she was done she looked…like an overweight, older woman in a black party dress. Nothing special. What had Rudy seen in her, anyway?

At the last minute she put on her jewelry, dabbed perfume behind her ears and on her wrists and slipped into the black heels. They were ten years old. She'd almost forgotten how to walk in heels. She checked herself in the long mirror hanging on the closet door. Now she looked…like an overweight, older woman in a black party dress.

William arrived half an hour before Rudy was due.

"How do I look?" Catherine asked him.

"You look good," he said. "Where are you going?"

"I'm not sure."

"You don't even know where he's taking you?"

"It doesn't matter where he's taking me." She'd go anywhere with Rudy Nichols.

"Keep your cell phone on in case."

"In case what?"

"In case you need to call me. And don't stay out too late."

"When's my curfew?" she teased.

"Not funny, Mom. You watch yourself."

"I will," she assured him.

He nodded, then went to fetch Cookie's crate.

"Have you told Lila about this?" he asked when he returned.

"No, but I will."

"She'll probably think it's great," he said irritably. "She reads too many romance novels."

"Every woman needs a little romance," Catherine said lightly, making him shake his head.

He and Cookie left and then it was just her, sitting in her living room, waiting for Rudy. Her and the butterflies.

At ten minutes to seven the doorbell rang and her heart shot clear up into her throat. He was here, this was it.

She swallowed hard in an effort to calm her nerves, got up, smoothed her dress and went to the door. She opened it and there he stood, holding a bouquet of pink roses and a bottle of champagne.

"You look beautiful," he said.

Not half as good as him. "Do I?"

"Oh, yes."

She stepped aside. "Come in."

He did, looking around as he went. There wasn't much to see in the hallway, only a hall table with a vase holding red silk poinsettias. A Kinkade print hanging on the wall. She led him into the living room.

"This is so homey," he said, taking in the tree and decorations. He handed her the bouquet and champagne. "I thought maybe for later," he said tentatively.

"That was so thoughtful of you. Let me just put these in water. Sit down and make yourself comfortable."

For later, she thought as she put the champagne in the refrigerator and found a tall cut-glass vase for the roses. She set it on her dining table, next to the glass globe his daughter had given her, then returned to the living room where he'd perched on the edge of the sofa. She sat down on the other end.

"You're probably wondering what I'm doing here," he said.

"A little."

"I missed you," he said simply.

"I missed you, too. How's Athena?"

"She's fine. She says hi, by the way."

"That was nice of her," Catherine said.

"She's a good daughter." He checked his watch. "I suppose we should go. I have reservations at Canlis for seven-thirty."

"Canlis?" she echoed. One of the most expensive and exclusive restaurants in Seattle. "Oh, you shouldn't have."

"Why? Isn't it good? I looked it up online and it seemed okay."

"It's very expensive."

He grinned. "That's all right. I can afford it. By the way, I'm spending this money with my daughter's permission," he added. "And that's saying something." He sobered. "Catherine, we left things pretty up in the air."

She bit her lip. Remembering their last conversation, she felt like a kite that had lost wind and crashed to the ground.

"I'm here because I want to be involved in your life."

"After everything you've been through?" It wasn't fair to ask him, really. "You know what I have waiting for me in the new year."

"I know. I also know that this is a very beatable cancer. The treatment your doctor has ordered is, most likely, insurance. If I'd been thinking I would have realized that."

"There are no guarantees. My oncologist will be checking

me every three months. It could come back." Simply saying the words was enough to freeze her blood.

He moved to sit next to her and took her hand. "You're right, it could, and there are no guarantees. I could have a heart attack tomorrow, get hit by a car. But that's life, isn't it? Unpredictable, full of good and bad and ups and downs. If you spend all your time worrying about the bumps in the road you'll never get anywhere and you sure won't have much of a life. I don't want to do that, Catherine. You're a special lady and I want to be with you. I think the bad times are done with us for a while and we might actually have some good times waiting ahead. Let's see where this leads."

She so wanted to see where it led, wanted to be with Rudy. But… "The next few months are not going to be pretty." Her lower lip began to wobble. "I won't have any hair."

A stupid thing to bring up. What did losing hair matter compared to the possibility of losing her life?

He kissed her hand. "It wasn't your hair that attracted me to you in the first place. It was your sweet smile and kind heart. I want to keep what we started going. Don't you?"

"Oh, yes," she said. "Yes!"

"Okay, then. Let's go check out that restaurant. I'm starving."

And so they did, eating at a window table, dining on prawns and grilled albacore, enjoying the view of Lake Union below. After their meal they returned to Catherine's house where she fed him cookies and they talked until nearly midnight.

"You're exhausted," he said. "I shouldn't have stayed so long."

"I'm glad you did," she said. "Shall we ring in the new year with some of that champagne?"

"One glass. Then I'll leave and let you get some rest. I'm here until the second if you'd like to get together tomorrow."

"I certainly would," she said. "Come over and I'll make a roast."

"I haven't had a roast since… It's been a long time. I'd love that."

He opened the champagne and poured it into two of her champagne glasses. "To the new road ahead of us," he toasted.

She could drink to that.

"Happy New Year, Catherine," he said after they'd sampled the champagne, then he kissed her.

And the butterflies went crazy.

Sierra was hosting a girlfriend New Year's Eve party, which had given Sophie permission to enjoy the party Trevor threw at his Portland condo. She'd liked his friends and had been happy to see some of the people who helped him run his company again. Many of them she'd met on her previous visit to Portland.

She'd also met his brother's girlfriend and was glad to see her and Kurt at the party. Sophie could easily envision doing things together as couples in the future.

"Having fun?" Trevor asked as the guests started getting their champagne ready to toast in the new year.

"Oh, yes," she said. "I like all your friends."

"And they like you. But then, what's not to like?" he added with a grin. He helped himself to another shrimp from a nearby platter and gave her one, too.

Shrimp, lobster mac and cheese, pork sliders, cookies, chocolate—she'd eaten enough food to last her for a week.

"Hey," someone called, pointing to the TV hanging over the fireplace. "Countdown's started."

Everyone chimed in, counting down the seconds. And then, just like that, it was a new year.

"Happy New Year," Trevor said to Sophie, and kissed her. With a kiss like that he should have had a fire extinguisher handy.

"Ecstatic New Year," she corrected him. "Seriously, where did you ever learn to kiss like that? Wait. Never mind. I don't want to know."

"That's just the warm-up. Wait till we get to the main event."

She was ready for the main event.

Or not. Suddenly she was feeling…

"Oh, my gosh!" She made a dash for the bathroom, still holding her champagne glass and sloshing champagne everywhere.

She barely made it to the toilet in time. Her poor, unhappy stomach. She shouldn't have had that shrimp. How long had it been sitting out? Food poisoning. She had food poisoning.

She could hear people talking out in the other room. Were they talking about her? She was going to die of embarrassment.

Or food poisoning.

She leaned her head against the toilet, bracing for round two.

Round two wasn't any more fun than round one.

She was still recovering from that when she heard a knock on the bathroom door, followed by Trevor's voice. "Are you okay?"

"I don't think so," she whimpered.

"Can I come in? Are you decent?"

"Yes." She spooled off some toilet paper and wiped her mouth. He was probably grateful he'd kissed her when he did. One disaster narrowly avoided, anyway.

He came in and saw her sitting in front of the toilet. "Uh-oh."

"I think I've got food poisoning," she told him. "The shrimp."

"I just ate some. Are you sure it was the shrimp?"

"I'm sure. We should call 911."

"Never mind that. I can get you to the emergency room faster." He held out his hand.

"You can't leave your guests," she protested.

"Kurt and Misty can keep 'em entertained. Come on." She took his hand and he pulled her to her feet.

They emerged from the bathroom, Sophie on shaky legs, feeling both miserable and embarrassed.

"Are you okay, Sophie?" asked Char, who was in charge of production at Cupid's Chocolates.

"I'm taking her to the emergency room," Trevor said. "Misty, can you grab her coat?"

"Sure," Misty said, hurrying to fetch it.

"Don't anybody eat any more of the shrimp," put in Sophie.

"Oh, my God, I just had six," said Trevor's buddy Mike.

"Oh, no," Sophie fretted as Trevor bundled her into her coat, then hustled her out of the condo.

"Never mind him. Let's take care of you," Trevor said, and rushed her out the door.

"Call us," Kurt called after him.

A moment later they were in his car and speeding down the street like a demon. He took a corner at top speed and Sophie's stomach did the wave. *Noooo. No barfing in Trevor's car.* She swallowed hard, determined not to make things any worse for him than she already had.

Her stomach got the message and behaved, and in another five minutes they were walking through the emergency room doors.

"She needs a doctor," Trevor said to the woman manning the check-in desk.

So did about half a dozen other people—all in various stages of dress. A woman in her twenties was wearing jeans and a parka and slippers, a foot with a makeshift ice bag propped up on her boyfriend's leg. A middle-aged couple sat in a corner, both thumbing through magazines and looking cranky. The man let out a phlegmy cough that had probably just sent a million attack germs into the air, and Sophie covered her face with her jacket sleeve.

An older woman and her daughter sat together, and the daughter's words drifted over to where Sophie and Trevor stood. "There's nothing wrong with you. We've gone through this before. It's just a panic attack."

Would that be Trevor talking to Sophie someday?

"That's easy for you to say," the mother retorted. "You're not the one panicking."

"Insurance?" the woman at reception asked Sophie.

She dug out her insurance card. She didn't feel all that bad anymore. She should never have made him bring her.

"Maybe we should go," she said to him. "I think I feel better." And she sure wouldn't feel good if she stayed around Mr. Germ much longer.

"We should check you out," he said. "Better safe than sorry."

The woman printed out a wristband and put it on Sophie and they found a couple of seats far from Mr. Germ.

"I'm sorry you had to leave your guests," Sophie said.

He put an arm around her shoulders and hugged her. "Hey, it's okay."

She looked to where the woman sat with her daughter and asked in a low voice, "Is that going to be me someday?"

"Nah. You'll be much better looking."

Trevor March had the best ever bedside manner.

One by one the other patients disappeared into exam rooms until it was only Sophie and Trevor in the waiting room. "All your friends will have gone home by the time we get back," she fretted.

"Are you kidding? Not that bunch, not on New Year's Eve."

"I really don't feel so bad now. We should go."

"We're here now. Let's stay and get you checked out. Better safe than sorry."

A sliding door to an exam room opened and a nurse stepped out, paperwork in hand. "Sophie Miles," she called.

"There you go. Be sure and tell her what you ate," Trevor said.

She nodded and went into the exam room. Had her temperature taken and blood pressure measured by the nurse. Got a blood test. And then, when the doctor appeared, told him what she'd eaten. Good Lord, had she really consumed that much?

"I think we can rule out food poisoning," the doctor said. "You have no fever, no stomach cramps, no diarrhea. No more nausea, right?"

She shook her head.

"And you're not dehydrated."

"But I ate shrimp."

The doctor nodded. "I understand. But you ate quite a few other things as well. I suspect they didn't play well together."

"So I'm okay?"

"You're good to go," he assured her. "Go home, drink some ginger ale and get some rest. Happy New Year."

Relieved New Year.

No, more like Embarrassing New Year, she thought as she rejoined Trevor.

"Everything okay?" he asked, standing up.

She nodded. Then sighed. "My sister's right. I am a squirrel."

"Everybody loves squirrels," he said easily. "They're cute."

"I'm really sorry I dragged you out. Gosh, what a pain in the neck I am."

"Do you hear me complaining?"

"Not yet."

"Not ever," he promised. He slung an arm around her and started guiding her out of the emergency room.

"It could have been food poisoning," she ventured. How did you know unless you went to the doctor?

"It could have," he said diplomatically. "From now on I'm going to keep a close eye on what you eat."

"Kind of hard to do when I live up in Seattle."

"So move to Portland. You can work anywhere, right?"

Hmm. She could.

"If I did..." she began.

"Let's leave the ifs out of it. Say you will."

"Only if you promise to cure me of hypochondria."

"That will require a lot of time on the couch," he said, and pulled her to him for a kiss.

New Beginnings

THERE HAD BEEN SOME BUMPS IN THE ROAD, BUT Rudy had been true to his word and helped Catherine win over everyone. On seeing how happy they were together, William had given his stamp of approval, and so had Lila.

Catherine's hair had grown back in, curlier than ever. In addition to her new curls she'd also gotten a lot more gray, but Rudy said her gray hairs made her look wise.

Come September, the two of them were celebrating another all-clear report from her oncologist with an Alaskan cruise. Denise and Charlie were joining them. Athena was going along also. Lila, too, had decided she wanted to come and Rudy had booked the owner's suite for the four of them.

Seeing its floor-to-ceiling windows and balcony nearly

took Catherine's breath away. "Oh, Rudy," she said. "You shouldn't have."

"Sure he should have," said Lila. "Thanks, Rudy. This is great."

"This is only the beginning of great," he promised.

He proved it that night when, at dinner, he produced a diamond ring for Catherine. "You will marry me, won't you?"

"Of course I will," she said, and kissed him.

Word spread quickly to the neighboring tables and soon a regular parade of fellow cruisers was stopping by their table to congratulate them and admire Catherine's ring.

"By the way," Athena said once the parade ended, "I have something for both of you. It's not from me, though." She handed the gift bag she'd brought into the dining room to Catherine.

"What on earth?" Catherine pulled out a large gold box with a cupid embossed on it. "Chocolates." She took the attached gift envelope and opened it, then read aloud. "'Everything's better with chocolate. Love, Trevor and Sophie.'"

"It sure is," said Lila. "Let's open 'em."

Catherine passed over the treat and smiled at Rudy. "I don't see how my life could get any better."

"Same here," he said.

Later that night, when she went to bed she found more than a chocolate on her pillow. Rudy had left her a charm—a sterling-silver heart. She picked up the little piece of ship's stationery where he'd scrawled a note. *Looking forward to another wonderful cruise, and a wonderful life together.*

And it would be.

★★★★★

Dear Reader,

When this story was first completed people (including myself and my husband) were taking cruises, seeing the world and having a wonderful time. They were going to concerts and plays and school functions and the last thing anyone was thinking about was stocking up on toilet paper and hand sanitizer.

COVID-19 changed all that. As I'm writing you this letter no one is going anywhere. I sincerely hope that by the time this book gets to you the bad times will be behind us, that people will be happily gathering again for concerts and holiday parties, that they'll be out shopping and even taking a cruise like the wonderful one my husband and I enjoyed last Christmas.

We never know what the future holds, but my wish for you is that yours will hold many opportunities to make lovely memories. Wishing you happy and healthy holidays!

Sheila